D0529469

EVERYONE LOVES MAX!

PRAISE FOR *THE ANGEL EXPERIMENT*

"**Book of the week**....Pace, action, mystery, and cool." —*London Times*

"Like the best sort of video game or action movie, in book form. It **shows the promise of becoming a favorite**." —*Cleveland Plain Dealer*

"**Speed, suspense, excitement**....Nonstop action carries this page-turner breathlessly from start to finish." —*Kirkus Reviews*

"The claim of '**addictive**' is completely true....The writing is quick, fresh, funny, [and] smart." —*Toronto Sun*

"A never-ending series of twists and action....A fantasy romp that's **hard to put down**." —*Virginian-Pilot*

PRAISE FOR *SCHOOL'S OUT—FOREVER*

"**Five stars**! An action-packed, thrilling, and truly amazing book!" —BookReporter.com

"Readers are in for **another exciting wild ride**...leaving [them] breathless for the follow-up." —*Kirkus Reviews*

"Patterson's **super-fast pace** keeps the action moving and the suspense tense." —*Star-Ledger* (NJ)

PRAISE FOR *MAX*

"Filled with humor....Patterson has brought Max and flock into a new direction and given them wings....This group of kids is going to be having **one massive fun ride** well into the future."
—EdgeBoston.com

"This one is the best yet."
—BestsellersWorld.com

"Will leave fans anxious for more of Max's adventures."
—BookLoons.com

"This book **will please all Fang lovers immensely**. For all the girls who have been dreaming about Mr. Tall, Dark, and Winged, your prayers have been answered."
—not-so-cg.blogspot.com

PRAISE FOR *FANG*

"Patterson has created **another thrilling adventure** that is sure to capture readers' imaginations....[His] quick-paced tale of adventure, betrayal, and redemption is full of **vibrant and memorable characters**. It **truly has bite**."
—*School Library Journal*

"This **will excite the legions of fans** waiting for this installment in the flock's story."
—*Booklist*

"[B]reath-taking....Maximum Ride fans will not be disappointed in *Fang*. **The high-flying plot and new twists leave the reader begging for more** of Max and the flock."
—*Burlington Times-News*

PRAISE FOR *ANGEL*

"Even reluctant readers won't be able to put down this **intense thriller**."
—Barnes & Noble

"A strong installment in the series....**Fantastic flying descriptions...will make readers wish they had wings**."
—The Associated Press

Dedicated to Kelly and Kevin Okun.

And everybody out there who might love books,
if they were given books that loved them back.

━━━━━━━━━

Many thanks to Gabrielle Charbonnet, my conspirator,
who flies high and cracks wise.

Little, Brown and Company

Hachette Book Group
237 Park Avenue, New York, NY 10017
Visit our website at www.lb-teens.com

Little, Brown and Company is a division of Hachette Book Group, Inc.
The Little, Brown name and logo are trademarks of Hachette Book Group, Inc.

The publisher is not responsible for websites (or their content) that are not owned by the publisher.

First Paperback Edition: January 2008
First published in hardcover in May 2007 by Little, Brown and Company

Cover design by Larry Rostant

ISBN 978-0-316-15427-7

HC 10 9 8 7 6 5 4 3 2 1
PB 11

RRD-C

Printed in the United States of America
The text was set in Life.

SAVING THE WORLD

AND OTHER EXTREME SPORTS

WITHDRAWN

A MAXIMUM RIDE NOVEL

JAMES PATTERSON

LITTLE, BROWN AND COMPANY
New York Boston

To the reader:

The idea for Maximum Ride comes from earlier books of mine called *When the Wind Blows* and *The Lake House*, which also feature a character named Max who escapes from a quite despicable School. Most of the similarities end there. Max and the other kids in Maximum Ride are not the same Max and kids featured in those two books. Nor do Frannie and Kit play any part in Maximum Ride. I hope you enjoy the ride anyway.

PROLOGUE

NO MORE MISTAKES!

Itexicon American Headquarters
Florida, United States

"We have meticulously crafted the skeleton of our new world," the Director proclaimed from the large TV screen in the conference room. "Parts of this skeleton are scattered across the globe. Now the time has come to connect those parts, to become one! And, as one, we will commence our Re-Evolution!"

The Director stopped speaking when she noticed that the phone was vibrating in the pocket of her white lab coat. Frowning, she pulled it out and looked at a message. The situation in Building 3 had become critical.

"It's time," she said, glancing at a colleague offscreen. "Seal Building Three and gas everything inside."

Across the conference table, Roland ter Borcht smiled. Jeb Batchelder ignored him as the Director turned her attention back to the camera.

"Everything is in place, and we're commencing the By-Half Plan as of oh seven hundred tomorrow. As you know, Jeb, the *only* puzzle piece not fitting in, the *only* fly in the ointment, the *only* loose end not tied up is your obnoxious, uncontrollable, pathetic, useless, flying *failures*."

Ter Borscht nodded gravely and shot Jeb a glance.

"You begged us to wait until the bird kids' prepro-grammed expiration date kicked in," the Director went on, her voice tight with tension. "But you no longer have that luxury, no matter how soon it will happen. Get rid of those loose cannons *now*, Dr. Batchelder. Do I make myself clear?"

Jeb nodded. "I understand. They'll be taken care of."

The Director wasn't so easily convinced. "You show me proof of extinction of those bird-kid mistakes by oh seven hundred tomorrow," she said, "or you will be the one to become extinct. Do we have an understanding?"

"Yes." Jeb Batchelder cleared his throat. "It's already in place, Director. They're just waiting for my signal."

"Then give them the signal," the Director snarled. "When you arrive in Germany, this foolishness must be over. It is a momentous day . . . the dawn of a new era for humankind . . . and there is no time to waste. There is much to do if we're to reduce the world's population by one-half."

PART 1

IN SEARCH OF HOT CHOCOLATE-CHIP COOKIES

"Lay off the freaking horn!" I said, rubbing my forehead.

Nudge pulled away from the steering wheel, which Fang was holding. "Sorry," she said. "It's just so much fun — it sounds like a party."

I looked out the van window and shook my head, struggling to keep my irritation in check.

It seemed like only yesterday that we'd done the pretty impossible and busted out of the very creepy and deeply disturbing Itex headquarters in Florida.

In reality, it had been four days. Four days since Gazzy and Iggy had blown a hole in the side of the Itex headquarters, thus springing us from our latest diabolical incarceration.

Because we're just crazy about *consistency,* we were on the run again.

However, in an interesting, nonflying change of pace, we were driving. We'd made the savvy decision to borrow an eight-passenger van that had apparently been a love machine back in the '80s: shag carpeting everywhere, blacked-out windows, a neon rim around the license plate that we'd immediately disabled as too conspicuous.

There was, for once, plenty of room for all six of us: me (Max); Fang, who was driving; Iggy, who was trying to convince me to let him drive, although he's *blind;* Nudge, in the front seat next to Fang, seemingly unable to keep her mitts off the horn; the Gasman (Gazzy); and Angel, my baby.

And Total, who was Angel's talking dog. Long story.

Gazzy was singing a Weird Al Yankovic song, sounding exactly like the original. I admired Gazzy's uncanny mimicking ability but resented his fascination with bodily functions, a fascination apparently shared by Weird Al.

"*Enough* with the constipation song," Nudge groaned, as Gazzy launched into the second verse.

"Are we going to stop soon?" Total asked. "I have a sensitive bladder." His nose twitched, and his bright eyes looked at me. Because I was the leader and I made the decisions about stopping. And about a million other things.

I glanced down at the map on the laptop screen in my actual lap, then rolled down the window to look at the night sky, gauge our whereabouts.

"You could have gotten a car with GPS," Total said helpfully.

"Yes," I said. "Or we could have brought along a dog that doesn't talk." I gave Angel a pointed look, and she smiled, well, angelically at me.

Total huffed, offended, and climbed into her lap, his

small, black, Scottie-like body fitting neatly against her. She kissed his head.

Just an hour ago we'd finally sped across the state border, into Louisiana, meticulously sticking to our carefully plotted, brilliantly conceived plan of "heading west." Away from the laugh riot that had been our stint in south Florida. Because we still had a mission: to stop Itex and the School and the Institute and whoever else was involved from destroying us and from destroying the world. We're nothing if not ambitious.

"Louisiana, the state that road maintenance forgot," I muttered, grimacing at hitting yet another pothole. I didn't think I could take this driving thing much longer. From the Everglades to here had taken for*ever* in a car, as compared with flying.

On the other hand, even a big '80s love van was less noticeable than six flying children and their talking dog.

So there you go.

2

I wasn't kidding about the flying-kids part. Or the talking-dog part.

Anyone who's up to speed on the Adventures of Amazing Max and Her Flying, Fun-Loving Cohorts, you can skip this next page or so. Those of you who picked up this book cold, even though it's clearly *part three* of a series, well, get with the program, people! I can't take two days to get you all caught up on everything! Here's the abbreviated version (which is pretty good, I might add):

A bunch of mad scientists (mad *crazy*, not mad *angry* — though a lot of them do seem to have anger-management issues, especially around me) have been playing around with recombinant life-forms, where they graft different species' DNA together.

Most of their experiments failed horribly, or lived horribly for only a short while. A couple kinds survived, including us, bird kids, who are mostly human but with some bird DNA thrown in.

The six of us have been together for years. Fang, Iggy,

and I are ancient, at fourteen years old. Nudge the motor-mouth is eleven, Gazzy is eight, Angel is six.

The other ones who function pretty well and last more than a couple days are human-lupine hybrids, or wolf people. We call them Erasers, and they have an average life span of about six years. The scientists (whitecoats) trained them to hunt and kill, like a personal army. They're strong and bloodthirsty but lousy about impulse control.

The six of us are on the run, trying to thwart the white-coats' plan to destroy us and most of humanity, which makes the whitecoats crazy. Or crazi*er*. So they have been going to extreme and sometimes pathetic lengths to capture us.

There you have it: our lives in a nutshell. Emphasis on *nut*.

But if the above whipped your imagination into a frenzy, here's something even more interesting: Fang started a blog (http:maximumride.blogspot.com). Not that he's self-absorbed and trendy or anything. Nope, not him.

We "acquired" a wicked-cool laptop when we escaped from the Itex headquarters, and get this — it has permanent satellite linkup, so we're always online. And because Itex is a world-class, top-secret, paranoid techfest, the linkup has constantly changing codes and passkeys — its signal is completely untraceable. It's our key to every imaginable piece of information in the world.

Not to mention movie times and restaurant reviews. I crack up every time I think about it.

But anyway, with our lovely laptop, Fang is upchucking every bit of info we manage to gather about our past, the School, the Institute, Itex, etc. out onto the Web. Who knows? Maybe someone will contact us and help us solve the mystery of our existence.

In the meantime, we can locate the nearest Dunkin' Donuts in, like, *seconds*.

3

Navigating roads and potholes felt like way more work than it was worth, so I convinced the flock to surrender our wheels and travel by wing.

Back to basics.

By midnight, we had crossed from Louisiana into Texas and were approaching the sprawling, fuzzy glow of lights that was Dallas. Focusing on the least-lit area we could see, we dropped altitude, coasting in slow, wide circles, lower and lower.

We landed in a state park, where it took about a minute to find some welcoming trees to sleep in.

And I mean *in* the trees, not under them. Let's hear it for government funding, people! Take it from me: State parks are a valuable natural resource! *Let's protect them!* If only for the sake of the mutant bird kids in your area.

"So, have you narrowed the plan down any?" Fang asked me, after we'd done our hand-stacking good-night ritual and the other kids were asleep. I was draped across a wide branch of a fir tree, swinging one leg, wishing I could take a hot shower.

"I keep putting two and two together and coming up with thirty-seven," I said. "We have the School, the Institute, Itex . . . us, Erasers, Jeb, Anne Walker, the other experiments we saw in New York. But what's the bigger picture? How does it all fit together? How am I supposed to save the world?"

I never would have admitted not knowing to the younger kids. Kids need leaders, need to know someone's in charge. I mean, *I* don't. But most kids do.

"I can't help feeling like the School is the place to start," I went on, ignoring the instinctive tightening of my stomach muscles at the thought of it. "Remember when Angel said she overheard people at the School thinking about the horrible disaster coming up, and afterward there would be hardly any people left?"

Yeah, you heard me right. Angel "overheard people thinking." Another clue that we're no ordinary cast of characters. Angel doesn't just read minds; sometimes she can actually control them too.

Fang nodded. "And we'd survive 'cause we have wings. And I guess fly away from whatever disaster happens."

I was quiet for a minute, thinking so hard my head hurt.

"Two questions," Fang said. His eyes looked like part of the night sky. "One, where's your Voice? And two, where are all the Erasers?"

"I've been asking myself the same things," I said.

Those of you not in the know will be thinking, *What* Voice?

Why, the little Voice inside my head, of course. You mean you don't have one? I did.

Well, I hadn't lately, but I figured that was just a technical hitch. It wasn't like my Voice punched a time clock or anything. It was too much to hope that the Voice might be gone forever, but at the same time I was a little freaked out by how *alone* I felt without it.

"The only thing I can think of is maybe the Voice is transmitted inside my head somehow, and now we're out of range?"

Fang shrugged.

"Yeah. Who knows? And then the Erasers, I don't know that either. This is the longest we've ever not seen them," I said, giving the sky around us a quick scan. I still had a microchip in my arm that I was sure was leading them to me, but we hadn't seen a single Eraser in four days. Usually they popped up out of nowhere, no matter where we were or what we were doing. But it had been ominously quiet on the Eraser front. "It's creepy, and it makes me feel like something worse is coming. Like there's a one-ton iron safe hanging over our heads, waiting to drop."

Nodding, Fang said slowly, "You know what it reminds me of? Like when there's a storm coming, and all the animals somehow know to disappear. All of a sudden there's no birds, no noises. And you look up, and there's a twister headed right for you."

I frowned. "You think the Erasers aren't here because they're fleeing before an impending disaster?"

"Um, yeah," he said.

I leaned back against my tree, searching the sky again. Even ten miles outside of Dallas, the city lights dimmed the stars. I didn't know the answers. Suddenly I felt like I didn't know anything at all. The only certainty in my life was these five kids around me. They were the only things I was sure of, the only things I could trust.

"Go to sleep," said Fang. "I'll take the watch. I want to check on my blog anyway."

My eyes drifted shut as he pulled the laptop out of his bag.

4

"Fans still hanging on your every word?" Max asked sleepily some time later.

Fang looked up from his blog. He didn't know how much time had passed. The slightest tint of pink on the horizon made the rest of the world seem blacker somehow. But he could clearly see every freckle on Max's tired face.

"Yep," he said. Max shook her head, then relaxed into the crook of a large branch. Her eyes drifted shut again, but he knew she wasn't yet asleep — her muscles were still tight, her body still stiff.

It was hard for her to relax her guard. Hard for her to relax period. She had a lot to carry on those genetically enhanced shoulders, and all in all, she did a dang good job.

But no one was perfect.

Fang looked down at the screen he'd flipped off when Max had leaned closer. He thumbed the trackball, and the screen glowed to life again.

His blog was attracting more and more attention — word was spreading. In just the past three days, he'd gone from twenty hits to more than a thousand. A thousand people were reading what he wrote, and probably even more would tomorrow.

Thank God for spell-check.

But the message on the screen now was particularly odd. He couldn't reply to it, couldn't trace it, couldn't even delete it without its mysteriously reappearing moments later.

He'd gotten one just like it yesterday. Now he reread the new one, trying to decipher where it came from, what it meant. Looking up, Fang glanced at the flock, now all sleeping in various nearby trees. It was growing lighter with every second, and Fang was pretty whipped himself.

Iggy was slung across two branches, wings half unfolded, mouth open, one leg twitching slightly.

Nudge and Angel had curled up close to each other in the crooks of wide live oak limbs.

Total was nestled on Angel's lap, one of her hands holding him protectively in place. Fang bet it was incredibly warm with that furry heat source snoozing on her.

The Gasman was tucked almost invisibly into a large hole made by long-ago lightning. He looked younger than eight, dirty, pale with exhaustion.

And then Max. She was sleeping lightly, characteristically frowning as she dreamed. As he watched, one of her hands coiled into a fist, and she shifted on her branch.

Again Fang looked down at the screen, at the message just like the one he'd received yesterday.

One of you is a traitor, it read. *One of the flock has gone bad.*

5

We'd never been to Dallas before, and the next day, we decided to visit the John F. Kennedy memorial, as part of our "Highlights of Texas" tour. Or at least the other kids had decided, and they had outvoted me and my wacky "lie low" suggestion.

Now we wandered around the outdoor site, and I have to tell you, I could have used a couple of explanatory plaques.

"This thing is going to fall on our heads any second," Total said, examining the four walls towering over us and looking around suspiciously.

"It doesn't say anything about President Kennedy," the Gasman complained.

"I guess you're supposed to know already when you come here," Iggy said.

"He was a president," Nudge said, trailing one tan hand along the smooth cement. "And he got killed. I think he was supposed to be a good president."

"I still think there was a second shooter." Total sniffed and flopped on the grass.

"Can we go now?" I asked. "Before a busload of schoolkids comes on a field trip?"

"Yeah," said Iggy. "But what now? Let's do something *fun*."

I guess being on the run from bloodthirsty Erasers and insane scientists wasn't enough fun for him. Kids today are so spoiled.

"There's a cowgirl museum," said Nudge. How did she know this? No clue.

Fang opened his laptop to a Dallas tourist site.

"There's a big art museum," he said, with no convincing enthusiasm. "And an aquarium."

Angel sat patiently on the ground, smoothing her teddy bear Celeste's increasingly bedraggled fur. "Let's go to the cowgirl museum," she said.

I bit my lip. Why couldn't we just get out of here, go hide someplace, take the time to figure everything out? Why was I the only one who seemed to feel a pressing need to know what the heck was going on?

"Football game," said Fang.

"What?" Iggy asked, his face brightening.

"Football game tonight, Texas Stadium." Fang snapped the laptop shut and stood. "I think we should go."

I stared at him. "Are you *nuts*? We can't go to a football game!" I said with my usual delicacy and tact. "Being surrounded, crowded, by tens of thousands of people, trapped inside, cameras everywhere — God, it's a freaking nightmare just thinking about it!"

"Texas Stadium is open to the sky," Fang said firmly. "The Cowboys are playing the Chicago Bears."

"And we'll be there!" Iggy cheered, punching the air.

"Fang, can I talk to you privately for a second?" I asked tersely, motioning him out of the memorial.

We stepped through an opening in the cement wall and moved a couple yards away. I put my hands on my hips. "Since when are you calling the shots?" I demanded. "We can't go to a football game! There's going to be cameras everywhere. What are you *think*ing?"

Fang looked at me seriously, his eyes unreadable. "One, it's going to be an awesome game. Two, we're seizing life by the tail. Three, yeah, there's going to be cameras everywhere. We'll be spotted. The School and the Institute and Jeb and the rest of the whitecoats probably have feeds tapping every public camera. So they'll know where we are."

I was furious and didn't know what to think. "Funny, you didn't *look* insane when you got up this morning."

"They'll know where we are and they'll come after us," Fang said grimly. "Then we'll know where the tornado is."

Comprehension finally dawned. "You want to draw them out."

"I can't take not knowing," he said quietly.

I weighed Fang's sanity against my determination to remain the leader. Finally I sighed and nodded. "Okay, I get it. One major firefight, coming right up. But you *so* owe me. I mean, my God, *football!*"

6

This may surprise you, but people in Texas are *very into* their contact sports. I saw more than one infant wearing a Cowboys onesie.

I was wound tighter than a choke chain on a rottweiler, hating everything about being here. The Texas Stadium was, shock, Texas size, and we were surrounded by more than sixty thousand popcorn-munching opportunities to go postal.

Nudge was eating blue cotton candy, her eyes like Frisbees, looking at everything. "*I* want big hair!" she said excitedly, tugging on my shirt.

"I blame you," I told Fang, and he almost smiled.

We sat down low, by the middle of the field, about as far from any exit as we could be. I would have been much happier, or at least slightly less miserable, in the nosebleed section, close to the open sky. Down here, despite the lack of roof on the stadium, I felt hemmed in and trapped.

"Tell me again what we're doing here," I said, running a continuous scan of our surroundings.

Fang popped some Cracker Jack into his mouth. "We're here to watch manly men do manly things."

I followed Fang's line of sight: He was watching the Dallas Cowboys Cheerleaders, who were not doing manly things, by any stretch of the imagination.

"What's going on?" Iggy asked. Unlike the others, he was as tense as I was. In a strange place, surrounded by loud, echoing noise, unable to get his bearings — I wondered how long it would take him to crack.

"If anything happens," I told him, "stand on your chair and do an up-and-away, ten yards out and straight up. Got it?"

"Yeah," he said, turning his head nervously, wiping his hands on his grubby jeans.

"I want to be a cheerleader," Nudge said wistfully.

"Oh, for God's sake," I snapped, but a look from Fang shut me up. It meant, don't rain on her parade. No matter how ill-conceived and sexist that parade might be. Inside, I was burning up. I never should have agreed to this. I was hugely miffed that Fang had insisted on it. Now, watching him practically salivate over the horrifically perky cheerleaders, I got even madder.

"They're wearing tiny little shorts. One of them has long red hair," he was murmuring to Iggy, who nodded, rapt.

And we all know how much you like long red hair, I thought, remembering how it had felt, seeing Fang kiss the

Red-Haired Wonder back in Virginia. Acid started to burn a hole in my stomach.

"Max?" Angel looked up at me. I really had to get these kids into a bath soon, I realized, looking at her limp blond curls.

"Yes, honey? You hungry?" I started to wave down a hot-dog vendor.

"No. I mean, yeah, I'll take two hot dogs, and Total wants two too — but I meant, it's okay."

"What's okay?"

"Everything." She looked up at me earnestly. "Everything will be okay, Max. We've come this far — we're supposed to survive. We'll survive, and you'll save the world, like you're supposed to."

Well, reality just shows up sometimes, doesn't it?

"I'm not comfortable in this stadium," I explained, trying to look calm.

"I know. And you hate Fang looking at those girls. But we're still having fun, and Fang still loves you, and you'll still save the world. Okay?"

My mouth was agape, and my brain was frantically trying to process which statement to respond to first — Fang loves me? — when I heard someone whisper, "Is that one of those bird kids?"

7

Angel and I looked at each other, and I saw a world of comprehension in her gaze that made her seem much older than six.

It took only seconds for the rest of the flock to hear the whispers and to realize that the whispers were growing and spreading.

"Mom! I think that's those bird kids we saw in the newspaper!"

"Jason, look over there. Are they the kids in the pictures?"

"Oh, my goodness!"

"Rebecca, come here!"

And so on and so forth. I guess some photographer must have gotten picures of us flying away from Disney World and splashed them all over the newspapers. God forbid we should be able to watch a lousy football game with nothing extreme happening.

Out of the corner of my eye, I saw two blue-uniformed security men starting down the aisle toward us. A fast 360 revealed no one morphing into Erasers, but there were many eyes on us, many mouths wide open in surprise.

"Should we run?" Gazzy asked nervously, watching the crowd, mapping exit routes like he'd been taught.

"Running's too slow," I said.

"The game hasn't even started," Total said bitterly from under Iggy's seat. "I have money on the Bears!"

"You're welcome to stay here and see how the score ends up." I stood, began grabbing backpacks, counting flock members. The usual.

Total crawled out and jumped nimbly into Iggy's arms.

I tapped Iggy's hand twice. In an instant, we climbed onto our chairs. The muttering of voices was swelling, rising all around us, and the next thing I knew, our faces were twenty feet high, being projected onto the enormous stadium screens. Just like Fang had wanted. I hoped he was happy.

"Up and away on three," I said. Two more security guards were approaching fast from the right.

People were moving away from us, and I was glad the stadium had a namby-pamby no-weapons policy. Now even the cheerleaders' eyes were on us, though they didn't pause in their routine.

"One," I began, and we all leaped into the air, right over everyone's head.

Whoosh! I unfurled my wings hard and fast. My wingspan is almost thirteen feet, tip to tip, and Fang's and Iggy's are even wider.

I bet we looked like avenging angels, hovering over the astonished crowd. Kind of grungy avenging angels. Angels in need of a good scrub.

"Move it!" I ordered, still scanning the audience, checking for Erasers. The last batch of Erasers had been able to fly, but no one seemed to be taking to the air except us.

A couple of hard downstrokes and we were level with the open edge of the roof, looking down at the brightly lit field, the tiny faces all staring at us. Some people were smiling and punching the air. Most seemed shocked and scared. I saw some faces that looked angry.

But none were elongating, becoming furry, growing oversize canine fangs. They were all staying human.

As we shot off into the night, flying in perfect formation like navy jets, I wondered: *Where have all the Erasers gone?*

8

"It sucked, but it was way cool at the same time," Gazzy said. "I felt like the Blue Angels!"

"Yeah, except the Blue Angels are an extremely well funded, well equipped, well trained, well fed, and no doubt squeaky-clean group of crack navy pilots," I said. "And we're a bunch of unfunded, unequipped, semitrained, not nearly well fed enough, and filthy mongrel avian-human hybrids. But other than that, it's exactly the same."

I knew what he meant, though. As mad as I was about our being in that situation in the first place, and as much as I hated being on the run yet again, and as vulnerable as that last little stunt had made us, still — the feeling of flying in tight formation, all of us with wide, beautiful, awesome wings . . . it was just incredibly cool.

Gazzy gave a hesitant smile, picking up on my tension, not knowing if I was trying to be funny. I sat down, stuck a straw in a juice pouch, and sucked it dry, then tossed it aside and drained another one.

We were hiding in the Texas mountains, close to the

border of Me-hi-co. We'd found a deep, very narrow canyon that protected us from the wind, and now we were settled on the bottom, in front of a small fire.

I hadn't been this mad at Fang for this long a period of time since — never. Sure, I'd agreed to his lame-butt idea, but actually, now that I thought about it, it was about six times stupider than I'd realized.

"Hmm," said Fang, looking at the laptop. "We're every-where — TV news, papers, radio. Seems a lot of people got photos."

"There's a surprise," I said. "I bet that explains those helicopters we were hearing."

"Are you okay, Max?" Nudge asked timidly.

I gave Nudge an almost convincing smile. "Sure, sweetie. I'm just . . . tired."

I couldn't help shooting a glance at Fang.

He looked up. "I got a hundred and twenty-one thou-sand hits today."

"Whaaat? Really?" He had that kind of audience? He could barely spell!

"Yeah. People are organizing, actually trying to find out info for us."

Iggy frowned. "What if they get caught by whitecoats?"

"What are you writing about?" I admit I hadn't been reading his blog. Too busy trying to stay alive, etc.

"Us. Trying to get all the puzzle pieces out there, see if anyone can help us put the big picture together."

"That's a good idea, Fang," said Angel, turning her hot dog over to burn the other side. "We need to make connections."

What did she mean by that?

Connections are important, Max.

The Voice was back.

9

I was so startled by the Voice's sudden reappearance that I jumped and practically fell against the rock wall.

Instinctively I put a hand to my temple, as if I could feel the Voice running under my skin like a river.

"You okay?" Iggy reached out and touched my jeans. He'd felt me jump.

"Yeah," I muttered, walking away from the group. I felt them all looking at me, but I didn't want to explain.

Voice. Long time no annoy, I thought.

You were doing pretty well on your own, it replied. As before, it was impossible to tell whether it was young or old, male or female, human or machine. I was instantly aware of a schizoid reaction: Part of me felt irritated, invaded, suspicious, resentful — and part of me was flooded with relief, like I wasn't so alone.

Which was dumb. I lived with my five best friends and a dog. They were my family, my life. How could I possibly feel alone?

Everyone is always alone, Max, said the Voice, chipper as always. *That's why connections are important.*

31

Have you been reading Hallmark cards again? I thought. I walked out to the end of the canyon and found myself a mere ten feet from a ledge that dropped sharply into a much deeper, bigger canyon.

Connections, Max. Remember your dream?

I frowned, not knowing what the Voice was talking about.

You mean my dream of becoming the first avian-American Miss America? I thought snidely.

No. Your dream that the Erasers are chasing you, and you run through the woods until you come to a ledge. Then you fall off the ledge but start flying. And escape.

My breath left my chest with an audible *oof*. I hadn't had that dream since . . . well, since my dream had been replaced by a reality that was much worse. How had the Voice known about it?

"Yeah, so?" I said out loud.

This canyon is very much like your dream. It's as if you've come full circle.

I had no clue. No idea what the Voice meant.

Connections. Putting it all together. Your dream, Fang's laptop, people you've met, places you've been. Itex, the School, the Institute. Isn't it all connected?

Okay, but how? I practically shouted.

I almost thought I heard the Voice sigh, but probably just imagined it.

You'll see. You'll figure it out. Before it's too late.

That's comforting, I thought angrily. *Thanks.*

Then I had another thought. *Voice? Where are all the Erasers?*

Granted, the Voice had never answered a direct question — no, that would have been too easy. You don't just give the rat a piece of cheese — you make her work for it, right?

Shrugging, I turned and headed back to the others.

They're dead, Max, said the Voice. *They've all been . . . retired.*

I stopped in my tracks, frozen by shock. The Voice was always coy with information, but as far as I knew, it had never lied to me. (Which meant nothing, I realize.) But — dead?

Dead, the Voice repeated. *They've been retired. All around the world, every branch of the organization has been terminating their recombinant-DNA experiments. You're among the only ones left. And they're coming for you.*

10

Ooh, ominous music, right? "They're coming for you." Big whoop. They'd been coming for us for four years now. They hadn't done too well so far.

I strode back to the flock.

"You okay?" Fang asked.

I nodded, then remembered I was mad at him.

I looked away and deliberately sat next to Nudge, against the other canyon wall.

"I just heard from the Voice," I said.

"What did it say?" Nudge asked, eating a rolled-up piece of bologna.

Angel and Total watched me intently, and Fang stopped typing.

"It said we haven't been seeing Erasers because they're all dead," I said bluntly.

Everyone's eyes widened to, um, about the size of dinner plates.

"What did it mean, they're all dead?" Nudge asked.

I shook my head. "I don't know. If it's not pulling my

leg, then I would guess it meant . . . that all the Erasers are taking dirt naps." I thought about Ari, Jeb's son, who had been Eraserfied, and felt a tugging pain in my chest. Poor Ari. What a sucky life he'd been born into. And such a short one too.

"Who killed them?" Fang asked, getting to the point, as usual.

"The Voice said . . . all over the world, every branch of Itex and the Institute and the School — they were all terminating their recombinant-DNA experiments. And that we were almost the only ones left." It started to sink in, what that meant, and a cold shiver made me put my arms around my knees.

We were all silent for a minute, digesting this.

Then Total said, "Okay, if anyone asks, I can't talk, right?"

I rolled my eyes. "Oh yeah, that'll fool 'em."

"What are we gonna do now?" the Gasman asked. He looked very worried and came to sit closer to me. I reached out and fluffed up his mohawk, which had grown out.

"We have a mission," I began, ready to psych us all up for solving this puzzle. And possibly taking out a few whitecoats while we were at it.

"We need a home," said Fang, at almost the exact same time.

"What?" I asked, startled.

"We need to find a permanent home," Fang said seriously. "We can't last on the run much longer. I say screw the mission. Let them blow up the world. We can find a place to hide out where no one can find us, and we can just . . . *live*."

11

We all stared at Fang. That was the longest statement any of us had ever heard him utter.

"We can't forget the mission," I began, just as Angel said, "Yeah! We need a home!"

"A home!" said the Gasman, looking thrilled.

"A real home, better than our last one," Nudge agreed happily. "With no grown-ups, and no school or school uniforms."

"A home with a yard and lots of grass," said Total. "No more of this pebbles-and-dirt crap."

Why was I the only one who needed to know what was going on, who needed to understand what had happened to us and why? After everything we'd been through in the last few months, now they were ready to just throw it all away? I mean, Angel's kidnapping, going to New York, the subway tunnels, the beach, staying with Anne Walker, going to that school . . .

Oh. Well, okay. So they might be a little tired of the fear, pain, and mayhem, but still . . .

"Iggy?" I said, trying to keep the pleading out of my voice.

"Let's see," he said, holding out his hands as if they were a scale. "Hmm. On the one hand, we have constant, desperate, heart-pounding escapes, day after day, never knowing what's going to happen to us or whether we'll even be alive the next day . . ."

I frowned, seeing where he was going with this.

"On the other hand, a home: hidden, safe, sleeping in the same bed every night, relaxing, not having to fight for our lives at a moment's notice . . ."

"Okay, okay," I said. "You don't have to rub it in."

They watched me, waiting.

What was with Fang? Why was he undermining me like this? I used to feel so connected to him, like he was my absolute best friend in the world, someone who always had my back. Now I looked at him and felt as if I hardly knew him.

Reluctantly I shrugged one shoulder. "Whatever. A home, whatever."

The ecstatic cheering only made me feel worse.

12

"I'm not giving up the mission," I said, loud enough for Fang, several yards away, to hear me. We were only about eight thousand feet in the air, but it was really cold, probably below freezing. The wind in my eyes made them water constantly.

"I know."

"This is stupid," I said. Looking down, I saw the Pecos River winding like a thin, shiny snake through west Texas.

"Their hopes and dreams aren't stupid," Fang said, and I felt a flush warm my cheeks.

"That's not what I meant," I grumbled. "It's just — we were on a path. Now we're just leaving that path. One day I'm supposed to be saving the world, and the next I'm out looking for real estate. I don't get it. Plus, thanks to your little plan, we can't spit without being spotted and recognized. Where was my brain when I agreed to that one?"

Fang opened his mouth, but I interrupted. "*Plus*, now, thanks to you, we left the younger kids to be watched over by a blind guy and a talking dog. I must be insane! I mean, even more insane than usual. I'm going back."

I dipped one wing, ready to make a big wheeling turn, but Fang edged into my way, his face set.

"You promised," he said, making me scowl. "You said you'd give a quick recon, see if we could find a place."

I kept up the scowl, thankful that not once in my whole life had anyone felt compelled to tell me not to ruin my pretty face like that.

"Let them blow up the world, and global-warm it, and pollute it," Fang said. "You and me and the others will be holed up somewhere, safe. We'll come back out when they're all gone, done playing their games of world domination."

He had positively become a chatterbox lately.

"That's a great plan. Of course, by then we won't be able to go outside because we'll get fried by the lack of ozone layer," I said, getting worked up. "We'll be living in damp caves, eating at the bottom of the food chain because everything with any *flavor* will be full of mercury or radiation or something!"

I recognized Fang's face of exaggerated patience, which of course got on my last nerve.

"And there won't be any TV or cable because all the people will be *dead!*" I was on a roll now. "So our only entertainment will be Gazzy singing the constipation song! And there won't be amusement parks and museums and zoos and libraries and cute shoes! We'll be like cavemen, trying to weave clothes out of plant fibers. We'll have nothing! *Nothing!* All because you and the kids want to kick back in a La-Z-Boy during the most important time in history!"

I was practically frothing at the mouth.

Fang looked at me. "So maybe we should sign you up for a weaving class. Get a jump on all those plant fibers."

I stared at him, saw how he was trying to suppress his laughter at my vision of the apocalypse.

Something inside me snapped. My whole world had gotten turned on its head in the last twenty-four hours. Like, my old world had sucked so bad, and this world, amazingly, sucked *worse*.

"I hate you!" I screamed at Fang. Tucking my wings in, I aimed downward, diving toward the ground at more than two hundred miles an hour.

"No you dooonnn't!" Fang's voice spiraled away into nothingness, far above me.

Inside my head, almost drowned out by the roar of wind rushing by my ears, I heard the Voice make a *tsking* sound. *You guys are crazy about each other,* it said.

13

"Oh, yeah. No bedtime. It's a good thing," Gazzy sang, doing a little dance.

"Look, just because Max isn't here doesn't mean all the rules have gone out the window," Iggy said, facing him. "She left me in charge, and I'm gonna make sure to do everything she would —" He couldn't keep a straight face any longer and cracked up, bending over and clutching his stomach.

Nudge rolled her eyes, and she and Angel shared a smile. She picked up a small handful of pebbles and carefully started distributing them among other little piles.

"Mancala, huh?" Total said, lying down next to them. "Next time we're in a store, let's lift some cards. We could play Texas hold 'em. I would kick your butts." His small, shiny nose twitched as he watched them play.

"That's a good idea," said Nudge, as Angel distributed her pile, though she had no idea how Total would hold the cards. Unless he had opposable thumbs hidden under his paw fur. Which, come to think of it, he very well might. Checking behind her, she saw she had enough room to let her wings stretch out a bit, so she extended them, enjoying the feeling. "Ahh."

"*I* want wings," Total said, not for the first time. "If I could fly, no one would have to carry me. If they could graft wings onto those big lunking Erasers, they could definitely patch a pair onto me."

"It would hurt, Total," said Angel, studying the mancala game.

"Do you think the Erasers are really gone?" Nudge asked them. In the background, she heard Iggy saying, "No, see, you need the spark to ignite it. You need the flint to make the spark, see?"

Gazzy murmured, "Yeah, but what about the bleach?" and then their voices faded again.

Nudge sighed. This was the kind of thing she wished Max or Fang were here to handle.

"Hey, guys?" Iggy called. Nudge looked up.

"How about a little test flight?" he said. "A little wheeling-around like the hawks showed us. Okay?"

"Yeah, okay," said Angel. She smiled at Nudge. "You were about to win anyway."

Nudge grinned back. "I know." Standing up, she dusted off her jeans and pulled her wings in to walk to the end of the tiny canyon.

One by one, the bird kids leaped off the ledge, falling downward for a few moments before hauling out their wings, strong, light, and catching the wind in their feathers. Nudge loved this feeling, the sensation of power and freedom, the knowledge that she could rise up from the ground like an angel. Any time she wanted to.

She smiled over at Angel, who turned to smile back at her. Then Angel's eyes went wide, and her face took on a look of horror. Nudge whirled as a large shadow blotted the light from the flock.

A wide, thick swarm of Erasers was flying right toward them. They were back!

14

"Seriously, we have to talk," said Fang.

I sighed, looking up at the sky. "It's just like dolphins chirping," I said regretfully, talking out loud to myself. "I hear sounds, but none of them make sense."

I put my hands on my hips and surveyed the scene below us. "No water source. Let's go."

Without waiting for him, I launched myself off the low cliff, moving my wings powerfully, heading toward the sun. We'd stopped twice already, and neither place had all the stuff we needed: close-by food source, water, safety.

This was completely pointless, as opposed to my original plan, which was completely pointed.

Without turning my head, I glanced out of the corners of my eyes to see Fang's sleek wings behind me. He was acting weird. I didn't think Fang had been replaced by a clone the way I had at one point. Yes, folks, in my life, that's actually a legitimate concern. Take a moment and count your blessings.

Maybe he really does just want to talk, said the Voice.

Oh, yeah, 'cause Fang is all about the wordy sharing of feelings, I thought back. *Something's up, something he's not telling me.*

And I would get it out of him at the next place we stopped. This was one mystery I could solve, even if I had to beat it out of him.

15

"I knew it was too good to be true," Gazzy yelled. "The Erasers' all being dead!"

"I didn't *feel* them coming," Angel said, confused.

Nudge's heart was pounding, the blood rushing in her ears. These Erasers moved more in sync with one another than the others they had encountered, but still awkwardly, choppily. Nudge shot a last look at Angel, then soared upward just as the Erasers hit them.

Focus. That's what Max always said. Focus.

Concentrating, Nudge dropped down on an Eraser, smashing her sneakered feet against its head. Then, whirling, she cracked the hard edge of her hand against its windpipe. The Eraser made a weird noise and started to lose altitude.

"Nudge! *Watch it!*" Gazzy screamed.

Wham! An iron-hard punch to the ribs knocked Nudge's breath away, and she sucked in air soundlessly, trying not to panic. Instinctively she remembered to keep moving her wings, staying aloft long enough to regain her breath.

But there was no time — the Eraser came at her again, fist cocked back to punch. At the last second, Nudge dropped suddenly, so that its big, hairy arm swished through empty air.

"Take that, sucker!" she wheezed.

Surging upward, Nudge kicked it, aiming for its stomach but actually hitting somewhat lower. The Eraser doubled over without a sound, and Nudge clasped her hands together and brought them down on the back of its neck as hard as she could.

"Ow!" Angel's cry of pain made Nudge whirl, and she saw the smallest member of the flock being held by one arm as she ineffectually tried to kick her captor.

Nudge rushed over but was beaten there by Iggy, following the sound of Angel's voice. Together they pummeled the Eraser, and Iggy chopped down on the arm holding Angel. With a strange roar, the Eraser turned and pulled back its arm, and then made an odd strangled sound.

Looking down, Nudge saw Total chomping on the Eraser's ankle, shaking his head even as he dangled there, high above the ground — with no wings.

"Get him," she whispered to Angel, who nodded and quickly dropped ten feet. The Eraser shook its leg, but Total closed his eyes and clamped down harder, growling fiercely. Judging from the other muffled sounds, he was also swearing a blue streak.

"Yo!" yelled the Gasman, catching everyone's attention. "Fire in the hole!"

16

Nudge's side was killing her, and she still felt low on oxygen. But experience had taught that when Gazzy or Iggy said something like that, you ducked and covered as fast as you could. So she folded in her wings, immediately dropping like a stone.

A good thirty feet down, she unfurled her wings and shot to one side, just as Gazzy pushed an Eraser away from him with a muttered *"Oof!"* Angel had grabbed Total, Iggy had grabbed Angel, and they were hauling upward like pocket rockets.

There were five Erasers left — Nudge guessed they'd disposed of about half of them. Her ribs felt broken, she wished Max and Fang were here, and she didn't know wh —

BOOM!

"Gross!" Nudge shrieked, as bits of Eraser hit her. "Gross, gross, gross! Oh, God, Gazzy! Gross!"

Nudge worked her wings, moving up toward Iggy. She passed one main chunk of an Eraser dropping past her, and saw two others that had been wounded — one's wing was broken almost off, and the other appeared to be missing a leg.

But it was weird, the way —

"You have terminated me," one of them said in a strange, flat voice. "But I am one of many."

"Robots!" Iggy breathed, taking Total from Angel.

"One of many, one of many, one of many," the robot Eraser was saying. Now Nudge saw the red light in its eyes, saw how they were fading and winking out.

"Good!" spat the Gasman, kicking it hard. "Because we like to blow stuff up, blow stuff up, blow stuff up!"

Then all the remaining Erasers seemed to fold in on themselves, as if programmed, and dropped out of sight. A long, long time later, the flock saw the small poofs of dust and dirt showing that they'd finally hit the canyon floor.

"Well, that was different," Iggy said.

"And so *gross!*" Nudge said, still brushing Eraser shards off herself.

17

"What are you thinking about?" Fang's quiet voice barely carried to me over the crackling of the fire.

I'm thinking about how much easier it was when everyone just did what I told them, I thought sourly. "Wondering if the kids are okay," I said.

"That place was way secluded and easy to defend. And if the Erasers are all dead . . ." Fang pulled a stick out of the fire and blew on a crisp piece of roasted rabbit.

Yes, rabbit. We'd caught it, and now we were going to eat it. I won't go into all the steps in between. The thing is, when you have to survive, you have to survive. I hope you never need to find that out for yourself.

He handed the stick to me, and I started gnawing, grinning at how surprisingly few etiquette rules seemed to apply here. Then I started laughing.

Fang looked at me.

"Thanksgiving at Anne's," I said. "Sit up straight, napkin in lap, wait for everyone to be served, say grace, take small amounts, use the salad fork, no burping."

I waved a hand around the dusty cave, where we squatted by a fire, tearing off strips of Thumper with our teeth.

Fang gave a half smile and nodded. "At least it isn't desert rat."

Okay, you sissies in the back, the ones going *"Eew!"* Let's see you go without anything to eat for three days, especially if you're a biological anomaly who needs three thousand calories a day minimum, and then someone presents you with a hot, smoky, charred piece of rat *au jus*. You'd scarf it down so fast you'd burn your tongue. There would be no quibbling about ketchup either.

"You know what they say about rat," I began.

"Everyone gets a drumstick," Fang and I finished together.

I looked at Fang, his sharp, angular face cast with shadows from the fire. I'd grown up with him, I trusted no one more than him, I depended on him. And now we felt a little like strangers.

I moved away from the fire and sat down with my back against the cave wall. Fang wiped his hands on his jeans and came to sit next to me. Outside, it was nighttime, the stars blotted out by thick, rolling clouds. This place probably got only a few inches of rain a year, and it looked like it was about to get some. I hoped the rest of the flock was curled up safe and warm where we had left them.

"What are we doing here, Fang?"

"The kids want us to find a place to settle down."

"What about the School and saving the world?" I asked with scalpel-like delicacy.

"We have to quit playing their game," Fang said softly, watching the fire. "We have to remove ourselves from the equation."

"I can't," I admitted in frustration. "I — just have to do this."

"Max, you can change your mind." His voice was like autumn leaves dropping lightly onto the ground.

"I don't know *how*."

Then my throat felt tight, and I rubbed my fists against my eyes. I dropped my face onto my arms, crossed over my knees. This sucked! I wanted to be back with the oth —

Fang's hand gently smoothed my hair off my neck. My breath froze in my chest, and every sense seemed hyper-alert. His hand stroked my hair again, so softly, and then trailed across my neck and shoulder and down my back, making me shiver.

I looked up. "What the heck are you *doing?*"

"Helping you change your mind," he whispered, and then he leaned over, tilted my chin up, and kissed me.

18

At that moment, I had no mind to change, or not change, or throw against the nearest wall. My mind had shorted out as soon as Fang's lips touched mine. His mouth was warm and firm, his hand gentle on my neck.

I'd kissed him once before, when I thought he was dying on a beach. But that had lasted a second. This was . . . going on and on.

I realized I was getting dizzy, and then realized it was because I hadn't taken a breath yet. It seemed like an hour before we broke apart. We were both breathing raggedly, and I stared into his eyes as if I would find answers there.

Which of course I didn't. All I saw was the dancing flames of our small fire.

Fang cleared his throat, looking as surprised as I felt. "Forget the mission," he said, his voice barely audible. "Let's just all be safe somewhere together."

And boy, did that seem like a swell idea just then. We could be like Tarzan and Jane, swinging through a jungle, snagging bananas right off a tree, living at one with nature, la-di-da —

Tarzan and Jane and their band of merry mutants!

Fang's hand was making slow, warm circles between my wings, and that plus the hypnotic fire and the stress of the day all combined to make me tired and unable to think straight.

What does he want from me? I thought. I half expected the Voice to chime in here, sure it had been eavesdropping on this whole embarrassing scene.

Now Fang was rubbing my neck. I was both exhausted and hyperaware, and just as he leaned in — to kiss me again? — I jumped to my feet.

He looked up at me.

"I — I'm not sure about this," I muttered. How's that for silver-tongued rapier wit, eh? Overreacting impressively, I raced to the front of the cave and launched myself out into the night, unfurling my wings, feeling the wind against my burning face, hearing the rush of air all around me.

Fang didn't follow, though when I glanced back I saw his tall, lean form standing in the cave entrance, highlighted by the fire.

Not too far away, I found a narrow rock ledge, well hidden in the night, and I collapsed there in tears, feeling confused and upset, and excited and hopeful, and appalled.

Ah, the joys of being an adolescent hybrid runaway.

19

What was Fang going to do, *blog* about Max throwing herself out into space just so she wouldn't have to kiss him again? No! Instead he smashed his fist against the cave wall, then grimaced with the pain and stupidity, seeing his bloodied knuckles, the almost instant swelling.

He banked the fire, keeping a small pile of embers glowing in case she came back and needed help finding the entrance. Neither was likely.

He kicked most of the rocks off a Fang-sized place and lay down, rubbing his wings against the fine silt because it felt good. He didn't want to check his blog — he'd had almost eight hundred thousand hits earlier — didn't want to do anything except lie still and think.

Max.

God, but she was stubborn. And tough. And closed in. Closed off. Except when she was holding Angel, or ruffling the Gasman's hair, or pushing something closer to Iggy's hand so he could find it easily without knowing anyone had helped him. Or when she was trying to untangle

Nudge's mane of hair. Or — sometimes — when she was looking at Fang.

He shifted on the hard ground, a half-dozen flashes of memory cycling through his brain. Max looking at him and laughing. Max leaping off a cliff, snapping out her wings, flying off, so incredibly powerful and graceful that it took his breath away.

Max punching someone's lights out, her face like stone.

Max kissing that weiner Sam on Anne's front porch.

Gritting his teeth, Fang rolled onto his side.

Max kissing him on the beach, after Ari had kicked Fang's butt.

Just now, her mouth soft under his.

He wished she were here, if not next to him, then somewhere in the cave, so he could hear her breathing.

It was going to be hard to sleep without that tonight.

20

Before Fang took the computer with him, and before they'd almost gotten nailed by robot Erasers, Nudge had been reading camping recipes online. She was tired of Ding-Dongs and hot dogs on a stick.

She'd found out that you could do amazing stuff, like cooking whole meals wrapped in foil in the embers of a fire. She decided to get a frying pan next time she had a chance. It wouldn't be too hard to carry around one little frying pan, would it? And if they had a frying pan, Iggy could make almost anything. Just thinking about it was making her stomach rumble.

"That smells good," said Angel, coming over to kneel by the fire. "Is that what that foil was for?"

"Uh-huh," Nudge said, poking at the foil package with a stick.

The next second, *the waning sun blinked out.*

They both looked up in surprise, and Gazzy and Iggy stopped playing tic-tac-toe.

Angel drew in her breath so fast it sounded like a whistle. Nudge felt like her own breath had turned to a chunk of concrete in her throat, because she couldn't make a sound, couldn't move.

Hundreds of those robot things, the things that Iggy called Flyboys, were covering the sky above their canyon and coming in both ends. Nudge guessed the few that had survived the earlier fight had gone to get reinforcements. There must have been ten times as many this time.

The flock was trapped.

"Dinner's ready," said Angel. "And it's *us*."

21

"Up and away?" Iggy asked, and Gazzy answered, "No! They're above us too! *Everywhere!*"

Nudge's ears were filled with a horrible droning sound, like a thousand bees, and as the Flyboys dropped closer, it started to sound like chanting, like, "We are many! You cannot win!"

"We can sure as heck try!" Gazzy yelled. Leaning down, he grabbed a bunch of sticks from the fire and threw them into the air. Several of the Flyboys caught fire. Excellent. They were flammable!

Nudge raced over and grabbed some burning sticks too, but she held one too close and singed her hand. Still, she threw them into the air as hard as she could, watching in amazement as Flyboys burst into flame.

"Cool!" Gazzy grinned, forgetting to panic for a moment. "It's like they were dipped in gasoline!"

"They don't have minds," Angel said.

Nudge looked at her.

"They don't have minds," Angel explained again, upset. "I can't do anything."

"Well, I can bite 'em!" Total cried, racing in circles around their feet. "Let me at 'em! Let me get my fangs on 'em!" He made little leaps into the air, snapping his jaws.

"Total!" Angel said. "Be careful! Come back!"

"Let me teach 'em a lesson!" Total yelled.

The flock fought hard — of course. Max had taught them to fight, to never, ever give up. Unless running away made more sense, she'd always added.

Running away would have been so great, Nudge thought, but in this case there was nowhere to run. The canyon was clogged with Flyboys. They seemed to be mostly metal with a thin Eraser covering on the outside. The ones that had burned were all metal now, their skin and fur charred and shriveled against them, smelling god-awful.

Iggy threw every bomb he had (Nudge had no idea where he'd been hiding them, and she bet Max didn't know about them either), but all the bombs destroyed only fifteen or twenty Flyboys. Not enough, nowhere close to enough.

The flock was caught. Maybe if Max and Fang had been there, it would have taken the robots another minute or two. That's how bad it was, how hopeless.

Within twenty minutes, the flock had been duct-taped into unmoving bundles, even Total. Then Flyboys grabbed them and took to the air, flying like big toasters or something.

Nudge saw Iggy, Gazzy, Angel, and Total, their mouths taped shut like hers.

Don't worry. Angel sent the thought out to each of them. *Don't worry. Max and Fang will come back. They'll find us. They'll be really mad too.*

Nudge tried not to think, so Angel wouldn't be more scared, but she wasn't able to shut her brain down completely. So Angel might have felt her think: *Not even Max and Fang can get us out of this. No one can. This is the end.*

22

I went back to Fang the next morning and pretended that nothing had happened, that my little DNA-enhanced heart hadn't gone all aflutter and that I hadn't imagined myself in a hoopskirt, coming down the stairs at Tara like Scarlett O'Hara.

Nope. Not my style. Instead I showed up, skidding on my landing, sending grit and pebbles everywhere, and said, "Let's roll!"

Topping the list of thorns in my side for today were:

1) Weirdness between me and Fang
2) Worry about leaving the flock
3) Gnawing sense of pressure about getting back to the mission
4) The usual: food, shelter, safety, life expectancy, etc.
5) And then, of course, that whole actual saving-the-world thing

Gosh, it was hard to figure out what to worry about first. Everything wanting to contribute to my ulcer, Get in line and take a number!

"You're quiet." Fang broke into my thoughts. Below us,

barren miles of mountains, plains, Indian reservations, and desert looked like wrinkles on a dirt-colored tablecloth.

I glanced at him. "Enjoy it while you can."

"Max." He waited till I looked at him again. "The one thing we have is each other. The one thing we can depend on, no matter what. We have to . . . talk about stuff."

I would pretty much rather have been torn apart by wild animals. "I liked it better when you didn't talk," I said. "I mean, there's a reason people don't look under rocks, you know?"

"Meaning what?" He sounded irritated. "We're going to pretend nothing's going on? That's stupid. The only way to deal with any of this is to get it out in the open."

Ugh. "Have you been watching *Oprah* again?"

Now I had made him mad, and he fell silent. I was relieved, but I knew this subject wasn't closed. Then my eyes registered the particular area we were flying over at high speed. It was a little hard to tell where Arizona left off and California began — you'd think they would just go ahead and paint those blue map lines everywhere, divvying up the states — but I recognized this place.

"Going down!" I announced, angling my body and tucking my wings behind me.

Fang followed me without comment. I could practically feel the strong "wring her neck" vibes coming from him, but it wasn't the first time he'd been really angry at me, and God knew it wouldn't be the last.

I landed at the edge of a woods near a dinky little Arizona town and started walking west. After two minutes I stopped, looking straight ahead at a small, tidy house surrounded by a somewhat scraggly yard.

Max, you're making a serious mistake, said the Voice. *Get up and get out of here right now. Get back to your mission. I'm very serious about this.*

I ignored it, emotions starting to swirl inside me.

"Where are we?" Fang whispered.

"At Ella's house," I said, hardly able to believe it myself. "And Dr. Martinez."

23

"If we can all fly, why are we in the back of a semi?" Iggy whispered.

He was rewarded by having one of the Flyboys kick him hard in the ribs. *"Oof!"*

Nudge winced, practically feeling his pain with him. Since he was blind, he couldn't see her face or the sympathy she was trying to send his way.

Everything hurt. Nudge didn't know how long they'd been lying on the floor in the back of this big truck, feeling every bump in the road. They'd been tied up for hours, and she couldn't feel her hands anymore. Every time the truck bounced, her shoulder or her hip banged against the hard floor, and she was sure she'd have humongous bruises. They all would.

After the Flyboys had grabbed them, they'd put cloth hoods over their heads. Nudge had smelled something sickly sweet. She'd grown dizzy and then passed out. She'd woken up in the truck, heading God knew where. Well, probably the School. Or the Institute.

Either way, it was going to be a long drive. Which

meant she could lie here and dread what was coming minute after minute, hour after hour.

What was coming: a cage. Awful, scary, really painful experiments, usually involving needles. Nudge tried not to whimper, thinking about it. Chemical smells. Whitecoats. Flashing lights, scary sounds. Knowing it was happening to the rest of the flock. And no Max, no Fang.

And all of this, being bound, seeing the rest of her flock also bound and in pain, not knowing where Max and Fang were or even if they'd be able to find the flock again — all of that stuff wasn't even the worst part.

The worst part was that when she'd woken up, when she'd counted heads in the truck, there had been only three.

Angel was missing.

24

It wasn't as though they had saved my life or anything — Ella and Dr. Martinez. It was worse: They had shown me what life could be like in Normal Land. It had haunted me ever since I'd left them.

What day was this? No clue. Would Dr. Martinez be at work?

I let my mind focus on this question in order to avoid the bigger, scarier question: Would they even want to see me again?

Or, nightmare: Had something bad happened to them because they'd sheltered me before?

Just like the first time, I stood frozen on the edge of their yard, unable to will myself forward, to knock on the door.

Max, began the Voice, and I answered it inside my head. *You're the one who said connections were important,* I reminded it. *Well, I'm here to make some connections. Deal with it.*

"What the heck are we doing here?" Fang's tone of mild

curiosity meant that he was so stunned he was about to fall over.

I had no answer for him. I didn't even have an answer for myself.

Then, just like the first time again, fate stepped in; or rather, Dr. Martinez stepped out of her front door. She blinked in the bright sun, then turned to lock the door behind her. Then she paused, as if listening, or sensing something: *moi.*

Behind me, Fang instinctively faded into the woods, where he would be invisible among the shadows.

Slowly Dr. Martinez turned, while I stood tense and almost quaking at the edge of her yard. Her deep brown eyes swept the area and flashed on me almost immediately. Then her mouth opened soundlessly. I made out the word "Max."

25

Then Dr. Martinez and I were running toward each other, and it felt like it was all happening in slow motion. I had planned on a cool, casual "Yo? Wha's happ'nin'?" But that dream was gone, gone, gone, baby. Instead I clung tightly to her, trying not to cry, taking a weird, deep, terrifying satisfaction from the sensation of her holding me.

Her hand stroked my hair as she whispered, "Max, Max, Max, you've come back." Her voice sounded broken, and I didn't trust myself to speak.

Then I remembered I was indulging in this revolting display of saccharine emotion right in front of Fang. Who would probably never let me hear the end of it. I turned and looked toward the woods. With my raptor vision, I could barely make out his dim outline.

I raised my hand to him, and Dr. Martinez's gaze shot toward the woods.

"Max? Are you okay?" she asked, her eyes on the trees and shadows.

"Yes. I — I didn't mean to come back," I said hesitantly. "But — I . . . We were in the neighborhood. . . ."

Dr. Martinez's eyes widened when a stiff-faced Fang slowly emerged from the woods, as if a shadow had taken form and come to life. How's that for a little bird-kid imagery, eh? The soul of a poet, that's me!

"This is my . . . brother, Fang," I muttered, stumbling over the word *brother*. Because he'd kissed me. And no southern jokes, please. Ick.

"Fang?" Dr. Martinez said, giving him a slow smile, warming up my day. She held out her hand, and he came toward us as if dragged by an invisible rope, as tense and unyielding as I'd ever seen him. Which is saying something.

He stopped about two yards from us and didn't take her hand.

"Fang? Are you — like Max?" asked Dr. Martinez.

"Nope," he said, sounding bored. "I'm the smart one."

I resisted the urge to kick his shin.

"Well, come in, both of you," said Dr. Martinez, sounding excited and bemused and awestruck. "I was going to run to the grocery store before Ella got home from school. But that can wait."

Inside, the house seemed more familiar to me than Anne Walker's, though I'd only been here maybe forty-eight hours, months ago. Maybe because it had felt like home, the first real home I'd ever been in.

Behind me, Fang stood close to the door, taking in every detail, cataloguing exits, planning courses of action in case violence broke out. As it tended to do around us.

"Are you guys hungry?" asked Dr. Martinez, taking off her jacket and putting down her purse. "I could make you sandwiches."

"That would be great," I said, my stomach growling at the thought.

Fang sniffed the air. "What's that . . . scent, that . . ."

Dr. Martinez and I smiled at each other.

"Chocolate-chip cookies," we said at the same time.

26

"So, you have your price," I said to Fang, speaking around a mouthful of crumbs. "Your soul for a cookie."

Making sure Dr. Martinez wasn't looking, Fang shot me the bird and took another bite, clearly savoring the warm chewiness, the notes of vanilla, the semimelted chocolate chunks. I grinned at him, then stuck out my tongue.

Dr. Martinez sat down at the table with us and dipped a cookie into her mug of coffee. She patted my arm. "I'm really glad to see you again, Max," she said, with so much sincerity that I blushed. "You know, there have been reports about mutant flying children in the news lately."

I nodded. "Yeah. We keep forgetting the 'lie low and hide' part of our plan."

"Do you have a plan?" she asked, concern on her face. "What are you doing now? Are there more of you?"

Just like that, my natural instincts for secrecy and self-protection kicked in, and I felt my face shut down. Next to me, Fang stiffened in midchew.

Dr. Martinez had no problem reading my expression.

"Never mind," she said quickly. "Forget I asked. I just . . . wish I could help in some way."

Dr. Martinez was a veterinarian, and she'd treated me for a gunshot wound at her clinic. She was the one who'd discovered, when she did an X-ray, the microchip in my arm.

"Maybe you can," I said. "Remember my chip?"

"The one in your arm?" Dr. Martinez frowned. "Do you still have it?"

"Yeah. And I still want it out."

She finished her cookie and drank some coffee, thinking it through. "Since you left, I've examined your X-ray a hundred times." She smiled. "I didn't think I'd ever see you again, but it drove me crazy — I had to figure it out. I've looked and looked at it, trying to see if there's any way to take out the chip without damaging your nerves so badly that you'd lose the use of your hand."

"Did you come up with something?" I was practically quivering with anticipation.

Her shoulders sagged slightly. "I'm not positive. It seems like I could possibly do it with microsurgery, but . . ."

"Do it," I said quickly. *"Do it now."*

I felt Fang looking at me, but I stayed focused on Dr. Martinez.

"I want this chip out," I said, hating the pleading sound in my voice. "I don't care what it does."

You can't risk losing the use of your hand, said the Voice.

For some reason I was finding it particularly annoying

today. *Why?* I thought, sarcasm dripping. *You think I can't save the world with one hand tied behind my back?*

Dr. Martinez looked hesitant, too cautious to take risks.

Suddenly Fang grabbed my left hand and turned it over, baring my forearm on the table. The angry red scars from when I had sawed at my arm with a broken seashell flamed up at us, puckered and ugly. Heat flushed my face, and I tried to pull my arm away.

"Oh, that," I muttered, aware of Dr. Martinez's wide, horrified eyes.

"She tried to cut it out herself," Fang said tersely. "Almost bled out, on a beach. Take it out, so she won't be such a moron again. Or at least not in that same way. Maybe in a different way," he acknowledged realistically.

I frowned fiercely at him, hating the look of consternation on Dr. Martinez's face. Then I glared at her, daring her to express pity. I swear, I would knock their two heads together if —

"I can try," she said.

27

"Where's Angel?" Gazzy's whisper was barely a breath in Nudge's ear.

"Don't know," she breathed back.

The truck stopped, and the back doors opened. It was daylight. The Flyboys riding in the back with them climbed out, then slammed the heavy metal doors, making Nudge's ears ring.

Ages later, the doors opened again, and a Flyboy threw in some pieces of bread and some fruit that was half rotten. The doors slammed shut again. There was creepy laughter outside.

Despite the blackness inside the truck, Nudge could see pretty well, and so could Gazzy. They wriggled over to the pieces of bread. Nudge was so hungry she felt sick. Even with their hands tied behind their backs, they managed to wolf down every bit of the stale bread and all but the grossest parts of the fruit.

"When we get out of this, every one of those robots is gonna have fang marks on 'em," muttered Total. His paws were trussed with duct tape.

"We'll never get out of this one," said Iggy. "I have a really bad feeling."

Nudge couldn't remember hearing Iggy sound so defeated. He was one of the older kids, like Fang and Max. Most the time she forgot he was blind. He was strong, powerful, and a mean fighter. Hearing him say that made Nudge feel as though a cold fist gripped her fast-beating heart.

"We'll get out." Nudge wished for the thousandth time that the doors would burst open and Max and Fang would be standing there.

Iggy was silent.

"We have to find Angel," Gazzy whispered. "We can't let them do . . . all the stuff they did to her last time."

Angel had been a mess when they'd rescued her last time. It had taken her weeks to recover. And since then, she'd been different somehow. Sadder. Quieter.

The thought of what they might already be doing to Angel made Nudge shiver.

"We need a plan," she said under her breath. "Max and Fang would make a plan. Let's think."

"Why don't we ask Santa Claus?" Iggy sounded bitter. "Or the Easter Bunny?"

"I say we just bite 'em," Total said. "They open the doors, we're on 'em, snarling and fangs and everything. Or I could rush their legs, trip 'em, and then you guys attack them."

"We don't have fangs," Gazzy explained patiently, sounding tired and without hope.

"No, but we have teeth," said Nudge. "We should have been chewing off the tape all this time! Come on! Total will chew on mine, I'll try to get Gazzy's off, and Gazzy, you work on Iggy's. Then we'll kick some Flyboy butt!"

With a new bloom of hope, Nudge scooted across the dirty metal floor so that Total could reach her hands, in back of her.

She'd just felt his first whiskery approach when the metal doors slammed open again, and five Flyboys climbed in. They walked to the front of the truck, not caring if they kicked the bird kids on the way.

Nudge lay very still, her head resting on the floor. So much for her plan.

28

"Is he your boyfriend?" Ella had been incredibly happy to see me. We'd hugged for a long time, until I heard Fang sigh impatiently. Now we were in her room, where she was changing out of her soccer uniform into regular clothes, while Fang made lame, stilted conversation with Dr. Martinez in the living room.

Regular people's backs look so naked and . . . *flat* without wings. Just an observation.

"Fang? No! No, no," I said quickly. "No. I mean, we grew up together, so we're more like . . . uh, siblings."

"He's adorable," she said matter-of-factly, pulling on some jeans and a hoodie.

I was still processing this and my reaction to it when she looked over at me and smiled. "But not as cute as Shaw Akers, in my class."

I grinned back. Ella flopped next to me on the bed, and it was so normal, so like sisters or best friends or something, that my throat got tight.

"Shaw is seriously, amazingly adorable," Ella went on, her face softening. "He asked me to the Christmas dance, but someone else had already asked me, so I have to go with the first one. But there's always Spring Fling. . . ." She wiggled her eyebrows, and I laughed.

"Good luck with that." I had no Spring Fling in my date book. Mostly I had "kick Eraser butt," "destroy evil School," "save world," stuff like that.

A gentle tap on the door made us look up.

"Ready?" Ella's mom asked, opening the door.

"Ready as I'll ever be," I said.

29

Dr. Martinez drove us to her clinic. It was after hours, so she said we wouldn't be disturbed. She parked in the back, sort of behind the Dumpster, so her car wouldn't be noticed right away.

Inside the building, she didn't turn on the lights, and she locked the door behind us.

"We don't board animals, so there's no one on night duty here," she explained, leading us to the OR.

The operating table was meant for animals up to the size of, say, a large Saint Bernard, and my legs dangled off it. The metal was cold under my back, and the lights were way too bright. I closed my eyes.

Max, I forbid you to take out the chip. The Voice sounded uncharacteristically stern.

Yeah, forbid me, I thought tiredly. *That's always worked so well for everyone else.*

"First, I'm going to give you some Valium, just to help you relax," said Dr. Martinez, starting an IV in my nonchip arm. "I'm also going to take a chest X-ray and do some blood work, just to make sure you're not sick or anything."

Because of my less-than-socially-accepted bizarro child-hood at the hands of evil scientists, I have an overwhelming reaction to science lab–type smells, like alcohol, plastic tubing, floor cleaner, etc. When Dr. Martinez put the IV in, I had to grip the sides of the table to keep myself from leaping up and racing out of there, preferably punching a couple people first.

My heart was pounding, my breath coming shallower, and I could feel the white lightning of adrenaline starting to seep into my veins.

You know what? Turns out Valium just shuts that stuff right down!

"This is great," I said with cheerful grogginess. "I feel so . . . calm."

"You're okay, Max," said Ella, patting my shoulder.

"You still want to do this?" Fang asked. "Bark once for yes."

I stuck my tongue out at him. With any luck at all, whatever grotesque thing would probably replace the Erasers wouldn't be able to track us once the chip was out. And maybe the Voice would be gone forever too. I wasn't positive the chip was connected to the Voice, but it seemed likely. Even though the Voice had been kind of helpful sometimes, I still wanted everyone out of my head except me.

Which is such a pathetic sentence, one that probably not a lot of people need to say.

Then Dr. Martinez stretched out my chipped arm and fastened it to the table.

30

Instinctively I started to panic when Dr. Martinez strapped my arm down, and then the panic just melted away, la la la.

Someone took my other hand. *Fang.* I felt his calluses, his bones, his strength.

"I'm so glad you're here," I slurred, smiling dopily up at him. I took in his startled, worried expression but dismissed it. "I know everything's fine if you're here."

I thought I saw his cheeks flush, but I wasn't too sure of anything anymore. I felt a couple of needle pricks in my arm, and said mildly, "Hey."

"That's just a local anesthetic," explained Dr. Martinez. "I'll give it a minute to take effect."

"Oh, look, the lights are so pretty," I said dreamily, having just noticed them.

I smiled at the way the lights were dancing overhead, pink and yellow and blue. I felt some pressure on my arm and thought, *I should look over and see what's going on,* but then the thought was gone, sliding away like Jell-O off a hot car hood.

"Fang?"

"Yeah. I'm here."

I struggled to focus on him. "I'm so glad you're here."

"Yeah, I got that."

"I don't know what I'd do without you." I peered up at him, trying to see past the too-bright lights.

"You'd be fine," he muttered.

"No," I said, suddenly struck by how unfine I would be. "I would be totally unfine. *Totally*." It seemed very urgent that he understand this.

Again I felt some tugging on my arm, and I really wondered what that was about. Was Ella's mom going to start this procedure any time soon?

"It's okay. Just relax." He sounded stiff and nervous. "Just . . . relax. Don't try to talk."

"I don't want my chip anymore," I explained groggily, then frowned. "Actually, I *never* wanted that chip."

"Okay," said Fang. "We're taking it out."

"I just want you to hold my hand."

"I *am* holding your hand."

"Oh. I knew that." I drifted off for a few minutes, barely aware of anything, but feeling Fang's hand still in mine.

"Do you have a La-Z-Boy somewhere?" I roused myself to ask, every word an effort.

"Um, no," said Ella's voice, somewhere behind my head.

"I think I would like a La-Z-Boy," I mused, letting my eyes drift shut again. "Fang, don't go anywhere."

"I won't. I'm here."

"Okay. I need you here. Don't leave me."

"I won't."

"Fang, Fang, Fang," I murmured, overwhelmed with emotion. "I *love* you. I love you *sooo much.*" I tried to hold out my arms to show how much, but I couldn't move them.

"Oh, jeez," Fang said, sounding strangled.

"Okay, we're done," said Dr. Martinez finally. "The chip is out. I'm going to unfasten your arm, Max, and then I want you to wiggle your fingers."

"Okay." I wiggled the fingers that Fang was still holding.

"The other ones," he said.

"Okay." I wiggled those fingers.

"Go ahead and move them, Max," said Dr. Martinez.

"I am moving them," I said, moving them more.

"Oh," said Dr. Martinez. "Oh, no."

31

So there you have it, folks. The most *humiliating* admission I could possibly even *conceive* of, plus the loss of my left hand, all in one day. I mean, the hand was still there, but it was dangling limply. More decorative than anything else at this point.

Just like my pride.

Every time the hazy memory of my saying goofily, "I love you sooo much" popped into my head, I shuddered all over again. That one experience guaranteed that I will never, *ever* get hooked on Valium or anything like it.

Dr. Martinez was incredibly upset about my hand. She was in tears afterward and kept apologizing.

"Hey, I made you do it," I told her.

"You didn't make me. I shouldn't have tried it." She looked crushed.

"No matter what, I'm glad it's gone," I said. "I'm really glad it's gone."

The next day I was Voice-free and starting to learn to do everything with only my right hand. It was a total pain in the butt, but I was getting better. Again and again I tried to move the fingers on my left hand, and again and again I got not a twitch or a tingle. My arm ached, though.

Again and again I felt Fang's night sky eyes on me, to the point where I was about to climb the wall. When Dr. Martinez and Ella were outside for a moment, I cornered him.

"What I said yesterday didn't mean anything!" I hissed. "I love *everyone* in the flock! Plus, it was the Valium talking!"

An unbearable smug look came over his usually impassive face. "Uh-huh. You just keep telling yourself that. You looove me."

I took a swing at him, but he jumped back nimbly, and all I did was jar my left arm, making it hurt.

He laughed at me, then pointed at the woods outside the window. "Pick a tree. I'll go carve our initials in it."

Barely suppressing a shriek of rage, I flung myself down the hall and into the bathroom, slamming and locking the door behind me.

My superacute raptor hearing couldn't help registering his chuckles outside. Holding my head in my right hand, I muttered, "God help me."

Too late for that, Max, said the Voice. *Only you can help yourself now.*

Oh, no.

The Voice was not connected to the chip. It was still inside my head.

Which made today's total:

1) Useless left hand

2) Fang believing some mushy emotion I didn't even *mean*

3) Voice still with us

Given these revolting developments, there was only one thing to do. Leaving my bandaged left arm outside the shower curtain, I sat in the tub with the water pouring down on my head and cried.

32

"I don't think you should leave until your arm heals," said Dr. Martinez, looking worried. "I'm saying that as a doctor, Max."

"We've been gone too long as it is," I said. "Besides, with our zippy recombinant healing powers, I should be fine, in, oh, about twenty minutes."

She knew I was exaggerating, but she also knew me well enough to know that little things like healing up and common sense don't usually affect my decisions.

"I don't want you to go," said Ella miserably. "Either of you."

"I know," I said. "But we have to. We've got to get back to our, uh, situation."

"Max, is there anything we can do to help?" Ella's mom's eyes were filled with a deep emotion that unnerved me.

Saving the world didn't feel like something I could delegate.

"No, I don't think so," I said politely.

Behind me, Fang stood waiting, hating being in the

open in their yard. He'd been weird all morning, and I wasn't sure if it was about my wonky hand, what I'd said *by accident,* or what. Anyway, I knew he was itching to be off, and part of me was too.

Part of me wasn't.

There were hugs, of course. These people couldn't spit without having to hug someone. It felt unbalanced, being able to hug back with only my right arm — that is, my left arm could move up, but it was pretty dead below the elbow. Awkward.

I saw Dr. Martinez step toward Fang, her arms out, but a glance at his face made her stop, then smile warmly and hold her hand out for shaking. He took it, to my relief.

"I'm so glad I met you," she said to him, looking as if she were visibly restraining herself from hugging him. He stood stiffly, not saying anything.

"Take care of Max."

He nodded, and his mouth quirked on one side. He knew the idea that anyone needed to take care of me would get my knickers in a twist. I scowled. We would discuss this, for sure.

"Later," he said to Ella and Dr. Martinez in that gushy, hyperemotional, overdramatic way he had.

Then he ran across the yard, leaping into the air and unfurling his wings right before he hit the woods. I heard them gasp at the sight of his fourteen-foot wings lofting him effortlessly into the sky, so dark they looked almost purple in the sunlight.

I smiled one last time at Ella and her mother, feeling really sad, but not as sad as I had last time, despite my ruined arm. Now I felt like, *I found them again; I can always come back.*

And I really thought I might, when all of this was over. *If* it was ever over.

33

Flying again felt as wonderful and life-giving as flying again always did. Fang and I didn't speak for maybe forty minutes, streaking back toward where we'd left the flock. I was filled with apprehension and started to think through the almost-certainly-impossible idea of us all getting cell phones so we could keep in touch during times like this.

Finally it couldn't be avoided any longer.

"So what's with you?" I asked brusquely.

As if he'd been waiting, Fang rose and held his speed so he was almost right on top of me. While flying, it was the easiest way to hand something to someone else.

I held up my right hand, and he reached down, pressing a small white square of paper into my hand.

I looked at it as he shifted slightly so we were side-by-side again.

It was a photo, and I recognized it.

It was the picture of the baby Gasman that Fang and I had found in a deserted crack house, like, a million years ago. I'd left it in my pack, hidden back with the others in the canyon. "Why'd you bring this?" I asked Fang.

"I didn't." His voice was calm as always, but I saw rigid tension in his frame. "I found it."

"What?" That didn't make sense. "Found it where?"

"Between two books in Dr. Martinez's home office," he said, looking at me, registering my shock. "Between a book about recombinant-DNA theory . . . and one on birds."

34

Well. If sudden knowledge had a physical force, my head would have exploded right there, and chunks of my brain would have splattered some unsuspecting schmuck in a grocery store parking lot down below.

Let's just say I was stunned, and it takes a fair amount to stun me, I promise you.

My jaw dropped open as I stared at Fang's grim face, and only the certainty that I would start eating bugs any second made me shut it again.

I'm not the leader for nothing. I mean, I'm the oldest, but I'm the leader because I'm smart, strong, fast, and determined. I'm willing to *be* the leader. I'm the decision maker. And now, with typical leaderly incisiveness, I put two and six together and came up with one single question that would get right to the crucial heart of the matter.

"Whaaat?"

"I found the picture in Dr. Martinez's home office," Fang began again, but I waved at him to be quiet.

"You searched her office?" I had never thought to do that. Not the first time, not this time.

His face was impassive. "I needed a paper clip."

"She had books on combining DNA?"

"And birds."

"She's a *vet*."

"Fine, she's a vet. But avian anatomy, *plus* recombinant-DNA theory, *plus* the picture of the Gasman . . ."

"Oh, God, I can't think," I muttered, putting my hand to my head.

Everything's part of the big picture, Max, the Voice helpfully supplied. *All you have to do is put the pieces together.*

Fortune cookie crap like that didn't do a thing for me. I mean, I could have gotten that anywhere, *without* having a freaking *Voice* in my head.

"Oh, really?" I snarled. "I just have to put the pieces together? Excellent! Thanks for the great tip! Wish you'd told me earlier, you —"

I realized I was talking out loud and shut up.

I didn't know what to think. And Fang was the only one I could admit that to. Any of the other kids, and I would've made something up to cover the truth.

I shook my head. "I don't know what the deal is. I know she's helped me, not once but twice."

Fang didn't say anything, in that annoying way of his.

We were practically to the canyon where we'd left the flock. I searched the area but didn't see any telltale sign of smoke from their fire. Which meant they were being smart for once, lying low, they were . . .

Fang and I dropped down into the canyon, but we already knew. We knew from two hundred feet up. I didn't need to touch the burned-out ashes or look around for clues, though I did, of course.

It was all horribly, sickeningly clear: The flock hadn't been here in a couple of days. The scraped canyon floor showed they'd been taken by force.

While I'd been happily stuffing my face with homemade chocolate-chip cookies, my friends had been getting captured, with all that that implied.

I dropped my head into my hand, holding up my left arm uselessly.

"Crap."

Massive understatement.

35

When Nudge finally opened her eyes, the truck was moving. She couldn't remember the last several hours, so she figured she'd been asleep.

Squirming around, she saw Gazzy and Iggy lying with their eyes closed, maybe sleeping. Even Total seemed worn out, lying on his side, not even panting.

Angel was gone. Max and Fang had no idea where they were or what had happened. Iggy seemed to have given up.

The Gasman hadn't said it, but Nudge knew he was more scared than he'd admit. Dried tear tracks streaked his dirty cheeks, making him look younger and more helpless than she'd ever seen him.

By moving slightly, Nudge could see five Flyboys sitting near the front of the truck, their backs against the truck walls. From here they looked almost like regular Erasers, but there was something slightly different about them. Basically, they were metallic robots with a thin Eraser skin over their frames. Their fur wasn't as thick. And they never morphed into looking semihuman — they stayed in wolf form all the time.

Nudge closed her eyes again, weary and aching all over, too tired to think. They needed a plan. Everything just seemed so overwhelming and scary.

The truck shuddered to a halt, the screech of the brakes hurting Nudge's ears. Then the ride grew very choppy, as if they had veered off the road and were rolling on dirt now. *Ow, ow, ow,* Nudge thought, biting her lip to keep from crying out. Gazzy and Iggy groggily opened their eyes, and Total stirred.

"I hope this is a potty break," he muttered.

There was shouting outside. The three bird kids struggled to sit up, their hands still duct-taped behind them.

The two back doors of the truck were thrown open with heavy, brain-rattling bangs. Sunlight flooding in made them blink and turn their heads away. The Flyboys in the truck with them strode to the opening.

There was more shouting, raised voices from the front of the truck. Nudge saw nothing outside except a long, empty dirt road with low brush lining it. No buildings, no electricity wires. No one around to help them. Nowhere to run to. Their wings had been bound flat against their backs.

"What's happening?" Iggy's whisper was barely audible, but a Flyboy kicked him.

"Shut up!" it growled, sounding like a recorded phone message.

Nudge heard many feet walking quickly toward the back of the truck. She braced for whatever was going to happen next.

Which no one ever could have predicted in a million years.

An overwhelming clump of Flyboys surrounded the back of the truck, furry faces frozen into identical sneers. Nudge swallowed, pretending to be braver than she was.

The crowd shifted restlessly, and Nudge saw that it was parting to let someone through. *Max?* Her heart jumped at the possibility. Even Max trussed up, in bad shape, thrown into the truck with them, would be fabulous, such a welcome —

It was Jeb!

Nudge felt a twinge around her heart as she looked at the face that had formed so much of her childhood. Jeb had rescued them. Then he'd died — or they'd thought he was dead. Then he had shown up again, clearly one of Them. Nudge knew that Max hated him now. So Nudge hated him too.

Her eyes narrowed.

From behind Jeb an Eraser, a real Eraser, stepped out to stand next to him. It was Ari! Ari, who had also been dead and then not really. Ari was the only real Eraser they'd seen in days and days.

Nudge put a bored expression on her face like she'd seen Max and Fang do a thousand times. *Yeah, yeah, Jeb and Ari,* she thought. *Show me something new.*

Someone else stepped out from behind Ari.

Nudge's eyes widened, and her breath seized in her throat. Her mouth opened, but no sound came out.

Instead her lips silently formed one word: *Angel.*

Nudge searched Angel's blue eyes, but they seemed like a total stranger's. Nudge had never seen her like this.

"Angel!" Gazzy's face looked happy but at the same time concerned.

"Angel?" Nudge finally spoke, fear trickling like ice water down her neck.

"Time to die," Angel said in her sweet little-girl voice.

36

"This is too easy," Fang muttered, frowning at the ground two thousand feet below us.

"I was thinking the same thing. They did everything except leave gigundo yellow arrows saying *This way, folks!*"

We'd flown in a mammoth circle and had picked up tire tracks within an hour. It looked like a big truck, lots of wheels, and it had left desert sand on the highway for almost half a mile. We couldn't think of any other reason a truck would have been hidden off-road and then driven out. Unless it belonged to, like, cactus poachers. Sand collectors. A movie crew.

This being the middle of Freaking Nowhere, USA, there was only the one road for miles and miles. So, one road with clear tire marks headed in one direction. Gee, obvious much?

"And we're falling for this because of our sudden, unexpected regression into unbelievable stupidity?" I said.

Fang nodded grimly. "We're falling for it because we've got no other choice."

"Oh, yeah. *That.*"

Three hours of fast flight later, we saw them: an eighteen-wheeled semi parked off the road in perhaps the most desolate, unpopulated spot in all of Arizona. You could not call 911 from here. You could not run for help. You could send off a flare every half hour for days and not be seen by *anyone*.

"Looks like the place," I said, sighing. "And look at that crowd down there. I thought all the Erasers were exterminated."

"So the Voice lied to you?"

"No," I said slowly, as we coasted on a current. "It's never actually *lied* to me. So if those things aren't Erasers, then they're the Erasers' replacements. Oh, joy."

"Yep." Fang shook his head, so *not* into this. "Five bucks says they're worse than the originals. And they probably have guns."

"No doubt."

"And of course they're expecting us."

"We did everything but RSVP."

"I hate this." Fang deliberately looked everywhere but at my useless left hand.

"That would be because you've still got a tenuous grasp of sanity."

I circled wide, trying to gear myself up for an impossible fight: We would be outnumbered a couple hundred to two, by something worse than Erasers. I had no idea if the rest of the flock would be able to help.

It was pretty much a suicide mission.

Again.

"There is one bright side to this," said Fang.

"Yeah? What's that?" The new and improved Erasers would mutilate us before they killed us?

He grinned at me so unexpectedly I forgot to flap for a second and dropped several feet. "You looove me," he crooned smugly. Holding his arms out wide, he added, "You love me *this much*."

My shriek of appalled rage could probably be heard in California, or maybe Hawaii. Certainly by the unknown army down below. I didn't care. I folded my wings against my sides and aimed downward to get away from Fang as fast as possible. Now that he had filled me with a blind, teeming bloodlust, I was ready to take out a couple thousand Eraser replacements, no matter what they were.

Which, I admitted to myself, may have been his point.

Amazingly, we were able to thump to quick-running landings on the roof of the semi without getting punched full of little unaerodynamic bullet holes.

Heads swiveled to look at us, Erasery heads, but there was something different about them. I couldn't quite put my finger on what.

"Iggy?" I yelled.

"Max!" I heard his strangled cry from the rear of the truck and trotted over.

"You guys ok —," I began, then I saw Jeb, Ari, and Angel standing on the ground. "Angel!" I cried. "Are you okay? I'm gonna take these guys apa —"

The look in Angel's polar-ice eyes stopped me.

"I *told* you I should be the leader, Max," she said with a chilling flatness. "Now it's your time to die. The last life-forms from the labs are being exterminated, and you will be too." She turned to Jeb. "Right?"

Jeb nodded solemnly, and then my world went blank in the wink of an eye.

PART 2

SCHOOL'S IN — FOREVER

37

My head was feeling as if had been used as a bowling ball, against solid marble pins.

My heart pounded, my breaths were ragged and shallow, and every muscle I had ached. I didn't know what was going on, but it was bad.

I opened my eyes.

The word *bad* was so grossly inadequate to describe the situation that it was like it was from another language — a language of naive idiots.

I was strapped to a metal hospital bed, wrists and ankles bound with thick Velcro.

And I wasn't alone.

With effort, I raised my head, fighting off the swift wave of nausea that made me gag and swallow convulsively.

To my left, also strapped to a metal bed, the Gasman breathed unevenly, twitching in his sleep.

Next to him, Nudge was starting to move, moaning slightly.

Turning to the right, I saw Iggy. He was lying very still, eyes open, staring up at a ceiling he couldn't see.

On his other side, Fang was straining silently against his Velcro restraints, his face pale and grimly determined. When he felt me looking at him, I saw relief soften his gaze for a split second.

"You okay?" I mouthed.

He gave a short, quick nod, then inclined his head to gesture to the others. I nodded wearily, summing up our situation with a universal "this is crap" expression. He tilted his head at a bed across from us. There was Total, looking dead except for the occasional muscle jerk, his small limbs bound like ours. He looked mangy, missing patches of fur around his mouth.

Moving my head carefully so I wouldn't hurl, I examined our surroundings. We were in a plain white room, which was windowless. I thought I saw a door beyond Nudge's bed, but I couldn't be sure.

Iggy, Fang, me, Gazzy, Nudge, Total.

Angel wasn't here.

I drew in a breath, readying myself to struggle against the straps, and it was then that it hit me: the smell. That chemical, antiseptic smell of alcohol, floor cleaner, plastic tubing. The smell that had filled my nose every day for the first ten years of my life.

Horrified, I stared at Fang. He gave me a questioning look.

Wishing desperately that I was wrong but with the terrified, sinking knowledge that I wasn't, I mouthed the answer: "The School."

Fang's eyes flared in recognition, and that was the only confirmation that I needed of this nightmare.

We were back at the School.

38

The School — the awful, terrifying place we had spent the past four years trying to get over, get away from. At the School, we'd been experimented on, tested, retested, trained. Because of this place, I would never be able to deal with people in long white coats and could never major in chemistry. Because of this place, when I saw a dog crate at a PetSmart, I broke into cold chills.

"Max?" Gazzy's voice sounded dusty and dry.

"Hey, sweetie," I said as quietly as I could.

"Where are we? What's going on?"

I didn't want to tell him, but while I was trying to come up with a convincing lie, the reality broke into his brain, and he stared at me, appalled. I saw him silently say, "The School," and I had no choice but to nod. His head flopped back against his bed, and I saw that his once fluffy blond hair was a dusty, matted gray.

"Hey!" Total said with weak indignation. "I demand a lawyer." But his characteristic belligerence was betrayed by the sad pain in his voice.

"Do we have a Plan B? Or C? Even Z?" Iggy's voice had

no life in it, no energy, and I got the impression that he'd given up and was only going through the motions.

I cleared my throat and swallowed. "Yes, of course," I said, scrabbling for any shred of authority I could muster. "There's always a plan. First, we get out of these straps."

I felt Nudge awaken and looked over at her. Her large brown eyes were solemn, her mouth stiffly trying not to quiver. A purplish bruise mottled her cheek, and I saw more on her arms. I'd always thought of her as a little kid, like Gazzy and Angel, but all of a sudden she seemed ten years older.

Because she *knew,* and it showed in her eyes.

She knew we were way, way up a creek, and that I had no plan, and that we had no hope.

Which pretty much summed it up.

39

I don't know how much later — after my arms had gone numb but before my ankles started burning with pins and needles — the door opened.

A little gray-haired woman in a white coat walked in, carrying a tray. Somebody's evil grandma.

A new scent filled the air.

I tried not to breathe it in, but it was unavoidable.

The woman walked right up to me, a smile on her pleasant face.

Get it together, Max. That was me talking. I hadn't heard the Voice since the melee in the desert.

I tried to look as unconcerned as a fourteen-year-old bird kid strapped to a hospital bed *in hell* could look.

"This is a first," I said coolly. "Torture by chocolate-chip cookie. Was this all your idea?"

The woman looked disconcerted but tried to smooth out her expression.

"We thought you might be hungry," she said. "These are hot out of the oven."

She waved the tray a bit, to make sure the incredible vanilla-tinged aroma of fresh-baked cookies reached all of us.

"Uh-huh," I said. "Because all you mad, evil scientists sit around whipping up batches of Pillsbury's finest during your coffee breaks. I mean, this is pathetic."

She looked surprised, and I felt anger warming my blood.

"I mean, points for the jail cell," I went on, motioning at the room with my head. "Kudos for the Velcro straps. Those were good starts. But you're sort of falling down with the chocolate-chip cookies. Like, did you skip school the day they taught hostage treatment?"

Pink patches flared on her cheeks, and she stepped back.

"Keep your lousy cookies," I said, narrowing my eyes and letting a snarl enter my voice. "Whatever you sick freaks have planned for us, get on with it. 'Cause otherwise you're just wasting our time."

Now her face was stiff as a mask, and she started to head to the door.

This is a plan, I thought. When they came in to get us for whatever, that would be our chance. And we would seize it.

She was almost to the door when Total raised his head weakly. "Not so fast," he croaked. "I'll take a cookie. I'm not proud."

Fang and I exchanged looks, and we rolled our eyes.

The woman looked startled when Total spoke and didn't know what to make of his request. So she just hurried out the door, and when it slammed behind her, I felt it in my bones.

40

"Okay, the second they undo us, make sure all heck breaks loose," I said when everyone was awake the next morning — at least I figured it was morning, since someone had turned the lights on again.

The flock nodded, but with none of the angry thirst for revenge they would need to escape.

"Look, we've had our backs against the wall before," I reminded them. "These guys always screw up, always make a mistake. We've gotten the best of them every time, and it'll be the same here."

No reaction whatsoever.

"Come on, guys, buck up," I coaxed. "Let's see some insane rage put apples in those cheeks."

Nudge smiled faintly, but the others seemed lost in their own worlds, tugging without purpose against their straps. Fang sent me an understanding look, and I felt so frustrated and stuck that I wanted to howl.

The door opened with a *whoosh,* and I quickly met everyone's eyes: This was it!

It was Jeb. Followed by Anne Walker, whom we hadn't

seen since we ditched her Martha Stewart farmhouse in Virginia. And the unholy trio was completed by a golden-curled little girl: Angel, who was eating a chocolate-chip cookie and calmly watching me with her big blue eyes.

"Angel!" Gazzy's voice broke as he understood that his sister had turned against us. "Angel, how could you?"

"Hello, Max," said Anne Walker, not smiling, not looking at all adoptive mom–like.

I sighed heavily and stared at the ceiling. *No crying. Not one tear.*

Jeb came and stood right next to my bed, so close I could smell his aftershave. Its scent awoke a slew of childhood memories, the years between ten and twelve years old, when I'd felt the happiest I ever had.

"Hello, Max," he said quietly, searching my face. "How do you feel?"

Which was a ten on the "imbecilic question" scale of one to ten.

"Why, I feel fine, Jeb," I said brightly. "How about you?"

"Any nausea? Headache?"

"Yep. And it's standing here talking to me."

His fingers brushed the covers on top of my leg, and I tried not to shudder.

"Does it feel like you've been through a lot?" he asked.

I stared at him. "Yeah. *Kind of.* And sadly, I'm still going through it."

Jeb turned and nodded at Anne Walker, and she made a noncommittal face back at him.

I started to pick up that something was happening here that I didn't fully understand.

Good thing I'm used to that feeling.

"Max, I've got something to tell you that I know is going to be hard to believe," Jeb said.

"You're not evil? You're not the worst lying, cheating, betraying jerk I've ever met?"

He smiled sadly. "The truth is, Max, that nothing is as it seems."

"Uh-huh," I said. "Is that what the aliens told you when you quit wearing your foil hat?"

Anne stepped forward. Jeb made a motion like, Let me do it, but she waved her hand at him. "The truth is, Max, that you're at the School."

"No freaking duh. And uh, wait — let me guess — I'm some kind of bird-kid *hybrid*. And you captured me. And, and, I'm strapped to a *hospital* bed. I bet I even have *wings*. Am I right?"

"No. You don't understand," she went on briskly. "You're at the School, Max, because *you never left it*. Everything that you think you've experienced for the past five months has all been a dream."

41

I gazed at Anne in admiration. "Gosh," I said. "This is a totally new tack. I truly did not expect that." Looking around at the flock, I asked, "Did anyone expect that?" They warily shook their heads no.

I nodded at Anne. "You've got me. Good one."

"It's true," she said. "You know you're an experimental form of recombinant DNA. You know that you've undergone testing during your limited life span. Part of the experiment has been to test your brains' imaginative capabilities, as well as how accurately we can manipulate and even create your memories. There are various experimental drugs that we've been authorized to use, drugs that allow us to, in essence, give you life memories that you never truly experienced."

Why was she doing this? Why go to so much trouble to spin this story?

"Does it really feel like you lived in Colorado with Jeb? That Angel was kidnapped? That you got her back? That you went to New York? That you killed Ari? That you lived with me in Virginia?" Her eyebrows rose.

Narrowing my eyes, I stayed silent. I was aware that the rest of the flock was paying intense attention to her every word.

"Max, we gave you those memories. We monitored your heart and lung rates while you imagined yourself in violent fights. *We* decided on New York, on Florida, on Arizona. Remember Dr. Martinez and Ella? Those constructs allowed us to test your psychological and physical responses to a warm, nurturing environment."

My blood turned to icy slush in my veins. They knew about Ella and Dr. Martinez. How? Had they harmed them? Killed them?

I fought to keep my face impassive, to slow my panicked breathing. I couldn't let them see that they were getting to me. This was the worst yet.

"What was the memory of living with you supposed to test?" I snapped. "How I would react to a two-faced control freak who didn't have a maternal bone in her body?"

Two red splotches appeared on Anne's cheeks. Score one for Max.

"You still don't believe us, sweetheart," said Jeb.

"Yeah. 'Cause I'm not a *lunatic*." My voice sounded a little choked.

Jeb gently took my left wrist. Instinctively I tried to pull away from him, but I couldn't. He carefully turned my hand inside the Velcro strap, so the underside of my arm was facing up.

"Look, Max," he said very softly. "I'm telling you, none

of it has been real. It was all a dream. You never left the School."

Remember that puckered red scar on my arm, from when I tried to cut the chip out myself? And then the surgery, just a few days ago? It had left clean, straight little lines, maybe half an inch long.

Jeb pushed back my sleeve so I could see farther up my arm.

There were no scars there. Not anywhere. My arm was smooth and unmarked. I tried to wiggle my fingers. They moved. There was nothing wrong with my left hand.

Next to me, Gazzy sucked in an astonished breath.

I tried not to breathe at all, tried not to swallow, tried to conceal my shock. Then something occurred to me: We'd gotten Total in New York. "What about Total?" I demanded triumphantly. "Was he a dream too?"

Jeb looked at me gently. "Yes, sweetheart. He was a dream too. There is no Total the talking dog."

He stepped aside so we could all see the bed across from us. It was empty. The sheets were smooth and taut and white. Total had never been there, had he?

42

Okay, color me *way* freaked. Either they were seriously messing with my mind or they were . . . even more seriously messing with my mind.

Very quickly, I ran through possible scenarios in my head:

1) They were lying (of course).

    a) Lying about us all having been in the School this whole time.

    b) *Not* lying about us all having been in the School this whole time.

2) This, even now, *this second,* was just another hallucination.

3) Everything up till now had in fact been drug-induced nightmares and dreams (an anorexically thin possibility).

4) Whether they were lying or no, whether this was a dream or no, I should just break loose, kick their sorry butts, and be done with it.

I lay back against my thin pillow. I glanced around at the flock. I had seen them age, seen them get taller, seen their hair grow. How could we have been tied up for years? Or had we been this big to begin with, been created this age?

I looked at Angel, wishing she would send me a reassuring thought. But nothing came from her at all. Oh, God.

I couldn't think anymore. I was hungry and in pain and trying to keep a steel lid on my rising panic. I closed my eyes and tried to take some steady breaths.

"How do you get some chow in this joint?" I finally asked.

"We'll get you something right now," Jeb said.

"Like, a last meal," said Angel in her little-girl voice.

My eyes opened.

"I'm sorry, Max," said Anne Walker. "But as you've probably figured out, we're shutting down all of our recombinant-DNA experiments. All of the lupine-human blends have been retired, and it's time to retire you too."

Which confirmed that we hadn't seen any real Erasers lately. Gazzy had explained about the Flyboy robot things.

"Retire as in kill?" I asked flatly. "Is that how you live with yourselves? By using euphemisms for death and murder?" I pretended to quote a newscast: "In today's news, seven people were 'retired' in a horrific accident on Highway Seventeen." I changed voices. "Jimmy, don't retire that bird with your shotgun." Then, "Please, sir, don't retire me! You can have my wallet!"

I gazed at Jeb and Anne, feeling cold rage turn my face

into a mask. "How's that working out for you? Able to look at yourselves in a mirror? Able to sleep at night?"

"We'll get you something to eat," Anne said, and she walked quickly out of the room.

"Max —," Jeb began.

"Don't you even talk to me!" I spat. "Take your little traitor with you and get out of our *death chamber!*"

Angel's expression didn't change as she looked from me to Jeb. Jeb took her hand and sighed, and they both left the room. I was shaking with emotion and in a last surge, strained against the Velcro straps with all my superhuman strength.

Nothing.

I flopped back against the bed, tears forming in my eyes, hating to have the flock see me like this. I wiggled my left fingers and looked for the scars. Nothing.

"So, that went well," said Fang.

43

Okay, here's a knotty little question: If you're dreaming that you're tied up by mad scientists in a secret experimental facility, and then you fall asleep and start dreaming, are you really dreaming?

Which one is the dream?

Which one counts?

How can you tell?

I'd been torturing myself with these pointless circular conundrums all day. Which raises another question: If I'm torturing my own brain by trying to figure stuff out, does that still count as Them torturing me? Because they caused the whole situation to happen?

At any rate, at some point I must have "fallen asleep," because at some point, a hand shaking my shoulder made me streak back to "consciousness."

As always, I leaped into wakefulness on full alert, automatically trying to assume a battle position. Pretty much impossible when you're all strapped down.

I see perfectly in the dark, and it took only a split second to register the familiar hulking bad news leaning over my bed.

"Ari!" I whispered almost silently.

"Hi, Max," Ari said, and for the first time in a long time, he didn't look that mental. I mean, every time I'd seen this poor screwup in the last couple months, he'd looked more and more as if he were standing on the edge of insanity with one foot on a banana peel.

But now he looked — well, not anything close to normal, but at least all the frothing at the mouth had stopped.

I waited for the first volley of venom.

But Ari had no snide remarks, no taunts, no threats. Instead he undid one of my arms, then pulled it down and strapped it to the arm of a wheelchair.

Hmm. Could I still fly if I was strapped into a wheelchair? I thought maybe I could. I guessed we would find out. In fact, if I could get some serious speed going on this thing, it might lend a significant boost to an exciting takeoff.

I sat down in the chair, and Ari strapped my ankle to the post by the front wheel. Just as I was tensing to make a break, he whispered, "They made this chair with lead bars. It weighs about a hundred an' seventy-five pounds."

Crap. Even though I was really tall for my age, I weighed barely a hundred pounds because of all the avian modifications to my bones and stuff. And the fact that I could almost never get enough food. So even though I was really, really strong, there was no way I could get a wheel-chair that heavy off the ground.

I looked at Ari with loathing. "What now, big guy? You taking me to your leader?"

He didn't rise to the bait. "Just thought I'd show you around a bit, that's all, Max."

44

"Gosh, a guided tour, from you? Now I *know* I'm dreaming," I quipped. But then a thought occurred to me. "They told me all the Erasers had been retired. And if I wasn't strapped down, I'd make air quotes around *retired*."

Ari looked sad. "Yeah. I'm the last one. They . . . killed all the others."

For some reason his quiet, sad confirmation of that terrible fact made my blood run cold. Despite what a walking chigger bite he was, there were still times when I could almost see the little kid he'd once been. They'd altered him when he was already three years old, and his results had been less than stellar, poor guy.

Oh, yeah, poor guy who tried to kill me a bunch of times. My eyes narrowed.

"The flock is supposed to be wiped out too," I said. "Am I the first to go? Is that why you came to get me?"

He shook his head. "I just have permission to take you around. I know you guys are supposed to be retired, but I don't know when."

I got an idea. "Listen, Ari," I said, trying for a cajoling

tone. Since snarling or threatening comes much more naturally to me, I wasn't sure how successful I was. "Maybe all of us should bust out of here together. I don't know what Jeb's told you, but you might be on the endangered list too."

I was about to go on, but he interrupted me.

"I know I am," he said, still very quietly. He pushed the wheelchair through the doorway, and we were in a long hall lit by fluorescent lights and tiled with the ever-popular linoleum squares. Suddenly he knelt down and pulled his shirt collar away from his neck.

I recoiled, but he said, "Look — I have an expiration date. We all do."

Totally grossed out but morbidly curious, I leaned forward. On the back of Ari's neck was a tattoolike line of numbers. It was a date. The year was this year, and I thought the month was this month, but I wasn't sure. Funny how time drags when you're being held captive.

I thought, *Eew.* Then, *Poor Ari.* Then, *This might be another trick, another way for them to yank my chain.*

"What do you mean, we all do?" I asked suspiciously.

His eyes, looking like the familiar kid-Ari eyes, met mine. "All of us experiments have built-in expiration dates. When someone's time is pretty close, it shows up on the back of their neck. Mine showed up a couple days ago. So my time is soon."

I looked at him, appalled. "So what happens on that date?"

He shrugged and stood to start wheeling me forward again. "I'll die. They would have exterminated me with the others, but my time is really close anyway. So they cut me a break. Because, you know, I'm Jeb's son."

His voice cracked as he said that, and I stared straight ahead down the hall.

This was a new low, even for mad scientists.

45

I don't know if you guys ever tour top-secret evil science labs, like for school field trips or something. But I got a tour that day, and if I had had to write a school paper about it, my title would have been, "Scarier and Far Worse Than You Could Possibly Imagine (even if you have a totally twisted imagination)."

I mean, we'd grown up here. (I thought.) Plus, we'd seen some horrific stuff at the Institute in New York. (I thought.) So it's not like devastating freaks of nature were new to me. But Ari brought me down halls and up and down in elevators, and we explored parts of the School I'd never seen, never knew existed. And let me tell you, the flock and I looked like Disneyland cast members compared with some of the things I saw.

They weren't all recombinant life-forms. Some were "enhanced" but not combined with another species.

I saw a human baby who wasn't even walking yet, sitting on the floor, chewing on a plastic frog while a whitecoat wrote a long, complicated, unintelligible mathematical problem on a wall-sized whiteboard.

Another whitecoat asked, "How long did this take Feynman to solve?"

The first whitecoat said, "Four months."

The baby put down the frog and crawled over to the whiteboard. A whitecoat handed her a marker. The baby wrote a complicated, unintelligible answer on the whiteboard, something with a lot of Greek squiggles in it.

Then the baby sat back, looked at the whiteboard, and started to gum the end of the marker. The other whitecoat checked the answer. He looked up and nodded.

The first whitecoat said, "Good girl," and gave the baby a cookie.

In another room I saw, like, Plexiglas boxes with some sort of grotesque tissue growing in them. Brainlike tissue floating in different-colored liquids. Wires were coming out of the boxes, connected to a computer. A whitecoat was typing commands into the computer, and the brain things were apparently carrying them out.

I looked at Ari. "Have brain, will travel."

"I think they were seeing if people would still need bodies or something," he said.

I saw a room full of the Eraser replacements, those Flyboy things. They were hung in rows on metal hooks, like raggedy coats in a closet.

Their glowy red eyes were closed, and I saw that each one had a wire plugged into its leg. Thin, hairy Eraser skin was stretched taut over their metal frames, and in some places it had torn, allowing a joint to poke through or a couple of gears and pulleys to show. The whole effect was pretty repulsive.

"They're charging," said Ari tonelessly.

I was starting to feel overwhelmed, even more overwhelmed than usual.

"They call this one Brain on a Stick," Ari said, gesturing.

I saw a metallic spinal cord, connected to two metal legs, walking around. It walked smoothly, fluidly, like a person. At the top of the spinal cord was a Plexiglas box holding — no, not a hamster — a brainlike clump of tissue.

It walked past us, and I heard sounds coming from it, as if it were talking to itself.

In the next room we saw a little all-human kid, about two years old, who had weirdly bulked-up, developed muscles, like a tiny bodybuilder. He was bench-pressing more than two hundred pounds — weights much bigger than he was, probably eight times his body weight or more.

I couldn't take any more of this. "So what happens now, Ari?"

"I'll take you back," said Ari.

We didn't speak as he navigated the halls and levels of this village of nightmares. I wondered, if his expiration date was real, how it must feel for him to know that the end of his life was coming soon, minute by minute, second by second. The flock and I had faced death a thousand times, but it had always had an element of "maybe we can slide out of this."

To have a date tattooed on your neck — it was like looking up and seeing a train's headlights coming right at you, and your feet just can't move off the track. I was going to check the backs of our necks as soon as I could.

"Max, I —" Ari stopped, pausing outside the door to the flock's ward.

I waited.

"I wish —," he said, his voice breaking.

I didn't know what he'd been about to say, but I didn't need to know. I patted his hand, perpetually morphed out into a heavy, hairy, Eraser-clawed mitt.

"We all wish, Ari."

46

The next day they let us loose.

"Is it time for us to die?" Nudge asked. She sidled closer to me, and I put my arm around her.

"I don't know, sweetie," I told her. "But if it is, I'm taking a bunch of 'em with me."

"Me too," said Gazzy bravely. I gathered the Gasman to my other side.

Fang leaned against a wall, his eyes on me. We hadn't had any time to talk privately since we'd gotten here, but I caught his gaze and tried to send him a look that had everything I was thinking in it. He was a big boy. He could handle the swear words.

The room's door swung open, with its peculiar air rush. A tall, sandy-haired man strode in as if he were the king of the world. He was followed by Anne Walker and another whitecoat I hadn't seen before.

"Dese are dey?" he asked, sounding like Ahnold in *The Terminator*.

Already he had me angry. "We be them," I said snarkily, and his pale, watery blue eyes focused on me like lasers.

"Dis vould be de vun called Max?" he asked his assistant, as if I couldn't hear.

"I not only *would* be Max, I *am* Max," I said, interrupting the assistant's answer. "In fact, I've always been Max and always will be."

His eyes narrowed. Mine narrowed back at him.

"Yes, I can see vhy dey've been slated for extermination," he said casually, as his assistant made notes on a clipboard.

"And I can see why you were voted 'least popular' in your class," I said. "So I guess we're even."

He ignored me, but I saw a tiny muscle in his jaw twitch.

Next, his eyes lit on Nudge. "Dis vun can't control her mouth or, obviously, her brain," he said. "Something vent wrong vis her thought processes, clearly."

I felt Nudge stiffen at my side. "Bite me," she said.

That's my girl.

"Und dis vun," he went on, pointing at Gazzy. "His digestive system has disastrous flaws." He shook his head. "Perhaps an enzyme imbalance."

Anne Walker listened expressionlessly.

"Dis vun — vell, you can see it for yourself," the man said, with a casual flick of his hand at Iggy. "Multiple defects. A complete failure."

"Yes, Dr. ter Borcht," murmured his assistant, writing furiously.

Fang and I instantly looked at each other. Ter Borcht

had been mentioned in the files we'd stolen from the Institute.

Iggy, sensing ter Borcht was talking about him, scowled. "Takes one to know one," he said.

"De tall, dark vun — dere's nothing special about him at all," ter Borcht said dismissively of Fang, who hadn't moved since the doctor had come in.

"Well, he's a snappy dresser," I offered. One side of Fang's mouth quirked.

"Und you," ter Borcht said, turning back to me. "You haf a malfunctioning chip, you get debilitating headaches, and your leadership skills are sadly much less than ve had hoped for."

"And yet I could still kick your doughy Eurotrash butt from here to next Tuesday. So that's something."

His eyelids flickered, and it seemed to me that he was controlling himself with difficulty.

Well, I get under people's skins. It's a gift I have, what can I say?

47

Ter Borcht looked at his assistant. "Let's get on vis de questioning," he said abruptly. Turning to me, he said, "Ve need to gather some final data. Den you vill be exterminated."

"Ooh," I said. "If I had boots on, I'd be quaking in them." I tapped my bare toes against the floor.

I saw a quick flare of anger in his eyes.

"No, really," I said, mucho sincerely. "Totally quaking, I promise. You're really a very scary man."

"First *you*," he barked suddenly at Gazzy, and Gazzy couldn't help jumping a tiny bit. I looked at him reassuringly and winked, and his narrow shoulders straightened.

"Vhat ozzer abilities do you haf?" ter Borcht snapped, while his assistant waited, pen in hand.

Gazzy thought. "I have X-ray vision," he said. He peered at ter Borcht's chest, then blinked and looked alarmed.

Ter Borcht was startled for a second, but then he frowned. "Don't write dat down," he told his assistant in irritation. The assistant froze in midsentence.

Glaring at the Gasman, ter Borcht said, "Your time is

coming to an end, you pathetic failure of an experiment. Vhat you say now is how you vill be remembered."

Gazzy's blue eyes flashed. "Then you can remember me telling you to kiss my —"

"Enough!" ter Borcht said. He turned suddenly to Nudge. "You. Do you haf any qualities dat distinguish you in any way?"

Nudge chewed on a fingernail. "You mean, like, besides the *wings?*" She shook her shoulders gently, and her beautiful fawn-colored wings unfolded a bit.

His face flushed, and I felt like cheering. "Yes," he said stiffly. "Besides de vings."

"Hmm. Besides de vings." Nudge tapped one finger against her chin. "Um . . ." Her face brightened. "I once ate nine Snickers bars in one sitting. Without barfing. That was a record!"

"Hardly a special talent," ter Borcht said witheringly.

Nudge was offended. "Yeah? Let's see *you* do it."

"I vill now eat nine Snickers bars," Gazzy said in a perfect, creepy imitation of ter Borcht's voice, "visout bahfing."

Ter Borcht wheeled on him as I smothered a giggle. It wasn't funny when Gazzy did a pitch-perfect imitation of me, but it was hilarious when he did it to other people.

"Mimicry," ter Borcht said to his assistant. "Write dat down."

Walking over to Iggy, he poked him with his shoe. "Does anysing on you vork properly?"

Iggy rubbed his forehead with one hand. "Well, I have a highly developed sense of irony."

Ter Borcht tsked. "You are a liability to your group. I assume you alvays hold on to someone's shirt, yes? Following dem closely?"

"Only when I'm trying to steal their dessert," Iggy said truthfully.

"Write that down," I told the assistant. "He's a notorious dessert stealer."

Ter Borcht moved over to Fang and stood examining him as if he were a zoo exhibit. Fang looked back at him, and probably only I could see his tension, the fury roiling inside him.

"You don't speak much, do you?" ter Borcht said, circling him slowly.

Fittingly, Fang said nothing.

"Vhy do you let a girl be de leader?" ter Borcht asked, a calculating look in his eye.

"She's the tough one," Fang said.

Dang right, I thought proudly.

"Is dere anysing special about you?" asked ter Borcht. "Anysing vorth saving?"

Fang pretended to think, gazing up at the ceiling. "Besides my fashion sense? I play a mean harmonica."

Ter Borcht locked his gaze on me. "Vhy haf you trained dem to act stupid dis vay?"

They weren't stupid. They were survivors.

"Why do you still let your mother dress you?" I countered snidely.

The assistant busily started writing that down but froze at a look from ter Borcht.

The scientist stepped closer to me, looking down menacingly. "I created you," he said softly. "As de saying goes, I brought you into dis world, and I vill take you out of it."

"I vill now destroy de Snickuhs bahrs!" Gazzy barked. Then the five of us were laughing — literally in the face of death.

48

"Oops," I said once we were alone again. "Guess they forgot to program us with any respect for authority."

"Those idiots," Gazzy said, scuffing his foot against the floor.

We were feeling victorious, but it was still clear: We were captive, and right now they held all the tarot cards.

"I miss Total," said Nudge.

I sighed. "If he ever existed."

"We didn't imagine the hawks . . . or the bats," Nudge said.

"Yeah," said Iggy. "We didn't imagine those creepy subway tunnels in New York."

"Or the headhunter, at that school," said Gazzy.

"I know. I'm sure we didn't," I said, though actually I wasn't, not a hundred percent, anyway.

Ari came and got me again that afternoon. This time I was actually allowed to walk. Wee-hah!

"I don't trust him. Keep your eyes open," Fang murmured as I was leaving.

"Ya think?" I whispered back.

"So what's this all about, Ari?" I asked, as we passed some whitecoats who looked at us strangely. "How come we're taking these little tours?"

Now that I wasn't strapped to a lead wheelchair, I was memorizing every hall, every doorway, every window.

He looked uncomfortable and still subdued. For a wolverine, anyway. "I'm not sure," he muttered. "They just said walk her around."

"Ah," I said. "So we can assume there's something they want me to see. Besides the brain on a stick and the super-babies."

Ari shrugged. "I don't know. They don't tell me anything."

Just then we passed wide double doors, and one of them swung open as we went by. A whitecoat hurried from the room beyond, but not before I'd caught a glimpse inside.

On a large video screen that took up a whole wall, I saw a map of the world. My raptor vision took in a thousand details in a second, which I digested as Ari and I walked. Each country was outlined, and one city in each country was highlighted.

Above the map was a title card, THE BY-HALF PLAN. I'd heard of that somewhere before.

On an off chance that it would actually get me somewhere, I asked Ari, "So, what's the By-Half Plan?"

Ari shrugged. "They're planning to reduce the world's population by half," he explained morosely.

I almost stopped in my tracks but remembered to

keep walking and to look disinterested. "Geez, by half? That's what, three billion people? They're ambitious little buggers."

My mind was reeling at the idea of genocide on that level. It made Stalin and Hitler look like kindergarten teachers. Okay, really evil kindergarten teachers, but still.

Ari shrugged again, and I realized it was hard for him to get worked up about things when he was going to die any day now.

I thought about what else I had seen, and it suddenly hit me: I'd seen some of this stuff before, like in a movie, or a dream, or in . . . one of those skull-splitting infodumps I used to get. For a while I'd had intensely horrible headaches, where it felt like my brain was imploding inside my skull. Then tons of images, words, sounds, *stuff* would scroll through my consciousness. I realized that some of what I was seeing, saying, doing right now — *I'd already seen it.*

Think, think.

I was still concentrating when we turned a corner and I literally ran into someone. Two someones.

Jeb and Angel.

49

"Max! Sweetheart," said Jeb. "I'm glad they're letting you get some exercise."

I stared at him. "So I'll be in really good shape when they kill me?"

He winced and sort of cleared his throat.

"Hi, Max," said Angel.

I just looked at her.

"You should really try one of these cookies," she said, holding out a chocolate-chip chunk of treason.

"Thanks. I'll make a note of it. You lying traitor."

"Max — you know I had to do what was right," she said. "You weren't making the best decisions anymore."

"Yeah, like the one when I decided to come rescue your skinny, ungrateful butt," I said.

Her small shoulders sagged, and her face looked sad.

Be strong, Maximum, I told myself. *You know what you gotta do.*

"I have lots of special powers," she said. "I deserve to be the leader. I deserve to be saved. I'm much, much more special than you or Fang."

"You just keep telling yourself that," I said coldly. "But don't expect me to get on board."

Her heart-shaped face turned mutinous. "I don't *need* you to get on board, Max." Her voice had an edge of steel in it. She'd learned that from me. What else had she learned? "This is all happening whether you're on board or not. You're going to be retired soon, anyway." She took an angry bite of cookie.

"Maybe. But if I am, I'm going to come back and haunt you, every day for the rest of your hard, traitorous little life."

Her eyes widened, and she actually took a step back.

"Okay, that's enough, you two," said Jeb, just the way he used to when some of us would mix it up back in the day.

"Whatever," I said in my trademark bored tone. I stepped around them, avoiding any touch as if they were poison, and headed down the hall. My heart was pounding, and I felt an unwelcome flush heat my cheeks.

Ari caught up to me. We walked in silence for a while, then he said, as if offering a consolation prize, "They're building an army, you know."

Of course they are, I thought, feeling depressed. "How do you know?"

"I've seen them. There's a whole hangar full of Flyboys, hanging up, charging. They have thousands, and they're making more all the time. They're growing Eraser skins in the lab."

"Why are you telling me this?" I asked.

He frowned, looking confused. Then he shrugged. "I don't know. I've always seen you fight. Even though I know you can't get out of this, it's like I still want you to know what you're up against."

"Are you setting me up?" I asked bluntly. "Is this a trap? I mean, even more of a trap than it obviously already is?"

He shook his head. "No. It's just . . . I know I'm never getting out of here. My time's over. I guess part of me hopes *you* still have a chance."

It made some sort of sad, pathetic sense.

"Oh, I'm getting out of here, I promise you." And maybe, just maybe, I would take him with us.

50

Under the general heading "Torturing the Bird Kids, Part Deux," you might find a whitecoat handing us a cardboard box that night.

We opened it carefully, expecting it to explode in our faces.

Inside, we found a slim wrapped package. It was a picture frame, book size but no thicker than a pencil. Of course Gazzy was the first one to press the red button on the side.

The frame bloomed into life, and there it was: that same picture Fang and I had found, once in a crack house in DC and once in Dr. Martinez's house. I swallowed hard, thinking about her. Wondering if she was real. Hoping she was okay. Trying to figure out what her deal was.

The picture was of baby Gasman, with his telltale cowlick, being held by a woman who looked kind of tired and washed out. He was plump and happy, maybe a few months old.

Then the picture started moving, not like a movie but like the actual picture was just . . . moving. The image zoomed in and rotated, as if we were walking around the woman and focusing on Gazzy. Then the picture pulled back and swung around. We saw an ugly room, with cracked walls and dirty windows. Was that the squatter's house we'd visited in Washington? Before it had become a bombed-out haven for thugs?

The camera focused on a wooden table, then on a slip of paper lying on the table. Again it enlarged and sharpened, enough so that we could read the paper.

It was a check. The name it was made out to was obliterated. The check was from Itex, for $10,000.

Gazzy coughed slightly, and I felt him trying to control himself.

His mother had sold him for $10,000 to the whitecoats at the School.

51

I didn't know why only Gazzy's life was in the picture frame, or why none of the rest of us got one. Those white-coats sure liked to keep us guessing!

We all checked one another for expiration dates, but none of us had them. Yet. But you know, when you've faced imminent death as often as we have, it gets a little old, frankly. Our room had no windows, so we had zero reference for time passing. We fought off boredom by coming up with plans to escape, courses of action to take. I led the flock through all kinds of scenarios, how we could use each one to our advantage.

That's what leaders do.

"Now, let's say they come get us," I started for the hundredth time.

"And, like, the halls are full of zebras," Iggy muttered sarcastically.

"And suddenly tons of *bubbles* are everywhere," said the Gasman.

"And then everyone starts eating beef jerky," Nudge suggested.

"Yeah," said Iggy, rubbing his hands together. "I'll grab a zebra; Gaz, you fill all the bubbles with your trademark scent, so people are choking and gagging; and let's throw beef jerky right into their eyes! Now, *that's* a plan!"

They all collapsed into laughter, and even Fang grinned at me as I gazed sourly at the flock.

"I just want us to be prepared," I said.

"Yeah — prepared to die," said Iggy.

"We're not going to die!" I snapped. "Not now, not any-time soon!"

"What about our expiration dates?" Gazzy asked. "They could show up any second. And what about stupid Angel, turning on us?"

There was a lot I wanted to say to him about that, but now wasn't the time.

I opened my mouth to spout some reassuring lies, but the door opened.

We tensed, turning quickly to see a whitecoat coming at us, armed with a clipboard. He checked his notes and pushed his glasses up on his nose.

"Okay," he said briskly. "I need the blind one and the one that can mimic voices." He looked up expectantly as we stared at him.

"Are you on *drugs?*" I asked in disbelief.

"Me? No," he said, looking confused. He tapped his pen against his clipboard. "We need to run some last tests."

I crossed my arms over my chest as Fang and I instinctively moved between the whitecoat and the rest of the flock.

"I don't think so," I said.

The whitecoat looked surprised at my noncompliance — obviously he hadn't read all of our case notes. "No, come along now," he said, striving for authoritative and achieving only weenie.

"You're kidding, right?" I asked. "Unless you're packing a submachine gun, you're flat out of luck, buddy."

He frowned. "Look, how about they just come along peacefully, and there won't be any trouble."

"Uh . . . how about, *no?*"

"What kind of trouble?" Gazzy asked from behind me. "I mean, *anything* to break the boredom."

The whitecoat tried to look stern. "Look, we're trying to explore other options to your retirement," he said. "You might be useful to us in other ways. Only people who are useful will survive the By-Half Plan. Actually, it's really more like the One-in-a-Thousand Plan. Only people with useful skills will be necessary in the new order, the Re-Evolution. You should want to help us find out if you're at all useful to us alive."

"Because we're probably not that useful dead," Nudge said thoughtfully.

"No," I agreed. "Well, maybe as doorstops."

The whitecoat made an "eew" expression.

"Or like those things in a parking lot that show where

the cars should stop," suggested Iggy. He closed his eyes and went stiff, to demonstrate what it would look like.

"Also an option," I conceded, while the whitecoat looked horrified.

"No," he said, scrambling for composure. "But China is interested in using you as weapons."

That was interesting. "Well, you tell China to bite us," I said. "Now, skedaddle on out of here, before we turn *you* into a doorstop."

"Come for testing," he tried firmly one last time.

"Come back to *reality*," I said, just as firmly.

He turned angrily and headed for the door. Gazzy looked at me, like, Should we rush him, push past him? I shook my head: Not now.

"You'll pay for this," the whitecoat said, flashing his ID card at the automatic lock.

"Boy, if I had a nickel for every time I've heard that," I mused.

52

See, when you're an evil, endlessly funded insane scientist, you have both the means and the motive to, say, suddenly gas a whole room of hostage bird kids.

Causing said bird kids to pass out without even realizing it and then wake up in a metal cage in the middle of a field.

At night.

Some of you have probably jumped ahead and are already at the place where you realize this happened to us, and I'm not just rattling on hypothetically, so good on ya!

"Unhhh," Gazzy moaned, starting to stir.

I forced myself to sit up. There were no lights. Even the moon and stars were blocked by thick, low-lying clouds.

"You are avake, yah?" said a voice in a horribly recognizable accent.

"Yah," I muttered, rubbing my head. "And you are still a butthole, yah?"

"It's time for you to be eliminated," ter Borcht said, sounding gleeful. "You don't cooperate vis de tests, you are useless to us."

I helped Nudge sit up, rubbing her back as she cleared her throat.

"I don't believe this," Fang muttered, rolling his shoulders. He looked around at our cage. It was big enough to hold us, as long as we didn't want to do anything frivolous, like stand up or move around.

"Believe it," said ter Borcht, clapping his hands together. "Tonight ve implement our Re-Evolution Plan! Vhen ve are done, ve vill haf a world of less dan a billion people. Each country vill be under our control! Dere vill be no illnesses, no veakness. De new strong, smart population vill save dis planet und take us into de tventy-second century!"

"Yeah," I said. "And if you look in the dictionary under 'delusional megalomaniac,' you'll see your picture."

"Nussing you say vill bozzer me," ter Borcht said more calmly. "It is time to eliminate you. You haf failed all de tests. You are not useful."

"No, but we're dang cute," I said, willing my brain to start churning out ideas. I scanned the sky and the field as best I could through the bars, but I saw nothing. *Come on, come on,* I thought.

"Max?" Nudge whispered. She edged closer to me and took my hand. I squeezed hers reassuringly, but I was thinking that maybe our time really was up. The five of us were hunched back-to-back inside the cage, all of us looking out.

Then a clumpy blob was coming toward us, growing larger. It took only a second for me to see that it was a group of people walking across the field. Probably here to get good seats for the fun. Some of them were wearing white coats, of course, but not all of them. My eyes picked out Jeb and Anne Walker.

"How can we break out of here?" Gazzy whispered so only the flock could hear.

"There's a plan," I murmured back. "There's always a plan." Well, it *sounded* good.

"Children," said Jeb when he was close enough. "It doesn't have to be this way."

"Okay," I said. "Let's have it be different. Let us out of the cage!"

He pressed his lips together, giving his head a tiny shake.

Next it was Anne's turn. Inside the cage, we were practically vibrating with tension.

"Do you know what's really sad?" she asked.

"That pin-striped pantsuit?" I guessed. "Those sensible shoes?"

"We gave you every chance," Anne said.

"No, see, giving us every chance would be opening this cruel and inhuman cage and letting us *out*," I said, ready to explode. "That would be *every* chance. This way, you've only given us *some* chances. You see the difference?"

"Enough!" ter Borcht barked. "Dis is pointless. Ve're just vaiting for de executioners. Say your good-byes."

"Good-bye," said a sweet little-girl voice.

And then a shiny metal bar swung through the air and smacked ter Borcht's head with a sickening, melonlike splat.

53

Well. It certainly got exciting as heck after that.

"Angel!" Nudge screamed, echoed closely by Gazzy. Fang and I threw ourselves against the cage bars, shaking them hard, searching for weak points.

Angel nimbly bobbed and weaved, her white wings beating as fast as my heart. She dive-bombed the group of scientists, who scattered, screaming for Flyboys to come to the rescue.

"I can't break it!" Fang said, slamming his fists against the cage.

"But I can!" The gravelly voice from behind made us spin in time to see Ari do a full morph into a good ol' old-fashioned Eraser. I'd forgotten how wolfish he could get, and his face, with its full snout packed with yellow, dripping teeth, was horrible up this close.

"Get back!" I shouted, pushing the flock away from him. Two ragged-clawed paws gripped the metal bars, and Ari lunged at us, fangs snapping.

I gasped as his teeth crunched down on the bars — and

then, with grisly twisting-metal sounds, he started to chew through.

Outside, Angel hovered like a demonic hummingbird, swinging her bar, keeping everyone and everything away from us.

"She's going to let Ari eat us!" Nudge cried. She braced herself against the cage and clenched her hands into fists. "But it won't be easy for him!"

Time-out. Okay, now, tell the truth: When's the last time you had to decide to make it hard for someone to eat you? That's just the zany, roller-coaster life of a lab rat on the run.

It was time to spill. "Angel's not a traitor," I said. "She and I agreed that she would do this so she'd be on the inside and could get us out if anything happened. She's been my *spy*."

Time halted as four dumbstruck bird kids turned to gape at me.

"We came up with this plan in case the worst happened," I said fast. "Which it did, of course. Angel's not a traitor — never was."

Smash! Time sped up again as Ari managed to gnaw through one of the bars. It was stomach churning to see — the ripped metal cut his mouth up something awful, and blood mingled with foul Eraser spit was flying everywhere.

Crack! Ooh — Angel had whacked another whitecoat. Like ter Borcht, this one dropped like a stone. In fact, ter

Borcht hadn't gotten up — he was rolling on the ground, moaning.

Riiip! Ari broke through another bar of the cage, and his unnaturally strong arms began to wrest the surrounding bars apart. His face was a repulsive bloody-meat picture as he snarled and grunted with the effort.

"I'll take him out," Fang whispered tensely in my ear. "Then you grab the others and get out of here."

I quickly tapped everyone's hands twice. They caught my eye and nodded, and we all braced for Fang's move.

With a final, wrenching, earsplitting screech, Ari forced the bars apart, making an Eraser-sized hole in the cage wall.

"Ready." Fang's voice was deadly quiet in the screaming chaos around us.

We all tensed, ready to spring out as soon as Fang took Ari down — but instead of coming in after us, Ari backed away quickly.

"Come on!" he shouted. "Get out of there! We'll hold these guys back!"

Wha?

"He's on our side!" Angel yelled from above. "He's with me! He's getting you out! Ari! *Release the secret weapon!*"

Ari fumbled with his jacket, and a small coal-colored shadow popped out of it and began to race around, growling and snapping.

Was it — could it be?

"Move it or lose it!" Total shouted. "Let's go, go, go!"

54

Fang shot through the hole in the cage, grabbed Total, and was up in the air before three seconds had passed. Amazingly, Ari stood off to the side and let him go.

I shoved Nudge through next, and she took a running leap, faltered for a moment, then stroked hard and rose into the air.

Still Ari stood back.

Watching him closely, I pushed Iggy out. "Four steps, up at ten o'clock," I hissed. He nodded, then followed my instructions.

"Come on, Gasman, you're last," I said, and practically threw him out of the cage, wincing as the torn metal scratched him. A minor concern at this point.

Ari watched him go.

Angel was keeping the humans at bay, and it was my turn. Ari and I had a troubled history — okay, we usually wanted to kill each other, and one time I did kill him — but I couldn't worry about it right now. I leaped from the cage, took a step on the ground, then snapped my wings out and was up in the air within one breath.

Oh, God, it felt so good to be *up,* flying, away from a world that held only pain and death for us.

"I'm so glad to see you guys," said Total, sounding a little choked up. "I thought you were dead! I didn't know what I'd do without you."

"Glad to see you again too," I said, surprising myself by actually meaning it.

Below us, Angel dropped the metal bar and zipped upward, streaming like a comet, her small face serene and beautiful. I blew her kisses through the air, my faithful partner in deception, and she beamed at me.

It was at that point that the executioners arrived and started shooting at us. I saw Jeb grab one of their arms, trying to mess up his aim, but the guy just clubbed him down with his gun, then kept firing.

We were already out of range. They would need a missile launcher to hit us now.

"Nyah, nyah, nyah," I said quietly, looking down at them. I sucked in sweet lungfuls of night air, counted my flock, and took a moment to focus my direction, *feeling* where we were, which way was north, where we should go.

Then I saw Ari, still on the ground. The men with guns were running toward him.

"Ari!" I suddenly screamed without thinking. "Get out of there! Come up! Come with us!"

"What?!" Fang exclaimed. "Are you nuts? What the heck are you thinking?"

Ari probably couldn't hear exactly what I said, but when he saw me waving my arms, he must have understood. He ran clumsily, a seven-year-old freak in a huge linebacker body, and forced himself into the air. A bullet grazed one of his unwieldy patched-on wings, but he kept flying awkwardly, rising upward slowly but steadily.

"Max, you are way out of line," Fang said furiously. He tossed Total through the air at Gazzy, who gave a startled cry and grabbed the little dog. "There's no way he's coming with us!"

"He saved our lives," I pointed out. "They're going to kill him."

"Good!" Fang said, a savage expression on his face. "*He's* tried to kill *us* a hundred times!"

I'd actually never seen Fang like this.

"Max, Ari's really mean," Nudge said. "He's tried to hurt you, and he's tracked us — I don't want him with us."

"Me neither," said the Gasman. "He's one of *them*."

"I think he's changed," I said, as Ari flew toward us.

"He helped get you guys out," Angel reminded us. "And he found Total for me."

Fang gave me an enraged, disgusted look and flew off before Ari got to us. Looking doubtful, Nudge and Gazzy went with him. Iggy heard their direction and followed.

Leaving me, Angel, and Ari behind.

55

"Thanks, Max," Ari said when he was within earshot. "You won't regret this, I promise. I'm going to keep you safe."

I frowned at him, trying not to look at his ruined, gory face. "We all keep each other safe," I said shortly, then swung into a steeply pitched right turn. I saw Gazzy and the others swooping over the School's large parking lot. An entrance there led to additional, underground parking.

"Where's Iggy?" I demanded.

The Gasman pointed downward, and I saw Iggy leaning over the open hood of a car.

"Oh, no," I muttered, as Iggy slammed the hood shut, then pushed the car toward the sloping entrance to the underground parking.

"Oh no, oh no," I continued as the car smoothly, silently rolled through the opening and disappeared. Iggy shot upward, looking happier than he had in weeks.

"And a-one, and a-two, and a-thr —," he began.

Boom! A massive explosion blew part of the top off the parking garage. We quickly flew out of range as streaming chunks of glowing red asphalt, glass, and concrete rocketed through the night sky. Alarms went off. Outdoor emergency lights flashed on.

"Way to be!" the Gasman crowed, slapping high fives with Iggy.

"Yeah," I said. "Way to be loud and obvious about where we are and what we're doing."

"High four!" Total said, holding up a paw. "That rocked!"

I felt Fang looking at me furiously, but I avoided his eyes. Ari hung back on the periphery.

I needed several moments to get a grip. Why had I asked Ari to come with us? Now everyone was mad at me. But it had seemed like the right thing to do. On the other hand, it required a perhaps ill-fated leap of faith on my part that he wouldn't suddenly turn bad again. I'm not real good at leaps of faith.

Then again, Ari was going to die soon anyway.

I wheeled around and faced the flock, their forms dimly lit by the fireball below.

Boom! Another explosion, even bigger than the first, blew out another section of the garage. I looked at Iggy, and as if he could sense it, he shrugged.

"Big garage full of big cars with big gas tanks."

Whatever. "Okay, guys, let's head north," I said briskly. No idea why, no idea where, but it seemed like the right thing to do.

Sometimes all you have is instinct, a gut feeling. It's important to pay attention to them.

I almost groaned aloud. *Look what the cat dragged in,* I thought. *Hello, Voice.*

Hello, Maximum. I'm glad you're okay.

No thanks to you, I thought as I leveled out and started flying directly north.

I've missed talking with you.

Well, I can't say that I've missed you, I thought. *But I sort of missed you too.*

Now I'm back.

Yep.

And you know what else was back? I saw it when I waved for the others to follow me more closely.

The scars on my arm. From taking out my chip.

PART 3

BREAKING UP IS HARD TO DO

56

What do you know? It wasn't all a dream after all. And somehow my hand still worked now. So, bonus.

First thing we did was circle back and pick up the gear that Fang and I had stashed before we'd been caught in the desert. Then we flew through the cold night air, north, and then northeast. I can't explain how I know where to go — it's like I have an internal compass or something. At the School, when we were little, they'd done tons of experiments searching for our magnetism sensors, which tell us where magnetic north is.

They didn't find them.

The farther north we went, the higher the mountains got, and the more snow was on the ground. Was it still December? January? Had we missed Christmas? I'd have to check a newspaper the next time we were in civilization.

Fang was still radiating fury, not looking at me, flying ahead of us, not talking to anyone. Nudge, Gazzy, and Iggy were also avoiding me, Angel, and Ari. I sighed.

Long flights are a good time to think things through. I guess that's true for people on airplanes too. I went on autopilot, my wings moving powerfully through the cold, my lungs pumping air in and out. Every so often we'd hit a current and coast for a while, moving our wings in marginal fractions to take advantage of nature doing the work for us.

I was born to fly. And yeah, I know tons of people before me have said that, thought that.

But I was *literally* born to fly, *made* to fly, created with the purpose of being able to propel myself through the air as effortlessly as any bird.

And I'm fabulous at it, let me tell you.

"Max?"

Nudge had dropped back next to me, but she still wasn't looking me in the eye, and she was as far away from Ari as possible.

"Yes?"

"I'm hungry. We already went through everything we had in the packs. I think the others are hungry too. Total keeps whining — you know what he's like."

"Uh-huh."

"So, uh, is there a plan to stop somewhere? Get some food?"

I looked at her. "There's always a plan."

And just like that, boom: I had one.

57

Not too long ago (though it felt like several lifetimes), Fang, Nudge, and I had found a vacation house in Colorado. No one had been using it then, but now it was ski season, and snow lay thick on the ground. Still, it was worth checking out.

Because the others were ahead of me, I sped up to be in front. Then I changed direction slightly, knowing exactly how to get there from here.

Taking a chance, I glanced at Fang.

"Where are you going? A little hideaway that Ari knows about?" Icicles crackled on his words.

"The ski house we found. Maybe it's still unoccupied. Be a place to rest up."

He shook his head. "No way! You know the rules — never return to a place you've been! If someone's been there, they know it was broken into and will have beefed up their security. If no one's been there, we pretty much cleaned out all the food anyway."

God, I just *hated* it when he was reasonable and logical.

I mean, if there was ever anything calculated to make me see red . . .

"I've thought of that," I said calmly. "But we need some downtime, and it's our best option."

"It is not!" he said. "We should find a canyon or cave somewhere and hunker down — "

"I'm tired of caves and canyons!" I surprised both of us by snapping. "I'm tired of desert rat, medium rare! I want a roof and a bed and food that I don't have to catch and skin!"

He stared at me, and instantly I felt embarrassed, as if I had just admitted I wasn't tough as nails.

Well, too bad. That was how I felt.

I sped up, leaving Fang behind, and headed right for the vacation home.

58

Imagine, if you will, a somewhat run-down, not very much used vacation hacienda. For those of us without even an everyday hacienda, the notion of having a vacation one makes us positively giddy. Even an unrenovated one.

Just like before, we came down in the woods a distance from the house and crept stealthily nearer. As we got close, we heard voices and the purr of a car engine. Fang glared at me like, I told you so. People were here.

"Okay, did you lock up?" one voice said.

"Yeah. And the fire's out."

"Good. I can't wait to come back."

"Maybe Saturday, right?"

So there you go. Car doors slammed, and the voices were muffled. We pressed against tree trunks, trying to hide our breath coming out like smoke.

I looked back at Fang and raised my eyebrows in triumph. They were leaving. It was perfect. We waited for ten minutes after the car drove away, then, unrepentant little felons that we were, broke in.

I did try to do as little damage as possible, though. Must be all that girly sensitivity they wired into my DNA.

"It's warm!" said Angel happily.

"Let's check out the kitchen!" Nudge hurried toward it.

"This is great," said Ari. Fang shot him a venomous glance, then scowled at me. I ignored him and headed to the kitchen. It was time for some serious chow.

"Oh, thank God they're not vegetarians," Nudge said with feeling, pulling out some cans of beef stew.

"What's that one that's worse than vegetarian?" Gazzy wrinkled his nose.

"Vegan," I answered him. "Let's crank those babies open." I rummaged for an opener.

"Look, they even have some dog food!" the Gasman said, holding up a paper sack.

Total looked at him. "You're kidding me, right?"

The fridge had some actual fresh food in it — cheese and apples. Jam. Butter.

"Oh, pig heaven," Nudge breathed.

Ari had a hard time eating — he had ruined his mouth. I didn't say anything. We all make choices, and we all have to live with them.

Have you thought about your choices lately, Max? asked the Voice. *Are you making choices for the greater good or just for yourself?*

Nothing like a disembodied voice inside your head to dull your appetite. *Clearly I'm not making choices just for myself,* I thought acidly. *If I were, I'd be reading a good book in a comfy hammock. Someplace warm.*

"What did that guy mean, that China wanted to use us as weapons?" Iggy asked, pouring half a box of cereal into a bowl. Without spilling any.

"I don't know." I frowned. "I guess we could be spies? We couldn't carry heavy arms or anything. I mean, who knows what those head cases have cooked up? Probably moronic stuff, like us duct-taped to a bomb, programming it at the last second or something." .

Gazzy laughed, and I looked around, thinking, *My flock is together and safe. For now.*

Well, my flock and Ari, the walking circus sideshow. And a talking dog. But still.

"Can I talk to you?" Fang was standing over me, his body radiating tension.

Oh, great. "Can it wait?" I ate the last piece of canned ravioli, then scraped the can with my fork.

"No."

I debated it, but there was really no ignoring Fang when he was like that. Sighing, I pushed back my chair and stalked outside. On the porch, I crossed my arms over my chest.

"Okay, let's have it out," I said, trying not to show that he was upsetting me.

"Choose now," he spat, his eyes practically shooting sparks. *"Me or him."*

59

"Gosh, Fang, you romantic fool," I said sarcastically. "How incredibly sexist-pig of you."

He snorted in exasperation but didn't look as dumb doing it as you'd think. "Not as a *boyfriend,* you idiot! I meant as a member of this flock! God, full of yourself, aren't you? I mean, either *he* goes or *I* go. I'm not going to stay while you let someone who's tried to kill both of us, more than once, stay!"

"I know if I think about it, I'll figure that sentence out," I snapped. "But I don't have to choose between you! People change, Fang. Face it, he helped save our lives. He worked with Angel. And while we were there, he let me in on some of the stuff going on at the School."

"Yeah, and I'm sure he had no ulterior motive for *that!* I'm *sure* he's not wired, not tracking us, not telling everyone where we are right this second! I'm sure seven years of brainwashing and training *just wore off* once you batted your eyes at him!"

I gaped at him. "He's seven years old, you jerk! And I'm

not batting my eyes at anyone! Not you, not him, not anyone! He doesn't even think like that!"

I'd never seen Fang so angry. His lips were pressed tightly together, and the skin around his mouth was white.

"And I'm sure you're making the biggest mistake of your life!" he shot back. Years of living in hiding, flying under the radar both literally and figuratively, meant that even now, when we were both spitting fire, our voices were low, pitched to reach only each other. "Ari's a killer!" Fang said. "He's toxic! They've polluted him and screwed him up so much he can't even think. He's a total liability, and you're out of your mind if you think it's fine that he's here!"

I hesitated. He was my right-hand man, my best friend, the one who always, always had my back. He'd die to save me, and I'd throw myself in front of a train for him without a second's thought.

"Okay," I said slowly, rubbing my temples. "I really think he's changed, and his expiration date is gonna kick in soon, anyway. But I know his being here is bumming everyone out."

"You picked up on that, huh, Sherlock?"

My eyes blazed. "I'm trying to meet you halfway, nimrod! I was going to say let me think about it. In the meantime, I'll keep an eagle eye on him. First sign of anything suspicious, I'll kick his butt out myself. Okay?"

Fang stared at me in disbelief. "Are you nuts? Did they finally send you around the bend? Ari needs to go *now!*"

"He doesn't have anywhere else to go! He helped us, remember? They're not gonna let him back in. Plus, I keep telling you, he's only seven years old, no matter how big he is. How's he gonna survive?"

"I don't give a crap," Fang said icily. "I'm fine with him not surviving at all. Remember this?" He yanked up his shirt to show the pink lines of his healed scars, the ones from when Ari had sliced him up like a tenderloin and almost made him bleed to death.

I shuddered just thinking about that awful day. "I remember," I said quietly. "But I can't just kick him out into the cold with no place to go, no way to survive. Not knowing that the whitecoats will be gunning for him now. It's only for a few days — just till he expires."

It felt weird saying it like that. Like *retire*. *Expire*. All different words for *die*. He was seven years old and wasn't going to live to see eight.

And his first seven years had sucked, big-time.

Fang poked me hard in the chest.

"Hey!" I said.

He leaned very close, several inches taller than me, and got right in my face. But this time he didn't kiss me.

"You're making your worst mistake," he snarled. "And it's gonna cost you. You'll see."

With that, he turned and jumped off the porch, not even hitting the ground before his wide, dark wings took him soundlessly into the night.

60

You are reading Fang's Blog. Welcome!
Today's date: Already Too Late!
You are visitor number: 28,772,461

TO EVERYONE, EVERYWHERE
WARNING
HEADS-UP
EVIL SCIENTISTS WILL END LIFE AS WE KNOW IT

And even as we don't know it.

I know what it's called now, folks. It's called the Re-Evolution Plan. And the By-Half Plan. We got out of the School (anyone who wants to bomb them, feel free). Now we're in hiding, ha ha. While we were there, we found out that the plan is to basically KILL anyone with any kind of disease or weakness. The only people left will be perfectly healthy and have useful skills. So everyone bone up on something useful! Or go into hiding. And if you have the sniffles, crawl under a rock and don't come out.

What would be useful, you ask? I've made a chart.

USEFUL	NOT USEFUL
Plumber	Politician
Carpenter	Publicist
Boat builder	Art history buff
Farmer	Celebrity chef
Sanitation crew	Interior designer
Cattle rancher	Pet psychic
Scientist	Celebrity rock/pop/hip-hop star
Military	Teen idol
Medical personnel	Life coach

So this would be a good time to examine your career goals.

Last time I checked, more than 28 million people had hit this blog. Way to go, people. Save yourselves. Save your brothers and sisters. Don't let the whitecoats get you.

And if you see any flying kids, keep your mouth shut.

— Fang, from somewhere in America

61

I was shaking after Fang and I fought. It's not that we never fought — we did all the time. But not like this. This was the maddest I'd ever seen him. After he took off, I stayed outside a minute, until I could paste a fake smile on my face. No sense in worrying the others.

When I went back inside, the flock and Ari and Total were all sprawled on the furniture or floor. They had that glazed look that comes from getting all the food you want, for once. I examined Ari. He was in a chair by himself. None of the others were anywhere near him. His clothes were still covered in blood.

I raided a closet and threw a flannel shirt at him. He looked up in surprise. "Thanks."

"Okay, who wants first watch?" I said.

"Where's Fang?" Gazzy asked.

"He went out for a while. He'll be back," I said shortly. Of course he would be back.

"I'll take first watch," Ari said.

I made an executive decision. "No, that's okay. I'll do it. The rest of you get some sleep." I didn't meet Ari's eyes.

While the others slept, I went through the fridge and pantry and took everything that wouldn't spoil and wasn't too heavy. I repacked all of our packs and set them close to the door. I walked around silently, turning off lights, then went outside and flew up onto the snow-covered roof.

I perched by the brick chimney, which radiated heat.

Everything was quiet.

Ages later, Fang returned. I tried not to breathe a sigh of relief. I hadn't been that worried, anyway. He flew up, saw me, and landed, flapping his wings for balance as he tried to find a place on the roof.

None of us are real big with the apologies, the heartfelt hugs. I glanced at him, then went back to keeping watch, doing regular 360 scans, listening, waiting.

"Twenty-eight million people have clicked on the blog," he said.

Good Lord. "Huh."

"I'm putting everything I know about what's going on out there," he went on. "Maybe if enough people get a heads-up, they can stop whatever's happening."

Stopping it is your job, Max.

"I thought *we* were supposed to stop it," I said.

"What, with one hand tied behind your back?" Fang scoffed. "You don't *have* to save the world, Max, no matter what they tell you."

For some reason that stung — like he didn't think I could do it. I'd always thought he'd be on board for anything I had to do.

"So now you and your blog are going to do it? I can go to bed and sleep in?" The words came out more caustic than I intended.

Fang shot me a sideways glance, his eyes unreadable. He shrugged and looked away.

Okay, now I was mad all over again. I hated it when Fang and I fought, but I hated even more him thinking that I — you know, wasn't able to save the world by myself.

I'm sure a lot of you girls out there worry about the same thing, huh?

"Next you'll be telling me you've got a Voice in your head," I said sarcastically, standing up. I balanced on the roof, holding my wings out for help. Like a squirrel does with its tail. Only thirteen feet across.

"Maybe," he said coolly, not looking at me.

I was speechless. Which is, as you know, very rare.

"Fine. You're on second watch," I muttered, and jumped down from the roof. I landed in the soft snow and went around to the porch.

Inside, Ari had not ripped everyone's throats out while they slept. It occurred to me that Angel was telepathic, and she would have picked up on any evil intent that Ari had.

I was pretty sure, anyway.

I made the rounds, checked on the sleeping flock, then positioned myself in an armchair right next to where Ari slept heavily on the floor. That way, if he moved, he'd wake me up.

I was burning up over Fang. I couldn't believe how full

of himself he was. Him and his blog. Fine! Let him save the world! I still had my mission.

You both have hard decisions to make, Max. Decisions that will affect the whole world, your future. Everyone's future.

Oh, good, so no pressure, I thought. I punched the cushion of the armchair into a better shape and closed my eyes.

I wasn't going to sleep a wink.

62

In the morning, Fang and I broke up.

And just to set the record straight, *I* left *him*. A split second after he left me.

He told me he wanted to do his own thing, follow his own mission, as he put it. He wanted to act on leads that people were sending in to his blog.

I stared at him. "You're basing your plan for human salvation on *e-mail?*"

He looked back at me. "You're basing yours on a Voice inside your head. A Voice that isn't actually just you talking to yourself. Right?"

Well, when he put it that way . . .

I just couldn't comprehend what was happening.

And then we had to tell the kids. I went over a hundred conversations in my reeling head. What would they say? How could we explain this?

"I've decided to go my own way," Fang told the flock abruptly. He cast a glance at Ari, then went on. "Almost anyone's welcome to come with me."

Go with him! Over my dead body.

"I think we should all stick together until Fang comes back," I said calmly. *Because if any of you pick him instead of me, I'll kill you.*

Four pairs of flock eyes, one dog, and Ari stared at us, back and forth.

"Holy crap," said Total.

"You guys shouldn't do this," said Nudge, looking worried.

I shrugged, my face flaming. Fang was the one doing it.

"You crazy kids," Total muttered. He paced back and forth on his short legs, then went and sat on top of Angel's feet. She reached down absently and stroked his head.

"We have to choose?" Gazzy squeaked. He looked at Fang, then at me. Then at Ari.

Crap, I thought.

"I'll go with Fang." Iggy's face was expressionless, but his voice hurt my heart. Shocked, I was glad he couldn't see my face.

I swallowed, unable to talk.

"I'm going to stay with Max," said Nudge unhappily, putting her hand in mine. I squeezed it, but I saw how she looked at Ari out of the corners of her eyes. She didn't trust him, didn't want him with us.

"I'll go wherever Angel goes," Total said. "If I must."

The Gasman and Angel were silent. Angel must have been communicating with him telepathically because he shook his head and looked like he was concentrating hard.

Finally Angel nodded her head decisively and nudged Total off her feet to come stand next to me.

"I'm going with Max," she said.

"Yeah, whatever," said Total grumpily, flopping back onto Angel's feet.

"I'm going with Fang," said Gazzy. I stared at him in astonishment.

Ari was the only one left, a glaring outsider to our family.

"No-brainer," Ari mumbled, coming to stand by me. His face was starting to heal very fast, the way our wounds did. "Max."

Please, please, don't let me regret this, I prayed to a higher power. *I mean, any more than I already regret it.*

"Fine," said Fang, slinging on his pack.

"Fine," I said, tilting my chin up, wishing with all my strength that he wouldn't do this, and making darn sure he couldn't tell I was wishing it.

And that was that. The flock was split in two. And I really had no idea if I would ever see Fang and his group again.

63

A sign of leadership? Facing your remaining flock with a calm face and a confident air when it's all you can do not to barf your guts up in the snow from stress and misery.

Half my flock was gone. Fang was gone. My right-hand man. How could he do this? Didn't he need me?

I straightened my shoulders. I didn't need *him*. Not anymore.

"Okay, guys," I said to Nudge, Angel, and Ari. And Total. I could see that Nudge and Angel were trying to keep stiff upper lips. Possibly Ari and Total, but it was harder to tell with them.

"I can't believe they went," Nudge said, typically blurting out something I was thinking but would never say aloud. "We shouldn't split up. We promised to never split up again. We need to all stick together."

Tell that to Fang. "It's not what I hoped would happen, but we're fine," I said authoritatively.

"What are we going to do now?" Angel asked. "Do we have a plan?"

I gave her a lofty look. "There's *always* a plan. How many times do I have to tell you guys?" *Come on, Max, pull a plan out of your hat, quick.*

Go to Europe.

Oh, thank God. Goddess. Whatever. The Voice finally had something constructive to say and not just more fortune-cookie crap.

"We're going to Europe," I said firmly. I handed out packs, and only then realized that Ari or I would have to carry Total, mostly. Neither Nudge nor Angel would be able to take his weight for very long.

Great. I just had to hope that Ari wouldn't eat Total.

"Europe!" Nudge sounded excited. "I've always wanted to go to Europe! Where are we going? I want to see the Eiffel Towel!"

"That's tower," I said. "Eiffel *Tower*. Actually, we're headed to . . ."

England, first. Start with England. Look for Schools.

"England," I said, holding my arms out for Total. He gave a little hop, and I zipped him inside my jacket. Only his small fuzzy face peeked out at the neck. He still looked a little mangy, and I hoped his face fur would fill in soon. "We're going to look for Schools, gather information. Learn everything we can about this Re-Evolution Plan. And we're going to have to move fast."

"I'm on your side," Ari said, sounding sincere. "I'm going to protect you no matter what." He looked down, and

I caught a glimpse of the scared seven-year-old he was inside. "Until my expiration date, anyway."

I nodded, not letting any softer emotions through.

"Okay, then," I said, starting to run down the driveway for a fast takeoff. "We head east!"

As always, I felt much, much better once we were high, high in the air. The land below us was a patchwork of green and brown, with tiny silver threads of rivers and gray clumps of cities. It was cold, and the wind made my eyes water, but I felt calmer, more in control, in the air.

It started to occur to me that England was really far away, over a honking big bunch of water. We'd flown for seven, eight hours straight a couple times, but it was hard, and we'd been wiped afterward. And God knew Ari wasn't that strong a flier. Not with those weird taped-on wings. Hmm. No place to land and rest over the Atlantic Ocean.

Go to Washington DC. There's a direct flight from Dulles.

Like, a plane?

Exactly like. Right down to the shiny silver outside.

Us . . . on a plane. That seemed so wrong, somehow. Redundant.

Plus, there was the whole cooped-up, claustrophobia issue.

You'll be fine.

"We're headed to Washington DC," I told my new miniflock. "We're going to take a plane from there."

Everyone looked astonished. I wondered how we would

get Ari, with his bizarre and scary appearance, through a busy airport.

"We're going to take a plane?" Nudge asked, her voice practically squeaking.

Total frowned. "Isn't that redundant?"

I sighed.

64

Flying west without Max was like flying with one wing missing, Fang thought. He kept seeing her face, furious, confused, and, even though she would never admit it, scared. He'd seen that face just about every day of his entire life. He'd seen it filthy with caked-on dirt, bruised and bloodied, snarling, laughing, sleeping, telling complicated lies with total sincerity . . . looking down at him with that light in her eyes, that communication between them. . . .

But she had his back against a wall. What did she expect him to do? Just lie back and take Ari? Like, oh, sure, he'd just *forget* how many times Ari'd tried to kill them, how likely it was that he was wired and tracking them, how dangerous he was to have around. He was a disaster of patched-together body parts, upgrades, twisted emotions, psychological torture. A walking, flying time bomb about to explode.

Fang looked at it this way: If you knew you were checking out in a couple days no matter what, well, what did it matter what the heck you did? You could do crazy stuff, dangerous stuff, break any law, kill anybody. None of it would matter because you'd be cold and stiff in a couple days. Friends didn't matter, loyalty didn't matter. You could burn any bridge.

That was who Max was choosing to spend time with. Who she was letting hang around the younger kids.

Fang would have followed Max to the end of the world, wherever and whenever that was. If she'd dropped into the cone of an active volcano, he would have backed her up, no matter what.

But he couldn't go along with Ari.

"Fang?" The Gasman's voice was subdued. None of them liked being split up. If they felt as though half of them were missing, it was because they were.

Fang looked at him and raised an eyebrow.

"Where are we going?"

"West Coast," Fang said. The opposite of wherever Max was going.

"What's there?" Iggy asked.

Funny you should ask. "The biggest information-dissemination system in the world," Fang said. "A place to get out news fast."

The Gasman frowned. "What, like, some computer place? Some kind of tower?"

Fang shook his head. "*People* magazine."

"Is this part of the 'lie low and be inconspicuous' plan?" Iggy asked pointedly.

"No," Fang said, angling his wing tips just a hair to lead them into a twenty-three-degree turn. "This is part of the 'blow the story open, post the blog, tell the world' plan."

"Oh."

Yep. Always pretend there was a plan. A lesson he'd learned so very well from Max.

65

"I hate you! You're such losers!" Iggy's face was a picture of anger and frustration. "You're just being jerks."

Fang rolled his eyes. Then, remembering, he said, "I'm rolling my eyes, Iggy."

"I'm shrugging my shoulders," said the Gasman, taking a stupendous bite of hot dog. "I have no idea what the heck you're talking about."

"*Describe* the people on this beach," Iggy said again. "This is Venice Beach! Part of LA. Home of Freak University! And you guys are, like, looking at maps and stuff!"

"Is there really a college named Freak University?" The Gasman looked thrilled.

"No," Fang told him. So much for Gazzy's dreams of higher education. Fang smoothed the map out on the slatted bench in front of them and started looking for landmarks.

Until Iggy kicked him.

"Ow! Dang it! What's wrong with you?"

Unerringly, Iggy's hand shot out and grabbed a fistful of

Fang's shirt. He pulled Fang's face close to his own. *"Describe. The. People."*

"There's a million people," Fang said, irritated. "Why? Are you meeting someone in particular here? Should I be looking for a man with a rose in his teeth, holding a *New York Times*?"

"This is Venice Beach," Iggy said again. "Home of roller disco. I smell coconut oil. I hear high-pitched giggles. I know we must be surrounded by beach bunnies, and you're looking at a *map!*"

Oh.

"What's a beach bunny?" the Gasman asked, his mouth full.

Fang glanced around. "Beach bunny, schmeach bunny. Who cares? As long as they're not Flyboys."

Iggy groaned so loudly that several people nearby turned to look. Fang kicked his shin lightly, telling him to cool it.

"Who *cares?*" Iggy whispered, sounding outraged. "Who cares? I do! You can see them. I can't. And God knows I won't be able to get familiar with them by *touch.* Just do me a favor!"

What would Max do in this case? Fang wondered. Actually, he didn't think Iggy would have talked to Max about it. This was a guy-guy situation.

Sighing, Fang looked around. "Um, okay. There are two girls over there. One's in a white bikini. One has 'Utopia' written across her butt. They have big blond hair. Um, over there is an Asian girl, skating on Rollerblades, with her dog, like a greyhound or something, running beside her. Oops, she almost took out that stroller."

"What's she wearing?" Iggy asked.

"A striped bikini."

"And knee guards," the Gasman put in.

"Oh, man," Iggy breathed. "More, more."

He never would have done this in front of Max, Fang thought. She would have been all over him like ugly on an ape, telling him what a sexist pig he was.

But they were all guys here.

"Um, there's a girl meeting her friend," he went on. "Her friend is giving her an ice-cream cone. Oh — it's dripping. Huh. It, uh, dripped on her . . . chest."

Iggy drew in a hissing breath.

"It's gonna stain for sure," the Gasman said. "That's chocolate."

"Hmm," Fang said, watching the girl dab at her chest with a paper napkin.

"What's that sound?" the Gasman asked.

"Huh?"

"That sound," the Gasman insisted. "What's that sound? *Fang.*"

Fang blinked a couple times and looked down, where the Gasman was yanking on his sleeve. "Sound?"

Then he heard it. A droning hum. A teeming chorus of metallic voices.

Oh, crap.

"Up and away!" he said. "It's Flyboys. *They've found us!*"

66

You are reading Fang's Blog. Welcome!
Today's date: Already Too Late!
You are visitor number: 972,361,007

Busted-up Hollywood

So, for those of you in the LA area, I need to fess up about the major wreckage over at the big Hollywood sign. A million hopefuls have fixated on that sign as a symbol of future movie careers, and I sure do apologize about it being destroyed.

But it wasn't my fault.

The Gasman, Iggy, and I were minding our own business somewhere in the greater LA area (which extends from Tijuana up to Pismo Beach), and suddenly, out of nowhere, a couple hundred Flyboys dropped down on us. How did they know where we were? I always assumed they tracked us either by Max's chip or by Angel's dog.

Which, as you've probably heard, are with us no longer.

So how'd they know where to find us?

Unless one of us three is telling them?

Which is impossible, of course.

Anyway, like I told you before, Max saw thousands of Flyboys back at the School, hanging in rows, charging up. So today they let a bunch of 'em go for a test-drive. I have to tell you people, those things are fast. They're strong. They can go for a long time without stopping.

But smart? Not so much.

Gaz, Iggy, and I shot up, fast, from where we'd been innocently hanging out. We're always better off in the air. Of course jaws dropped, eyes popped, small children screamed, etc., when we suddenly whipped out wings and took flight. I guess we're unusual even for LA.

The three of us against a couple hundred Flyboys? I don't think so. Sure, maybe sixty, or even eighty, no problem. But not two hundred. Not even if Max were there.

Well, okay, maybe if Max were there. Maybe the two hundred. But she wasn't there.

Anyway, Gaz, Iggy, and I instinctively implemented a tried-and-true plan of action, Plan Delta, which we've used any number of times and have down to an art.

Basically it means "run like hell." Or rather, "fly like hell."

We flew. We zipped out of there like lightning. The Flyboys don't seem to have altitude problems — they followed us easily up into 747 cruising altitude, where even I was getting a little short of breath. Like the Erasers, they're not too nimble, but they're wicked fast and scarily strong.

One of Iggy's newest explosives took out about fifty of them, and sorry to all those folks showered by bits of Flyboy metal and flesh matrix down at that MTV party on the beach. The rest of them tore after us, and we couldn't outrun them.

Then I saw the Hollywood Hills. We flew right for the sign and, at the very, very last second, screamed into a direct vertical climb. I mean, my belt buckle scraped one of the letters. But the three of us made it, shooting straight up like rockets.

The Flyboys were not so fortunate.

One after another, they plowed right into the sign, setting off electrical charges that shorted them out and made quite a few of them explode like metallic, furry popcorn. And if you think that's a gross description, be glad you weren't there, being pelted by the little pieces. I think only about six or seven of them managed to avoid the carnage, and I have no idea what happened to them.

After we'd busted our sides laughing, we blew out of there, and now we're hiding. Again.

Us: roughly 200. Hard to tell with all the parts flying.

Them: 0

Take that, you whitecoat schmucks. Now you owe California a new Hollywood sign.

— Fang, somewhere in the West

67

Post a Comment on Fang's Blog
Busted-up Hollywood
108 comments

Kewl dude 326 said . . .
O man Fang thats so awesome, i mean when u guys popped all the flyboys. i would a been bustin my gut 2. Keep flyin, man.
San Diego
11:51 AM

Sugargrrl said . . .
Dear Fang,
I'm so glad your alright. I hate those flyboys and hope they all crash and burn. If u need a place to stay in Roanoke, Virginia, just e-mail me.
12:14 PM

Heather said . . .
We should all make posses and search everywhere for labs and Schools and stuff! There are millions and

millions of kids in the world, and we can fix what the grown-ups have polluted and destroyed! Landfills and oil slicks and endangered species and wiping out forests and driving gas hogs and not caring about the environment and not caring about animals! Their time of destroying everything is over! It's time for Green Kids to unite!

Heather Schmidt
President, GreenKidsforaGreenerPlanet.org
12:57 PM

Streetfightr said . . .

Us kidz got 2 take over! De groneups hav recked everything! Dere destroyin r whole planet! De kidz shuld run everything! Dey want us 2 b quiet! We won't b quiet no more!

Brooklyn
1:20 PM

Chen Wei said . . .

Fang, I was wondering: do u have a girlfriend?
Hong Kong
P.S. I am 15 years old but look younger.
2:40 PM

Carlos said . . .

I say we burn all the science labs! Make all the grown-ups into slaves!

Texas
3:07 PM

Anonymous said . . .

Carlos, no, that's stupid. We need science. Science isn't bad by itself. It's just bad when bad people use it to do bad things. We can do good things with science. Like feed the world. I don't want to make all grown-ups slaves. My parents are grown-ups, but they're all right.

Concerned Future Scientist

Louisiana

4:21 PM

Adide said . . .

I am afraid the grown-ups are going to destroy our planet. I want them to stop. I wish they would use science to make better crops and make more rain. Instead of bombs, they should make more schoolbooks for children.

Uganda

4:26 PM

cobra said . . .

Fang, i think i saw u guyz flyin u wuz over my uncles deli in Lincoln Park.

Chicago

5:27 PM

Dita said . . .

I can't believe you and Max split up! You guys should stick together! Now I'm even more worried about all of you! Be extra careful!

Mumbai

6:08 PM

Sean said . . .

Fang, I want to be a bird kid. I don't care what it takes. I would go through anything to be able to fly and be with the flock. Tell me where to meet you. I want to join you today.

Manchester, England

6:35 PM

Sue_P said . . .

I want to join too! I would love to have wings but think it's too late for me. It would hurt. But I will fight for you on the ground! Just tell me where and when!

Palm Beach

6:38 PM

Fang turned off the computer after wading through thousands of messages like these. Max didn't think the blog could help, but he was sure it could. He bet he could raise an army of a hundred thousand . . . ordinary kids, who might be brave and committed, but who would have zero fighting skills and would quickly be slaughtered.

He sighed and lay back, resting his head on one arm. This leader stuff sucked.

68

My miniflock was doing all right, thanks to Angel. For future reference, here are some things you can do if you're a six-year-old genetic anomaly with the ability to control other people's minds:

1) Get business-class tickets for yourself and three other genetic anomalies, plus a dog, on British Airways.

2) Convince airport security that your talking Scottie is a service dog and therefore allowed everywhere, including the ladies' room, which frankly I was not thrilled about.

3) Make people not really notice the hulking, butt-ugly, damaged Eraser loping at your side.

4) Once on board, help people think it's normal for a dog to get his own seat *and* meals.

5) Arrange for us to each have three meals at a time. First-class meals, not that crap they serve to the poor schmucks in Economy.

"Total!" I whispered. "People *have* to pass you to get to the bathroom. Quit growling."

"Sorry," he muttered. "They're getting too close to my steak. Speaking of which, could you cut it into little pieces?"

I leaned over and quickly cut up the steak on Total's tray. I saw Angel grinning at me, and I couldn't help grinning back. Yes, my flock had been split apart: Half of my family was AWOL. We were homeless and on the run, as per usual. We were going to a strange place with no idea of what to do once we got there. And we were trapped in a big sardine can with a bunch of strangers who I was praying weren't Erasers or whitecoats.

And yet.

"Nice chairs," Ari said, patting the arms with his clawed, oversize paws.

"This is kind of fun," said Angel. She gave a little bounce in her seat and started flicking through her movies on demand.

"Max?" Nudge whispered from across the aisle. "Do you think these people are okay?" She nodded back at the other passengers.

"I hope so," I said, keeping my voice down. "But I'm not positive. I wouldn't put it past them for this all to be a setup, and we're surrounded by whitecoats who are going to turn on us. But Angel hasn't picked up anything, like, no evil intent coming from anyone on the plane. So I'm hoping it's okay."

"I've never been on a plane," Nudge said.

"None of us have. It's kind of weird, huh?"

"Yeah. It's really comfortable. These chairs turn into beds, you know? And the little TV and the magazines and the food and people getting you stuff."

I nodded. We were pretty dang pampered. I mean, compared with our usual glamorous life of sleeping in subway tunnels and eating out of trash cans.

"But it seems weird to be up in the air and not . . . outside, you know? And I miss —" She stopped, biting her lip.

"Me too," I said quietly. "But I'm sure they're fine. And I'm sure we'll see them again soon." Because I was going to track them down like *dogs* after my mission was over. I was gonna rag on Fang about this for the rest of his *life*. He couldn't get rid of me that easily.

"I hope nothing goes wrong with this plane," Nudge whispered. "It seems kind of . . . unnatural for a machine to be, like, up in the air. I don't get how it's staying up."

"It's got honking big engines on it," I said, decisively clarifying the situation for her in my leaderly way. "But I tell you what — if something happens to this plane, the four of us will be the ones who make it."

Nudge's face cleared. "Oh, yeah. I didn't think of that."

"Now, rest up before our British invasion."

69

Cushy seven-hour respite aside, it was time to get down to business once we landed at London's Heathrow Airport. We had gone the whole flight without anyone turning into an Eraser and attacking us, and the plane hadn't dropped out of the sky like a lead weight, so it was an excellent start.

For a few moments after we got off, I paused, hoping that maybe the Voice would cut me a break and give clear and followable instructions.

But no. The Voice was MIA, and we were on our own.

Which was *fine*. I'd gotten us all this far. The Voice was a recent phenomenon, and as far as I was concerned, it could stay gone.

"Okay," I said, clapping my hands. My miniflock gathered around me. "The first thing we should do is find an Internet café, get on the Web, and Google Itex in England. Even if we don't find them by name, we'll probably see other links that can help us."

"Whoa, whoa, hold the phone," said Total. "We're in *London*. Are you telling me we're not going to go see the Crown Jewels?"

"And the Tower of London?" Angel added.

"Ooh, look — Madame Tussauds!" Nudge said, pointing at a poster on a kiosk. "We've got to go there!"

Once again I was nonplussed by my flock's ability to completely put aside the fact that we were fighting for our *lives*. For the lives of the entire *world*.

Frowning, I pressed on. "Itex probably has its main offices in the suburbs, not right in the city."

"Buckingham Palace," Ari startled me by saying. "With the guys in the funny fur hats."

"Yeah, yeah, Buckingham Palace!" Nudge agreed without looking at him.

I drew in a breath, ready to start issuing commands.

You know, when you're right, that's all you get to be, said the Voice.

"What the heck does that mean?" I asked, irritated.

"Buckingham Palace," Nudge explained. "Where the queen lives. And Mr. Queen."

"No, no, not you," I muttered. I leaned against a wall and closed my eyes for a second. *You wanna explain that?* I thought. *Or is that one of those kung fu koans I'm supposed to meditate on at the top of a mountain? Ommm.*

"Max?" Angel asked. "Do you have a headache?" She sounded worried.

"No, I'm okay," I said. "Gimme a minute. And keep an eye out."

My flock waited patiently, unlike me. I was ready to rake my fingernails down the wall.

Yes, you should pursue your mission, said the Voice, miraculously answering me. *But you haven't learned how to balance your leadership. You have to lead, but you must also listen.*

And just let them do whatever they want? I demanded silently.

Max, they're children. They're just along for the ride. A strong leader can bend sometimes.

I opened my eyes. "Fine. We'll take a tour, hit the hot spots. Angel, get us on one of those double-decker bus tour things."

"Okay!" she agreed happily, while Nudge punched the air. We headed for the Ground Transportation area.

"I want to ride on top!" Total said, trotting at Angel's side. "But in Max's jacket, 'cause it's cold."

"Oh, yay," I said so no one could hear me. *You're wrong, Voice,* I thought. *They're kids, but they're not just along for the ride. I need every one of them if I'm going to succeed.*

70

"Those aren't the real jewels." I was certain of it. No way would they just have the real Crown Jewels of England hanging out in a glass case where anyone could knock it over.

"They're so beautiful," Nudge breathed, leaning as close as she could to them. "The Imperial State Crown. Golly. I would love to have a crown like that."

And I was so sure she would get her wish, because bizarre science experiments so often become crowned heads of state. Jeez.

"Get a load of the scepter," Total whispered. "How do you like that rock?"

"It says they're real," said Angel, pointing to a placard. "That's the real Cullinan diamond. I like the Orb."

"What, and the queen just comes and gets them when she's going to Parliament?" I scoffed. I turned to Ari. "What does that other sign say? On your side."

Ari looked at me, and for just a second he was almost recognizable as the little boy who used to follow me around so long ago. His face flushed, highlighting the scars that had pretty much healed over. "Don't know," he said, turning away. "Can't read."

"Let's go to Madame Tussauds," said Total. "We must!"

"I don't know who any of these 'famous' people are," said Angel, once we were inside Tussauds.

We were moving around a room full of wax celebrities, and frankly, the only way I would have been more uncomfortable was if I had rocks in my shoes. For those of us who grew up being subjected to evil scientists' tests, walking around lifelike figurines who *could leap out at us at any second* was totally unnerving.

I was watching the figures like a hawk (get it? li'l' flock humor for ya there), waiting for someone's eyes to move, someone's chest to rise and fall with breathing. So far, none of them had budged. Which didn't mean none of them would.

"Me neither," said Nudge, sounding disappointed.

"Me neither," said Ari. Next to all of these smooth wax figures, his rough features and voice stood out like a brick in a jewelry case.

"Um, I think this one is Brad Pitt," I said, pointing. "Who knew he was this tall?"

"Who's Brad Pitt?" Angel asked.

Total tsked and scratched behind one ear with a hind leg. "Only a world-famous movie star," he said. "Read a paper sometimes, will you?"

I let out a breath. "I'm sorry, guys. I'm trying to get on

board with the whole sightseeing thing, but this place gives me the willies."

"Is that the technical term?" asked Total. "The willies?"

"Yes," I said. "Anyway, one of these suckers is going to move, and then I'm going to take the whole room out. I have to get out of here."

"Oh, thank God," said Nudge. "I hate this place."

"Me too," said Angel.

Total shook his head, looking disgusted. "You people. This is modern *culture*."

71

Next up, the Itex Corporation. The major industrial giant that seemed to be behind all the recombinant-DNA experiments; as well as the Re-Evolution Plan, also known as the By-Half Plan; and who knew how many other lunatic plans of mass destruction and mayhem.

Basically, the last place any of us would ever, ever want to go voluntarily.

The place we *had* to go.

Their office was in . . .

"Threadgill-on-Thames?" Nudge read carefully.

"It sounds like a tweed theme park," said Angel.

"It's pronounced 'Tems,'" Total said, licking one paw. "Can I have another potato chip?"

I passed him a newspaper cone full of hot fried fish and french fries. Those wacky Brits called fries "chips." And potato chips were "crisps." And cookies were "biscuits." I had no idea what real biscuits were called. Wangdoodles?

"And the vinegar?" Total asked.

I sprinkled vinegar on it for him, then looked at the map again. The Internet cafés we'd found were for people with their own computers. Since Fang had taken our computer, we'd had to go to a library.

Of course, we'd found that Itex was everywhere, with branches in fourteen cities throughout the United Kingdom. But the *main* office seemed to be about a thirty-minute flight from London, west-southwest.

"I like fish and chips," Ari said. "They're yummy."

"Uh-huh," I said distractedly, tracing a line on the map.

I still couldn't believe I had to go kill the dragon without Fang by my side. He had abandoned me, Nudge, and Angel. Was he so pissed about Ari that he didn't care if we lived or died? Did he think his blog was really going to solve everything? It's not like a bunch of angry kids with pitchforks and torches was going to end Itex's reign of terror.

The word *terror* suddenly made me think about when Gazzy had told those FBI guys his name was Captain Teror. My eyes were hot and itchy in a flash, and I had trouble swallowing. Gazzy. Iggy. I missed them so much. I'd had dreams about them all night and woke up convinced something bad would happen to them and I wouldn't be able to help.

I was going to *kill* Fang. That was totally on my list, right after "save the world."

Jerk. Cretin. Oh, God. He was part of me; he was in my blood. My blood was in him, literally. How could he have done this?

I glanced over at where Ari was drawing the last of his

french fries through a mound of ketchup, his too-large hand making it look like a toothpick. I'd been watching him carefully, and so far he seemed loyal, sincere, not acting suspiciously. But what if I really had made my worst mistake?

I know what you're thinking: Of course you didn't, Max! It was Fang! He made the mistake!

And yes, we all know that my making a mistake is very, very rare. *Exceedingly* rare.

Still.

I was going to keep an eye on Ari.

"Max?" Nudge was looking at me. "Earth to Max."

"Huh? What?"

"We're going to fly there, right?" Nudge asked, pointing to Threadgill-on-Thames on the map. "Like, *fly* fly, not plane fly, right?"

"Right." I glanced out the window. "We'll go as soon as the sun sets. In the meantime, anyone want more tea?"

"Yeah, I'll have some," said Total. Of course.

72

"Oh, lovely," I breathed, peering through a tall bank of hedges. "Geez, they're not even pretending to gussy this place up, are they?"

"It looks so depressing," said Nudge softly. "*I* would hate to work there."

"You think?" I said. "*I* would hate to undergo cruel and unusual scientific experimentation there. It looks like the kind of forbidding, twisted place where evil scientists would do totally unthinkable, gruesome experiments. Like graft other species' DNA into innocent infants."

"For example," said Nudge.

"What are we gonna do here?" Ari asked. The rest of us were so slender and lithe, thanks to our birdlike bones, that Ari seemed especially hulking and clunky in comparison. Now he loomed over us in the dark as we took our first look at the Itex British headquarters.

Fittingly, the building used to be a prison. And boy, had the Brits cornered the market on dank and gloomy. Itex headquarters had an unmistakable eau de prison about it — looming, blocklike rectangular buildings made of dirty brown brick.

If the leader of Itex is reading this right now, I have two words for you: *seasonal plantings*.

The entire thing was surrounded by an electrified chain-link fence at least twelve feet high, topped with razor wire, in case getting repeatedly shocked with five thousand volts wasn't enough of a deterrent. And okay, if you're totally nuts, maybe it wouldn't be.

Of course, we were just going to fly over it anyway.

I heard Angel swallow in the quiet night and looked down at her. Her face was unusually pale, her eyes wide.

"What's up?" I asked her, going on alert.

She swallowed again and reached for my hand. I squeezed hers and knelt down to her level.

"I can feel thoughts and stuff coming from inside," she said brokenly. "From the whitecoats and also, like, minds without bodies."

Brains on a Stick, I thought.

"They're thinking awful stuff," Angel went on. "They're really bad. Like, evil. They want to do their plan and they don't care what they have to do to make it happen. They don't mind killing people. Or animals."

Or any combination thereof, I thought.

"How about other bird kids?" I asked. "Other recombinant life-forms, Erasers?"

She shook her head, her curls shining in the moonlight. "They're all dead. They killed them all."

73

So of course we had to get in there! I mean, why would we pass up a chance to break into a place where delusional mass murderers were targeting creatures just like us? What would be the fun of avoiding *that* situation?

"Do we really have to go in there?" Nudge asked. "'Cause, I mean, if we don't actually have to, then I'd rather not. I'd rather kick back somewhere."

I smiled at her and tried to smooth her unruly brown hair. "You and me both, kid. But I have this whole saving-the-world gig, and I kind of have to do this. You with me?"

She nodded, not looking happy, then put a fierce expression on. "I'm ready. Let's bust this place up!"

"Me too!" said Angel. "Those people are really evil. They shouldn't be allowed to hurt anyone else. We have to fix it so they can't."

"We have to end this now, here!" Ari said.

"That's right!" I said, holding my fist out to tap, like we did at bedtime. "We're gonna rain fire on this place! When we're done, there'll just be a greasy spot!"

Remember the Hydra, Max?

I almost jumped. Would I ever get used to an uninvited Voice inside my head? My guess at this point was no.

Hydra, Hydra, I thought. *Sounds like a . . . sprinkler?*

No. The Lernaean Hydra, one of the labors of Heracles. Every time Heracles cut off a head, two grew back in its place.

Oh. That. Yeah, I saw a cartoon about it once. What about it?

Think it through, Max, said the Voice. *It'll come to you.*

I frowned suspiciously. *Is this one of those metaphor things? Would it kill you to just come out and tell me?*

Silence.

Of course.

"Max?" Angel asked.

I held up a finger. "One sec. Voice imparting unnecessary knowledge."

Total flopped down in the grass and rested his head on his front paws.

Okay. Hydra, I thought. I remembered the cartoon I had seen, where a big muscular mouse dressed in a lion skin had been trying to lop catlike heads off this giant dragon thing.

But I wasn't getting the connection.

Oh, wait. A head got cut off, and two grew back in its place.

We were planning to destroy this Itex headquarters. Did that mean if we destroyed it, two would grow back in

218

its place? Or, like, two others would become more power-ful? Hmm.

The Hydra itself must be killed, Max. The whole thing at once. This is just one head. Find the body and kill it.

I thought. I remembered the map I had glimpsed through an open door back at the School, when Ari had been taking me around. It was a map of the world. Almost every country had had an Itex symbol somewhere on it, and many had had smaller stars as well.

Because I'm smarter than the average recombinant bear, I realized that we needed to check out some of the other Itex branches, in other countries, to find the heart of the beast. *Thanks a lot, Voice,* I thought a little sarcasti-cally, to no reply. *Will you make up your mind about just where the heck we're supposed to be going?* God, I was so tired. A world saver's work is never done.

I hunkered down next to the hedge and motioned everyone closer.

"Guys, I do believe that France is calling our names."

Nudge frowned. "They're yelling for flying bird kids?"

"Yes." I stood up and held out my arms for Total. He jumped up, and I zipped him into my jacket. "Does anyone know any French?"

"I know how to ask for a spunky Chablis," said Total, his voice somewhat muffled. I unfolded my wings and stretched them out, ready to take off.

"I know some Spanish," said Nudge. "*Cerrado* and *abierto*. Stuff like that."

"That'll be good in Spain. In France, I guess we'll find out if Angel can read minds in French."

Angel shook out her wings, looking intrigued. "I don't know," she said. "But you know what? I want some pastry while we're there."

"Ooh, I second that emotion," said Total.

I stifled a response — had Madame Tussauds taught them nothing? — and took off into the chilly night, kind of feeling like Harry Potter escaping from the Dursleys. Except in our world, Dursleys were everywhere, were heavily funded, and had a strong scientific bent.

74

Los Angeles, gangbangers, huh!

"If they're not the Crips or the Bloods, does that mean they're the Cruds?" Iggy asked in all seriousness.

"Shh!" Fang told him. "Keep it down! Don't throw gas on this particular fire, okay?"

"Okay," said Iggy, but Gazzy chuckled and slapped him a high five.

"Besides, they're the Ghosts," Fang reminded him. "They have it on all their jackets."

"Oh, I must have missed that," Iggy said sarcastically, and Fang mentally smacked his forehead.

"Yo," someone said, and he spun to see a guy named Keez walking toward them. That morning they'd been lying low in an empty lot in east LA, and they'd suddenly been surrounded by a big gang. Literally a street gang: the Ghosts. They'd all tensed to fight, but one of the gang, Keez, had recognized Fang, Iggy, and Gazzy from the news. He'd also been reading Fang's blog. The gang controlled this part of the city, and Keez had offered them a safe house.

Now he nodded at Fang. "This way, dude."

"We're famous," Iggy whispered, so low that Fang could barely hear him.

"So's swine flu," Fang whispered back.

They followed Keez to an abandoned building in the middle of a scary, decrepit block. People eyed them curiously, but with a simple hand motion from Keez, they looked away.

"I want a Ghosts jacket," the Gasman whispered to Fang. Fang felt the Gasman's hand start to reach for his, then drop. Since they'd split, the Gasman had been trying to be super tough. Fang had to remind himself that he was just a little kid. Max, though she was about the toughest person Fang had ever met, was weirdly good with all the mom stuff, putting bandages on, calming the kids down when they had bad dreams. He'd never realized how much extra work that took.

As they followed Keez up some broken brownstone steps, Fang reached out and took the Gasman's hand. The kid looked up at him, surprised, but then Fang felt the small hand tighten around his. So he'd done the right thing.

Two big guys were standing guard at the front door, but a nod from Keez made them step aside. Inside it was a lot like that burned-out crack house Max and Fang had found in DC, only with less cozy charm. But it was relatively safe and hidden, and those were two of his favorite things.

"Crash here." Keez motioned them into a shell of a room that looked as if one of Iggy's bigger experiments had exploded in it not long ago.

"Cool. Thanks, man," Fang said. Then he, Iggy, and the Gasman collapsed on the floor. It was time for Fang to step up and make a plan.

75

"*This* is your plan?" Iggy's voice held disbelief.

"Yep. Grab your backpack."

The Gasman didn't say anything, but Fang wondered if he was wishing he'd decided to go with Max. The first day it had seemed like an adventure. Now it was starting to seem just . . . painful. But there was no way Fang was going back — until Max ditched the cretin.

The offices of *People* magazine were on about four floors of a colossal building in downtown LA. Fang was sure that if Angel were here, it would be no problem for them to see the president of the whole company and convince him to publish an entire special issue about Itex and their evil ways.

But he was Fang, and he could work his own wiles. He held up a bag of deli sandwiches, and the front guard signed them in. "Delivery elevators in the back," he said in a bored voice.

"Let's take the stairs," Gazzy whispered.

"We're going to the twenty-seventh floor," Fang whispered back.

Basically, stepping into the elevator felt like volunteering for psychic trauma. It was small, enclosed, and full of other people, all of them better dressed and significantly more hygienic than the bird kids.

On the twenty-seventh floor, they practically leaped out of the elevators into a designer reception area bustling with people. Fang held on to his bag and approached the main desk.

A guy in his early twenties with mod rectangular glasses looked at them as though they were three scruffy homeless children.

"Can I help you?"

"I need to speak to your top reporter," Fang said coolly. "I have a story with worldwide implications. You print what I tell you, and this magazine will go down in history."

The reception guy was unimpressed. "Do you have an appointment? With *anyone?*"

Of course not. That would require a level of forethought that Fang hadn't mastered yet. He felt the deli bag had been a master touch. "I just need to speak to someone, right now."

The guy sneered. "I don't think so."

"If they find out you didn't let me talk to someone, you'll get canned so fast you'll feel like tuna."

That was when the guy pressed the button for security.

Fang tapped Iggy's hand twice. "Let's go! Now!"

76

Two burly security guards picked up their pace as soon as they saw Fang, Iggy, and Gazzy race toward the stairwell. Fang knew that when someone was chasing you, you never got on the elevator, twenty-seven floors up or no. They could lock you between floors, be waiting for you. You always took the stairs.

Fang yanked the door open, and the three of them flung themselves downward, four steps at a time. They pushed past startled employees and almost collided with someone delivering sandwiches. Behind them, they heard stairwell doors being opened and security guards yelling. On one floor, the door opened right as they passed, and Fang felt someone take a swipe at his jacket. He continued to leap downward, keeping track of Iggy and the Gasman out of the corners of his eyes. Unfortunately, there were no windows in the stairwell that they could escape through.

The stairs felt endless and went back and forth so tightly that Fang started to feel seasick. *Keep it together,* he told himself. *Keep it together. You've got a little kid and a blind guy depending on you.*

"Okay, about to reach bottom!" Fang alerted Iggy after endless minutes. "Eight more steps, then a hard left!"

"Gotcha," said Iggy.

Finally they reached bottom. If they could just make it out the front doors . . .

There were eight security guards waiting at the bottom of the stairs. Fang whirled to head back upstairs, but the door closest to them opened, and four more guards started thundering toward them. The three bird kids bolted into the lobby, trying to break through the line of guards.

Unsuccessfully.

"We're leaving!" Fang snarled, but a guard had the back of his jacket and his belt loop. He marched Fang to the big glass doors, muscled them open, and tossed Fang down the building's front steps.

"You don't weigh nothin'!" he said in surprise.

"Don't come back!" said another guard.

Iggy and the Gasman landed on the sidewalk next to Fang, and they quickly scrambled to their feet. After some of the situations they'd been in, getting thrown onto the sidewalk like trash wasn't that bad, but it meant that Fang's big plan had bombed. He dusted off his pants, opened the deli bag, and passed out squashed sandwiches as they made their way back to the safe house. *WWMD?* Fang wondered. What would Max do? Besides let a murderous creep into their lives, that is.

"No go, eh?" Keez was honing a switchblade on a spinning metal wheel.

"Nope."

"You shoulda whooshed out those wings, man," he said. "I saw you guys on the news once. You got them wicked wings, right? That woulda done it for sure."

"Uh, I didn't want to resort to cheap tricks," Fang muttered. Plus, he hadn't thought of it. Keez was right. That would have worked like a charm. Shoot.

On to Plan . . . *H?*

77

"The plan is hot dogs?" said the Gasman, enthusiastically wolfing down his second one. "I like this plan!"

Fang did a quick 360, but this section of El Prado had only the usual assortment of dealers, homeless people, and Ghosts. Nothing too threatening.

"The plan is not hot dogs," Fang said, wiping his fingers on his jeans. "We're just killing time till the real plan falls into place." Of course, there was no real plan — yet. But Fang was the leader of this particular flock, and leaders always had to look confident, even when they were blowing smoke. Another lesson he'd learned from Max.

"All right, my man," Keez said to the hot-dog vendor, and shook his hand. Fang gathered that Keez had just been comped about a dozen hot dogs in return for the vendor's safety on this street. Interesting.

Iggy was halfway through his fourth hot dog when he suddenly froze in midchew. Fang watched his face alertly.

"What?" he said.

"Crud," Iggy said, throwing down his hot dog. "Fly-boys."

"You guys scatter!" Fang told Keez quickly. "We've got trouble, but they're only after us."

"How do they keep finding us?" the Gasman wailed, then stuffed the rest of his hot dog into his mouth.

"We'll stay!" Keez said, pulling out his cell phone.

"No, man, you don't under —" was as far as Fang got before he heard the buzzing, and then it was too late.

There were about eighty of them, and they swarmed above the roof of a nearby building like a cloud of wasps.

"What the heck is that?" said Keez. Already other Ghosts were pouring out of buildings, running up the street.

"Robots," Fang said tersely, and unfolded his wings. "You guys should split."

He heard a couple of gasps, and one Ghost said, "Holy Mother."

"We're staying," said Keez, and he pulled out his switchblade. He waved his arms at his troops, yelling over the increasing noise. "Fan out!"

"Eighty Flyboys — coming from ten o'clock," Fang told Iggy. Iggy and the Gasman both snapped out their wings, causing more indrawn breaths and muttered exclamations. "On the ground, the Ghosts can help. We'll do what we can from the air."

Iggy nodded his understanding, and then Keez said, "Here!" and pressed a long crowbar into Iggy's hands. Iggy grinned and threw himself skyward.

One of his wings brushed a Ghost on the downswing, and the Ghost ducked, looking astonished.

Fang judged they had about four seconds before impact. "They're metal based," he said quickly. "Covered with skin. Knives won't do squat. Pipes and baseball bats would be better."

"Bats we got," said Keez, handing Fang one. "And we got something else too." Fang saw that three Ghosts had run up with what looked like a *bazooka,* maybe five feet long. There was no time to ask where they'd gotten that. Fang ran a few steps and leaped into the air, hoping to lead the Flyboys away from the gang that had protected him.

His heart pounding, blood roaring in his ears, Fang flew straight at the cloud of Flyboys.

78

"We will destroy you," the Flyboys droned. "You have no escape."

That was the most imaginative, threatening thing the whitecoats had programmed these 'droids to say? "Talk about lame," Fang muttered. Mechanical heads swiveled, laser-red eyes locked on to him, and a bunch of the robots split away from the main group to face him down.

Fang readied his aluminum baseball bat. A sudden whining, whistling sound made him backpedal hard. Fifty feet away, a ground-to-air missile flew directly into the mass of Flyboys. Its aim was off and it exploded too late, above them. But it still blasted about fifteen metallic heads off, and Fang had a moment to hope that the Gasman had enjoyed the display.

Then everything went into fight speed: super slow and super fast at the same time. Fang raced among the Flyboys and started swinging, feeling the numbing shock of hitting Flyboy metal as hard as he could. Within a minute he discovered that hitting a shoulder at a certain angle would pop an arm out of joint, and hitting a head sideways from one direction and then quickly downward would often snap it clean off.

Well, not *clean,* actually — it was totally gross, made worse by the sparks and dangling electrical wires he saw as the headless body plummeted downward.

"Oof!" Fang lost his breath when a Flyboy kicked him in the stomach. It was different from fighting Erasers. Erasers were clumsier but more adaptable. Flyboys were stronger and more precise, but their moves were limited.

Fang couldn't see the Gasman. He caught sight of Iggy, wielding the crowbar like a sword, slashing and bashing Flyboys with his long reach. His nose was bloody and one eye was swollen, but he was holding his own. Fang heard gunfire and small explosions on the ground, and he hoped the Gasman had gotten out of there.

Bam! Fang blocked a Flyboy's punch, then swung his bat furiously, landing a blow to the back of its head. The head made a simultaneous clunking and squishing sound, but the Flyboy wasn't seriously damaged.

Fang started to swing again but was blocked by another Flyboy coming in from the side. A hard, jaw-snapping kick right in Fang's kidney made him gasp, and he instantly folded his wings and dropped like a stone for about fifteen feet, long enough to recover. Then he poured on the power and shot straight up, swinging the bat with all his strength, managing to make two Flyboys drop. He damaged another so badly it flew crookedly away, smoke streaming from its neck.

And just like that, it was over. The remaining fifteen or so Flyboys got into formation, then they spun and flew off as one. Fang glided to where Iggy was hovering, listening for any remnant of sound.

"S'over," he told Iggy. "Let's go."

They flew down to El Prado, as police cars from all over the city raced toward the area.

On the ground, the street was littered with broken bits of Flyboys. They found the Gasman with Keez, and though they both looked beat up, they were standing.

"Police coming," Fang said. "We gotta go."

"All right, man," said Keez, holding out a swollen, bloody hand. "Whew! That was some action! This kid here is dangerous!"

The Gasman puffed his chest out.

"Thanks," said Fang. "Thanks for everything." Then the three of them took off. From above, Fang saw the Ghosts scattering into buildings, down alleys, into cars that screeched off. By the time the police got there, all that was left was a scattering of completely unexplainable chunks of metal.

79

Total squirmed inside my jacket like a gopher in a hole. We were super high, keeping a lookout for planes, making our way across France. We hadn't bothered with the Itex plant in England, since it was just a single head of the hydra. We knew there were about four different Itex plants in Germany, including its world headquarters, and that's where we were headed. But this little dog was about to make me lose my mind.

He squirmed again. I resisted the temptation to unzip my jacket and let him discover the joy and excitement of free-falling. He took a breath and sniffed a little.

Here it comes, I thought.

"It's like you have no *soul,*" Total said.

"Total, we've been over this," I said impatiently. "We checked out the Itex plant in Saint Jean-de-Sèvre." Total grimaced at my pronunciation, making me want to smack him. "We're on a mission to check out the main headquarters, in Germany. There is no Itex plant in Paris. Thus, going to Paris makes no sense."

"No, it's only the center of world culture," he said. "The

home of some of the best food on the planet. Fashion, art, architecture — ah, Versailles!" He sounded like he was about to cry.

I rolled my eyes.

"And yet, no Itex plant," I said pointedly.

"I wouldn't mind seeing Paris," said Nudge. "I saw this guidebook back at the library. They have little canal boats you can take tours on, and fancy gardens, and that Loovra museum, and palaces, and all kinds of stuff." She looked at me hopefully.

Total had taught both girls how to use crocodile tears, and now Angel turned grieving eyes on me. I steeled myself, waiting to feel her infiltrate my brain, but she didn't (that I could tell).

"Life is so short," Angel said sadly. "So short and so hard. The idea of seeing the City of Light, just once —"

"Oh, for God's sake," I muttered.

"It would almost make everything seem worthwhile," she finished.

"Yes, because what's a life of degradation and torture compared with a charming bistro on the Champs-Élysées?" I asked, sarcasm dripping. Total grimaced again.

"Exactly!" Angel said excitedly. "That's what I'm talking about. It all becomes unimportant when you're standing, like, at Sacré-Coeur!"

I knew I was beaten. If I didn't give in, not only would I have to listen to two children, a hulking disaster, and a dog whining at me all the way to Germany, but once we got there, no one would be able to concentrate on the mission. Plus, I was expecting the Voice to pop in at any second with some sage fortune-cookie advice like, See what Paris has to offer. Or, What's the lesson you could learn from this? Or, Maybe you'll find a bright, shiny clue to something right there at the Arc de Triomphe!

I looked down. Far below us, the millions of lights of Paris were obvious — it was the biggest city in the country and sparkled like a diamond. An expensive, time-consuming, no doubt pointless diamond.

I rubbed my forehead with one hand. "Oh, all right," I muttered. "Fine. We'll spend a couple hours in Paris."

I tried to block out the whoops of joy. Looking at Ari, I realized he hadn't weighed in. In general, he kept his thoughts to himself, as if he didn't deserve to have an opinion. Nudge and Angel still didn't look at him or interact with him. I also knew that Paris would be one of the last fun things he did in this life.

"Let's find someplace to sleep," I said, as we angled downward through the night.

80

Here's the weird thing: We hadn't seen hide nor hair of an Eraser or a whitecoat or a Flyboy chasing us since we'd split from Fang and the others. We still had me, Angel, Total, Ari — all of the "if" factors that could possibly be tracked. And yet the last several days had been one *grande vacance,* as we say here in gay Paree.

So what was different? Just that Fang, Gazzy, and Iggy weren't here. It was crazy. I wondered what they were doing, if they were, like, on a beach or partying somewhere or whatever. Completely forgetting about us. Not missing us.

Part of me was dying to find an Internet café and at least read Fang's latest blog entry. Maybe I could get some idea of where they were and what they were doing. But the bigger, self-righteous part of me refused to acknowledge my burning curiosity.

"OMG!" Nudge squealed, putting a filmy, arty scarf around her neck. "This is fabulous!"

And so suitable for an Eraser to grab and yank, thus breaking your neck, I struggled not to say. Instead I nodded unenthusiastically, hoping she would read between the lines.

"This is what I'm talking about," Total said happily. He leaned his front paws on the marble table and pulled his chocolate pastry toward him. "I'm sitting here, I'm eating, and Angel didn't have to control anyone's mind. *This* is civilization."

Dogs are allowed in most restaurants in Paris, in case you haven't picked up on that. We were sitting at a tiny marble-topped table outside a café. People streamed past us, not turning into Erasers or whatever would come after Erasers.

"It *is* really neat," Nudge said, looping her scarf around her neck so it wouldn't dip into her coffee. "How many of these can I have?" She was on her third pastry.

I shrugged. "However many you can eat without barfing." Okay, as a mom I'm unconventional, I admit. Especially since I'm only fourteen and didn't actually give birth to any of these guys.

"I wish —," Angel began, then stopped. She pulled her café au lait over and took a sip.

I wish everyone was here with us, I heard in my mind, and it wasn't the Voice. I nodded at Angel. *Me too,* I thought back.

"What are we going to do after this?" Nudge asked. "How about the Loovra?"

I shook my head. "Too enclosed, too much security, too many people. There isn't enough Valium in the world to get me in there."

"The Eiffel Tower is open, and high," said Angel.

I nodded. "It's a possibility." I checked my watch. "You guys have four hours, then we have to bug out of here."

Nudge snapped me a salute. *"Jawohl!"*

Total started choking with laughter, and Ari and Angel both grinned.

Everyone knows what the Eiffel Tower looks like. But in person, it's *so much* bigger — all this lacy steel and iron swooping up and up into the sky. It was so tempting to just fly to the top, but instead we waited in an endless line and took a crowded elevator to the top. And you know how much I like being packed into small spaces with other people!

But once we were at the top, the view was magnificent. Right below us was the Seine River, with its houseboats and tour boats. From up there we could see everything, all the major landmarks, like the Arc de Triomphe and the Louvre museum. Paris stretched as far as we could see.

I had to admit, Paris was really beautiful. The buildings all seemed so old and fancy and really pretty in a non-American kind of way. I wished the guys could see it. I hope you guys can see it some day too, if it's still standing after the whitecoats try to destroy the world.

Of course Nudge made us shop. At least street stands weren't as claustrophobia inducing as enclosed stores. All along the Seine were little stalls selling books and flowers, and I felt as if we were in a movie with subtitles. I waited with saintly patience as Nudge and Angel sorted through

T-shirts and hats and books in French that we couldn't carry, much less read.

Ari tried on a leather jacket — his old one was shredded and bloodstained. The stall vendor looked at Ari warily, then Angel distracted him and he didn't seem to notice Ari anymore.

"It's you," I said, watching him shrug it on. "Is it comfortable?"

He grimaced. "Nothing's comfortable when you're built like this." He gestured to his hulking, overdeveloped muscles, the lumpy wings that didn't fold in perfectly, neatly, like ours.

I stepped behind him to smooth out the collar, and that's when I saw it again: the expiration date on the back of his neck. His time was coming, very, very soon.

You know what? I was glad I'd shown him Paris.

81

You know the other strange thing about Europe? It's weensy. It was like, oops, I blinked, there goes Belgium! All of Western Europe could fit into America, east of the Mississippi. Flying from England to France took about thirty minutes. Crossing over France took about six hours. It had take us almost eight hours to cross Texas, back in America.

Anyway. Here's my one-note take on Germans: They're scrubbers. Hoo, boy, we're talking a tidy little country. France? Not so much.

"Okay, no one leave their socks lying around," I instructed, as we drifted to a landing outside a town called Lendeheim. "That would send them right over the edge."

Lendeheim seemed to have been designed by the "Germany" team at Epcot. I kept expecting Bambi to pop out from behind a bush. There was so much carved gingerbread on the houses that my stomach growled.

The one main road through town led uphill to an incredible medieval castle. You guessed it: *Itex*. Still lording it over the peasants, in their way.

"This is too cute," said Total, hopping down from my arms. "I want to start planting window boxes or something."

"The hiiillls are aliiive," Nudge warbled, spreading her arms wide, "with the sound of —"

"Okay, listen up," I broke in. "The castle is through these trees. Let's do a quick recon and then decide what to do next."

I set off into the woods, pushing aside the picturesque German underbrush. Frankly, I'd expected a German forest to be a little tidier than this.

"Wait, don't tell me," Total said, trotting after me. "We're gonna break in, steal some stuff, break some stuff, almost get caught, and then escape in some dangerous, dramatic way."

I set my jaw, trying to ignore Nudge's giggle. "Maybe," I said tightly. "You got a better plan?"

He was silent for a few moments. "Well, no."

I know you might not believe this, but slogging through a foreign European forest in the dead of night with an ex-Eraser, a talking dog, and two kids who depend on you for their lives — well, not as much fun as you'd think. But maybe that's just my negativity talking.

Once again, I was forcibly reminded of what slooow and hard work walking is, compared with flying. But I didn't want to take a chance of being seen, not this close to the castle. For all I knew, they had watchtowers or radar or searchlights. Possibly all three.

But we finally made it. Standing at the edge of the woods, looking across the moat at the thick, high castle wall, I felt like this was the most castley castle I'd ever seen. It was all pointy and chock-full o' turrets, with narrow slits for cute Robin Hood arrows, and other windows with many tiny panes of glass. Of course, the floodlights and razor wire at the top of the wall detracted a bit from its charm, but if you squinted, they faded a little.

"There's an iron gate," whispered Nudge, pointing. "We can see through it."

"Yep." Sticking to the shadows, we half crouched, half crawled toward the castle, checking carefully for trip wires or hidden traps. When we were within thirty feet of the gate, the sound of marching feet made us freeze, bellies to the ground.

My raptor vision showed me the next generation of Erasers goose-stepping in the courtyard. I saw just as clearly lines of people marching after them, fierce expressions on their faces. But there was something odd about them — something not entirely human. And then I saw my old clone double, Max II, who had tried to replace me, who Jeb had tried to make me kill. She was back.

82

Standing next to me, Ari had gone rigid, his eyes locked on the Max clone. I remembered that they had been an anti–real Max team and felt my stomach tighten. My vigilance about Ari cranked up a couple notches.

While I pondered this revolting development, Nudge elbowed me in the ribs.

"Oh, my God!" she whispered. "Do you see that?"

"Yep," I said, watching Max II grimly. "We meet again."

"What do you mean? We've never seen her before," said Nudge.

I turned and looked at Nudge. "Hello? You don't remember that topsy-turvy day when 'I' tried to *cook* and offered to *fix your hair?*"

Nudge frowned. "Yeah. That was Max Two. That's not what I'm talking about! Look, four rows behind her!"

I looked. Then I saw what Nudge meant.

There was a *Nudge II* — marching along with an un-Nudge-like solemnity. Other than that, she looked exactly like her.

"Holy moly," I breathed, hardly able to believe it.

"Uh-oh," said Angel quietly, then pointed. I swallowed a groan and dropped my head into my hands for a second. Excellent. Just what the world needed: another Angel. Because God knows, one six-year-old mind-controlling flying child just isn't enough.

"I don't believe it," said Nudge. "There's another me!"

"And another me," said Angel.

Was everyone here a clone? Maybe not, but they were all mutants of some kind, I was willing to bet.

"What, I'm not important enough to have a double?" Total sounded completely offended. " 'No, let's not clone the dog. He's just a dog, after all.' "

I rubbed his head behind his ears, but he huffed and flopped over on the grass.

"I don't have a double either," said Ari. So Jeb hadn't cloned his son. How sentimental of him.

"Are they going to try to replace us, like they did with you?" Nudge asked.

"Yes," I said. "But we'll catch on immediately when the new Nudge is silent and mopey, and the new Angel acts like an actual six-year-old."

They smiled, and I congratulated myself on my ability to keep their spirits up even in the face of this new atrocity.

"Actually," I went on, "let's come up with a code word or phrase to use with one another when we need to make absolutely sure we're the right ones. Okay?"

"Okay," said Nudge.

"Ooh, I've got one," said Angel, and we put our heads together as she whispered it.

"Perfect!" said Nudge, breaking into a smile.

I laughed silently and slapped her a very quiet high five.

Ari grinned and nodded.

Even Total's furry black face seemed to smile.

So what was the secret word?

Yeah, like I'm gonna tell *you*.

83

What with all the stomping and the fiercely staring straight ahead, none of the Flyboys or clones or other mutants seemed to hear us when we flew over the wall as silently as we could. We caught up with the troops and started marching right behind them, a last line of followers eager to herald the beginning of the Re-Evolution.

I'm so sure.

Anyway, gutsy little devil-may-care freaks that we are, we trooped right into the building with them, our feet moving in lockstep, arms swinging tightly at our sides. We would see how long it took someone to notice. My guess is that it wouldn't be long. Call it a hunch.

We filed between tall metal double doors, which swung shut behind us with an ominous clang. Inside, we were surprised by how the Marching Gang o' Mutants immediately split up. The Flyboys veered off down one dimly lit stone hallway, and the others split up into several streams heading in different directions.

It was like a stone rabbit warren, with many hallways

winding away from the main doors. Amber emergency lights barely lit the way.

Moving silently, we followed a group through another set of double doors, the surrealness of it giving me ill-advised giggles that I quickly swallowed.

Still no one seemed to notice us. We were heading deeper and deeper into one of Itex's most important strongholds without anyone getting in our way.

I looked down at Angel.

"Trap?" I said out of the side of my mouth.

She nodded. "Trap."

84

"Everyone on guard," I breathed, and then suddenly we were in an airplane hangar–sized room.

The ceiling was at least thirty feet high, and the only windows were narrow horizontal slits maybe a foot or two below the ceiling. The stone walls were hung with tremendous TV screens, several on each wall. The rest of the room was filled with gray metal bunks, each covered with a kicky olive drab army blanket suitable for bouncing quarters off.

You had to give it to them: These guys sure knew how to party!

The mutants filed off into the rows of metal bunks, and we found ourselves alone at the edge of the room.

Instinctively we formed a circle, our backs to one another, and cased the joint.

"This is so nice," said Total. "I want my room at home to look just like this. If we ever get a home."

"Shh," I said mildly. "Everyone keep an eye out, mark your emergency exits, and let's see what's going on."

All around us, everyone had moved with purpose to

what I assumed were assigned chores: The products of the finest scientific minds in the world were busily sweeping, dusting metal beds, polishing their boots.

Nudge and I looked at each other at the same time, and Angel read our minds. In the next moment we had each found boots in our sizes beneath various beds. Ari copied us, managing to find some extra-large ones. In seconds we had laced them onto our feet and hidden our filthy, shredded sneakers.

"Oh, yeah," said Total. "Now we blend."

I made a face at him and then turned my attention to the TV screens. There were three screens on each wall, and if they'd been showing, say, a soccer game, I would have been in pig heaven.

However, they were broadcasting the earnest face of a fair-haired woman who was speaking in consecutive languages. We tapped our feet through German, French, Spanish, Italian, and Japanese, with our room's occupants scarily shouting agreement and praise every so often.

Nudge frowned. "Who does she remind me of? I feel like I've seen her before."

I thought, then shrugged. "No idea."

Finally the whitecoat got to English. "The time of the Re-Evolution is here!" she said forcefully. Various voices in the room cheered.

"We have begun implementing the By-Half Plan! Even as you watch this, the weak, the unnecessary, the ones who drain our resources, are being eliminated!"

85

More cheers, while we five looked at one another in horror and then quickly remembered to cheer along with the others.

The woman looked out from the screen with the sincere zeal of a serious nut job. "We are creating a new world. A world where there is no hunger, no sickness, no weakness."

"Because they *killed* everyone," I muttered.

"The causes of war will be eliminated," she went on earnestly. "There will be plenty of food for everyone. There will be plenty of room for everyone. People will cease to fight over property, food, wealth, energy resources."

Everyone in the room cheered.

"Yep, no reason to fight," I whispered. "Unless, of course, you're persnickety about *religion*. I bet everyone will be so healthy and happy that it won't even matter anymore. It's not like people take it that *seriously*." I rolled my eyes and shook my head.

Every so often someone would walk past us, not giving us a second glance. We cheered with the others and tried to look busy by smoothing beds, lining up shoes, picking lint off blankets.

"Remember," said the whitecoat, "we can't achieve Re-Evolution without you, our chosen ones. The new order must be pure. All races are equal. All genders are equal. But illness, weakness, and other flaws must be eliminated."

"All genders?" whispered Nudge. "Aren't there just the two? Or did I miss something?"

I shrugged. "No idea. Maybe they've created others."

The thought was fairly repulsive, and we made "eew" faces at each other.

"So if you know of anyone who should experience the glory of martyrdom so that others may live in paradise, please inform your supervisor immediately," said the woman. "It will reflect well on you, and you will be praised."

I looked at the others, appalled. "Oh, my God," I said softly. "They want people to turn in anyone who isn't perfect. Which is, like, *everyone!* No one is perfect!"

I couldn't have said it better myself, Max, said the Voice.

So what now? I thought.

You're where you need to be, doing what you need to do, said the Voice. It was so rare that I got approval from the Voice that I was taken aback. *But are you sure you can do this alone?*

I've got Nudge and Angel and Total and Ari, I thought.

You're missing half your family, said the Voice. *Who are also half your army.*

Not my fault, I thought testily. *Not my decision.*

Does that mean it isn't your problem and you don't have to fix it?

I narrowed my eyes suspiciously. On the TV screen, the whitecoat had switched back to German.

And your point is . . . ? I thought.

You need the rest of the flock. You need more fighters on your side. Get them back.

I groaned to myself. Oh, just *heck.*

86

"We would be amazing spies," Nudge whispered into my ear, "don't you think so?"

The five of us were crawling silently through a ventilation duct, in search of a computer. So far we had passed another barracks, a cafeteria, bathrooms — I guess even perfect people have to "go" sometimes — and a couple of offices with workers in them.

We needed an empty room with a computer. And then, like, a bunch of hot food! And comfy beds! After what felt like miles of crawling on hard metal, we looked down into a room that was dimly lit by a computer screen saver.

As quietly as possible, we unscrewed the grate, then dropped one at a time down into the room, waiting for the blare of motion detectors. But it remained quiet.

"Okay, make this fast," I told Nudge. "There might be silent alarms, hidden infrared cameras, whatever. We probably have about a minute."

Nudge nodded and sat down in front of the computer. She put her hands on the keyboard and closed her eyes.

Seconds ticked by, with me getting more and more nervous and twitchy.

Suddenly she opened her eyes, looked at the computer keyboard, and started to type.

In seconds she had cleared the computer screen and pulled up an e-mail program.

"I have no idea how she does that," I whispered, and Total nodded.

"Okay," said Nudge. "I'm connected."

"Great job," I said, my heart hammering, and not only because I was expecting to be caught any second. "Tell Fang to come to Lendeheim right away, with everybody. Tell him things are really, really bad."

Nudge typed quickly.

"Tell him that the really evil stuff has started and that we have days, maybe hours, to throw a wrench in it."

"*Wrench* starts with *w*," said Total, reading over her shoulder.

"It doesn't matter," I hissed. "Just tell Fang to get his butt here, now!"

Nudge nodded and typed, then hit the Send button. And our message was off, hopefully to make its way to Fang's e-mail account.

True, he got a katrillion messages a day, but I hoped his eye would be caught by the all-cap THIS IS FROM MAX. READ IT NOW!!!! in the subject line.

"Well," I said, "that's all we can do. We just have to hope it gets through."

The computer screen blinked, and then the whitecoat we'd seen on TV earlier popped up, looking straight at us.

"Very good, Max," she said, sending chills down my spine. "You got further than I thought you would. I should have given you more credit."

Behind my back I made motions with my hands that meant, *Up and out of here, now!*

"No, there's no point in that," said the woman. "Look up."

So of course I looked up. The ceiling was absolutely covered with hovering, silent Flyboys, clinging like hairy bugs, their red eyes glowing.

"Oh, crap," I said.

"How eloquent," said the woman. And then, "Attack them!"

87

It wasn't pretty. We did manage to take out six or so Flyboys, but after all the metal springs and fur had settled, we were captured, our hands cuffed, our legs shackled.

My nose was bleeding, and a cut on the inside of my mouth stung. Ari had fared badly, and his recently healed face showed newly split skin and two black eyes. Both Angel and Nudge had nasty bruises, but nothing seemed to be broken. Total of course had done his best, biting the Flyboys, but he hadn't done much damage.

The Flyboys carried/dragged us through a series of tunnels, and I tried to memorize the route. We went up and down stairs, through a round tower, and finally came to a pivoting stone slab that became a secret door. Through this door was an office, like a business office. It looked totally out of place, with fluorescent lighting and a modern wooden desk, instead of, say, a medieval torture device.

The Flyboys dropped us roughly on the stone floor, which was padded here and there by Oriental carpets. None of us made a sound as our knees slammed against the stone, our shackled hands unable to break our fall. In a second we all scrambled up, standing with our backs to one another, searching for exits, counting guards, seeking out anything we could use for weapons. We're just funny that way.

My eye was caught by something on the big desk. A little plaque that said DIRECTOR.

Ooh, the Director! At last! The head honcho, big cheese, big kahuna! The one pulling all of our strings! The one in charge of everything and everyone! The completely insane psychopath who was trying to eliminate most of the world's population! Finally we would meet. And I would take him apart using only my teeth if necessary.

I elbowed the others and nodded my head at the desk.

"You know what to do," I breathed to Angel. Time for a little mind puppet.

The heavy stone wall pivoted again, and the fair-haired woman from the TV came in, followed by several other whitecoats. The whitecoats had the inevitable stethoscopes, blood pressure cuffs, etc. This was going to be amusing. A "totally horrible" kind of amusing.

"Hello, Max," said the woman. She was about my height, with a slender build. Glancing at the others, she said, "Angel, Nudge, Ari. And the dog."

I knew that killed Total, but he didn't say anything.

"I've been waiting to meet you for a long time," said the woman. "It's very important that we speak, face-to-face. Don't you think so?"

"Well, what's important is that *you* believe that," I said, and her eyes flickered.

"My name is Marian Janssen," she said calmly. "I'm the Director of Itex, and its research and development companies."

I kept my face very still. This was the Director? The Director was a woman? Oddly, it was disappointing that the person behind all of this destruction was a woman. This kind of schizo-steamroller behavior seemed more natural for a man, at least to me.

"Not only that," she continued, keeping her eyes on my face, "but I am your mother, Max."

PART 4

I DIDN'T JUST HEAR WHAT I THOUGHT I HEARD, DID I?

88

Frankly, it takes a lot to surprise me. I'm pretty unsurprisable. But I admit, that was pretty much the last thing I expected to hear. "Hoo, delusional much?" I said, proud that my voice was rock solid. Almost.

The Director walked to her big desk and set down several CD-ROMs.

"I know it's hard to believe, but look closely at me, Max. I'm an older version of you."

I stared at her blond hair, her dark brown eyes. I remembered that Nudge had said she reminded her of someone.

"Yeah?" I said. "Let's see your wings."

She gave me a smile. "I don't have any avian DNA. But you — you were the most brilliant success we ever had."

I was still reeling from shock, so I went on "smart retort" autopilot. "Then why do you and ter Borcht keep trying to *kill* us?"

"You're an older generation, Max," she explained. "You have no proven life span. There's no room for mistakes in the new world."

I was floored. "Here's a tip: Your protective maternal instinct sucks."

"I'm your mother, Max, but I'm also a scientist. Believe me, watching you grow up from afar, devising this entire game, this series of tests — there were times that I didn't think I could go through it."

"Funny, I felt the same way. For completely different reasons. But you had a *choice*," I pointed out, becoming more and more incredulous.

"I'm making the ultimate sacrifice to create a new world. I gave my only child to the cause."

"That's not the ultimate sacrifice!" I said, outraged. "Giving *yourself* would be the ultimate! Giving *me* up is like the second-to-ultimate! See the difference?"

She smiled somewhat sadly. "You're so smart, Max. I'm so proud of you."

"Which makes *one* of us," I said. "I mean, God! It's parents' career day at school. I stand up and say, 'My mother is an evil scientist who's planning a holocaust that will eliminate half the people on Earth.' How could I ever live that down?!"

She turned away and sat at her desk. "I blame Jeb for letting you be such a smart aleck."

I stared at her. "I blame *you* for altering my DNA! I mean, I have *wings*, lady! What were you *thinking?*"

"I was thinking that the world's population is destroying itself," she said in a steely tone I recognized. (I have one just like it.) "I was thinking that someone had to stand up and take drastic action before this entire planet is incapable of supporting human life. Yes, you're my daughter, but you're still just part of the big picture, part of the equation. I was thinking I'd do anything to make sure the human race survives. Even if it seems awful in the short term. In future history books, I'll be heralded as the savior of humanity."

Perfect. I *finally,* after fourteen years, meet my mother, and she's a raving *lunatic.* This day just could not get better.

I swallowed. "You give good megalomania," I said.

The Director motioned to the Flyboys hovering around the edges of the room. "Take them to the place that I prepared," she said. "You know what to do once you get there."

89

"I don't want to make you feel even worse, Max," said Total. "But I can't stand your mother."

I looked at him. In the English / mad-scientist dictionary, you can translate "place I prepared" as "dank, ominous dungeon." Literally a freaking dungeon! Cinderella's castle had come complete with a real dungeon. And the "you know what to do" part translated to "chain them all to the walls like medieval prisoners."

"Well," I said, "at least with my parents, I don't have to look hard for something to rebel against."

Anyway, we seemed to be the only occupants in the dungeon, though it stretched on, out of sight. Loudspeakers were hung on the walls, and they were playing the Director's brainwashing messages, which in itself was enough to drive anyone starkers.

Like, if the whole "chained to a wall in a dungeon" thing wasn't enough to send you around the bend.

All of us were flying creatures, except for Total, and sort of halfway Ari. So chaining us to the wall, underground, was one of the worst things you could do.

My mother had done this to us.

I shook my head, unutterably depressed. "I mean, why couldn't she have been a nice hooker, or a crack addict, like Fang's mom?"

"Speaking of Fang," said Nudge, "maybe he's on his way here right now."

A gleam of hope flared and was just as quickly extinguished. "Yeah, if our message got through. If he's gotten over Ari, which I doubt. If they can somehow get to Europe, like, *right away*."

"Max?" said Angel. "You're kind of making things worse."

I was. I was being a jerk. Later, when I was alone, I would lie down and sob my guts out from the raw, acid disappointment about my mother. Right now I had to stop taking it out on everyone.

"You're right," I said, my throat feeling tight. "I'm sorry. Actually, I do think that our e-mail got through, because Nudge is brilliant at that stuff. And he's Fang. They're on their way. I know it."

Silence.

"You lie really well, Max," Nudge said approvingly.

I laughed. "I've had a lot of practice. But seriously, I do bet they're on their way."

"How could they cross the ocean?" Ari asked, not meanly, just wondering.

"Maybe they got tickets on a plane, like us," said Angel.

"Or maybe they stowed away on a plane," suggested Nudge.

"Or maybe they, like, flew up into the sky, waited for a jet to pass by, then dropped down onto it and held on," I said dramatically, and we all laughed. I imitated Fang hanging on to a jet, mouth open from the wind drag.

Their chuckles seemed to make the walls recede a bit and the darkness not quite so dark.

The loudspeakers were most annoying when they were in English because we couldn't help listening. The Director — or Crazy Old Mom, as I liked to think of her — was again spouting something about the future of flawlessness.

"She is a seriously negative woman," I said.

"I'm sorry, Max," said Nudge. "I know she wasn't what you were hoping for."

"Yeah." I smiled wryly. "'Delusional mass murderer' wasn't really on my list."

Again I wanted to wail with disappointment, but I swallowed it down. I had finally found my mother, and she was my worst nightmare. This was really just too bitter to bear. On top of that, Nudge was trying to comfort me. It was *my* job to comfort *her*. Usually the only person who comforted me was Fang. Who had deserted me.

A slight scratching sound in the shadows made us all prick up our ears.

"Rats," said Nudge nervously.

But it wasn't rats. A tall figure appeared in the distance.

We all went on alert, ready for a fight, since flight was out of the question.

A voice spoke.

"Max," Jeb said.

And now my day of horror was complete.

90

"Well, well," I said, using every bit of strength I had to make my voice sound chipper. "Fancy meeting you. Come here often? How's the food?"

Jeb moved closer, till he stepped into the dim circle of light given off by the amber emergency fixture. He looked just the same — maybe more tired than usual. I guess torturing kids takes it out of you.

He gave me his trademark smile tinged with sadness. "Actually, no one knows I'm here."

I made my eyes round. "Gosh, I sure won't tell anyone!"

"So you met the Director?" he asked.

My facade crashed down, but I struggled to keep it together. "Yes. And what a picnic she turned out to be. Three billion women with ovaries on this planet, and I had to get the one voted 'most likely to become a delusional psychopath' as my mom."

Jeb knelt down on the filthy stone floor, looking at me. I felt Angel wound tightly with tension next to me and wondered if she was picking up anything from Jeb. He hadn't acknowledged the others, including Ari.

"You can still save the world, Max."

A sudden wave of exhaustion almost sucked me under. I wanted to roll up into a fetal position and stay there for the rest of my life, which I hoped would be mercifully short. I had been working so hard for so long, going at 140 percent. I had pretty much hit rock bottom.

I closed my eyes wearily and leaned against the dank stone wall behind me. "How?" I said. "Through Re-Evolution? The By-Half Plan? No, thanks. I'm getting off the madcap train of mass destruction."

Max, you have to trust me, said the Voice inside my head. *You were created to save the world. You still can.*

Give it a rest, Voice, I thought. *I'm beat.*

Max, said the Voice. *Max.*

Then it occurred to me that the Voice wasn't actually *inside* my head.

Oh, God.

I opened my eyes.

Jeb was still kneeling in front of me. "You've come a long way, Max," said the Voice, except that it was Jeb's mouth moving, the sound coming from *him*. "You're almost home. Everything will work out, but you have to do your best. And you have to trust me again."

It was Jeb, speaking with the Voice, the Voice I'd been hearing inside my head for months.

Jeb was the Voice.

91

Fang paused a moment, his fingers over the keyboard in the Internet café. Next to him, Iggy and the Gasman were sucking down lattes like there was no tomorrow.

Which maybe there wasn't.

"I feel like I could fly, like, to the space station!" the Gasman said enthusiastically.

Fang looked over at him. "No more caffeine for you, buddy." He glanced around to make sure no one had heard the Gasman. But they were off in a corner of this run-down coffee shop, and there weren't that many other people in here anyway.

Iggy drained his cup and wiped the foam mustache off his lip. "I liked it farther south," he complained. "The sunshine, the beach bunnies. Up north here, this place has too much of the damp-mist thing going on."

"It's really pretty, though," the Gasman said. "The mountains and the ocean. And the people look more real." He glanced over at Fang. "Are kids still reading your blog?"

Fang nodded. "Tons."

He scrolled down quickly, scanning the entries, and then he felt someone's eyes on him. Instantly he looked up and tracked his gaze left to right, taking in the whole café. It was times like this he missed Max the most — because she would have felt it too, and they would have exchanged glances and known what to do in a moment, without speaking.

Now it was just him on this coast, and her and that cretin wherever they were.

Fang saw nothing, so he moved his eyes more slowly this time, right to left. There. *That guy*. He was headed this way.

Fang shut the laptop and tapped Iggy's hand. The Gasman saw it and looked up, on alert. Eight years old and his fists were clenched, muscles tight, ready to fight.

When the guy was about fifteen feet away, still beelining for them, Fang frowned.

"We know this guy," he murmured. "Who is he?"

Casually the Gasman turned and looked over his shoulder. "Uh . . ."

"His footsteps," Iggy muttered. Fang couldn't hear his footsteps. Iggy went on, face pinched with concentration. "Those footsteps . . . We heard them . . . in a subway tunnel."

Fang's eyes widened, and he sharpened his focus.

Of course.

Now the guy was six feet away, and he stopped. Fang had never seen him in daylight before, only in flickering reflections from oil-can fires in the train tunnels below New York City. He was the homeless computer nerd who carried a Mac everywhere he went, the guy who'd claimed that Max's chip was screwing up his hard drive. When they'd asked him about her chip, he'd gone wiggy and run off. What was this guy doing *here?*

"You." The guy frowned and pointed at them but pitched his voice so only they could hear him. "What are *you* doing here?"

"Take a seat," Fang invited him, pushing one out with his foot.

The guy looked around suspiciously. "Where's your girlfriend? The one with the chip inside her."

"Not with us."

He seemed to relax, fractionally, and edged warily into the seat, looking around. Fang smiled to himself. Finally, someone more paranoid than they were. It was refreshing.

"What are *you* doing here?" Fang asked, gesturing to the coffee shop. "Above ground. On the West Coast."

The guy shrugged. "I get around. I see people here, there, all over. I just like to hang in New York mostly — it's easier to blend."

"Yeah," Fang agreed.

Then the guy's eyes fell on Fang's closed laptop, and Fang saw him shift his alert level from yellow up to orange.

"Nice 'book," he said.

"Thanks." Fang waited.

"Don't usually see one like that around."

"Guess not."

The guy seemed to make a decision, and he leaned forward across the table. "Where'd you get it? Or do I not want to know?"

Fang almost grinned. "You probably don't want to know."

The guy shook his head. "You people get into some serious stuff."

"Yeah," Fang acknowledged with a sigh. He looked up. "Would you know how to get a message through to *every* kid on the 'net, *everywhere* in the world?"

92

The guy looked at Fang. "Maybe. Probably. Guess it depends on the message."

"Would you need to know the message?" Fang asked, seeing a big wrinkle looming. This guy was, after all, pretty much a nutcase. Who knew how he'd react to Fang's message?

The guy thought about it, then said, "Yeah."

"There goes *that* plan," said Iggy, sucking down the last of his latte.

"Can I have a muffin?" the Gasman put in.

Fang pushed some money across the table. The Gasman took it and headed to the counter, keeping an eye out around him the whole way.

"What's your name?" Fang asked.

There was a long pause while the guy considered.

"Man, this guy's more paranoid than we are," Iggy said. "It's kind of refreshing."

The guy looked at Iggy and seemed to notice for the first time that Iggy was blind. He turned back to Fang. "Mike. What's yours?"

"Fang. He's Iggy. The little one's the Gasman. Don't ask why."

"Sit here long enough and you'll find out," Iggy muttered.

Mike's eyes went wide, and he tensed in his chair. Fang and Iggy tensed too, waiting.

"Is that your blog on the Web?" Mike asked in a whisper.

"Yeah."

The Gasman returned and put a plate of muffins on the table. He immediately picked up on the vibe and stilled, looking quickly from boy to boy. Since no one was pulling out weapons, he sat down and took a muffin, pushing the rest toward the others.

"So you're sayin' you have . . . like, wings?" Mike kept his voice low.

"Not just *like* 'em," said Iggy, talking with his mouth full. "We *got* 'em." He realized Fang hadn't answered the question and turned his head. "Oh. Was that a secret?"

"Not anymore," Fang said dryly.

"You're the bird kids everyone's talkin' about."

Fang shrugged. "Can you help me or not?"

"I'll help you if you're them. Convince me."

"I'll need more room," said Fang, looking around.

Mike took them upstairs, above the coffee shop, where he pulled out a set of keys and unlocked a door. Fang was on hyperalert and wished Angel were there to scan for any threats.

"In here." Mike ushered them into a large room, obviously used for storage. Boxes of various supplies were stacked along one wall, but the middle of the room was empty. "This enough space?"

Fang nodded and shrugged off his jacket. He made note of where the windows were and gauged whether they were single or double paned, in case he had to jump through one any time soon.

Slowly, Fang unfolded his wings, stretching his muscles, enjoying the sensation of extending them after holding them tight against his back for hours. He shook them out, feeling the feathers align. The tips of his wings almost touched the walls on both sides of the room. He wished he could take off right now and fly for hours, wheeling through the open sky.

Mike's mouth was slightly open. "Dude. That is so awesome." He looked at Iggy and the Gasman. "You guys got 'em too? What about those chicks that were with you?"

"We all have them," said Fang. "Now, howsabout sending that message?"

93

Mike's fingers flew over the keyboard of Fang's laptop. "I just gotta write a bit of code here," he muttered. "Get you in through a bunch of different back doors. Lotsa people got firewalls up, stuff like that, but this should bypass most of 'em."

He opened Fang's main blog page and scanned it quickly. "Okay, I've gotta try to get access to them through their IP addresses, since you don't have most of their e-mail addresses," he said. "This could be tricky, but I'll give it a shot."

"You are a criminal mastermind," the Gasman said admiringly.

"I try," Mike said.

"Wait," said Fang, reading over his shoulder. "Switch over to my e-mail for a sec. I just saw a pop-up alert on the bottom of the screen."

"Yeah, this one has three red flags for priority," Mike said, pointing.

Fang's heart sped up.

THIS IS FROM MAX. READ IT NOW!!!!

We're in Germany. Town of Lendeheim. Big castle
here, head of Itex. Lots of really bad stuff. Come as fast
as you can. (Hi Fang! From Nudge. I miss you!) Do NOT
blow this off. Come!!! We have days, maybe hours. I
mean it, you better get your butt over here. Max.

Huh. Fang sat back and nodded at Mike to keep
working.

So. Max wanted him back, eh? She didn't say whether
she still had Frankenbirdy with her. If she did, Fang didn't
want any part of it.

On the other wing, it had cost her a lot of pride to ask
him to come. She'd never even taken his blog that seriously, and now she was using it to beg him to come back.
Well, order him to come back. Which was as close to begging as Max would get.

What were they doing in Germany? How had they gotten to Europe? How did she expect him to get to Europe?

He looked at the date on the e-mail. Early this morning.
And Germany was about ten hours or so ahead. . . .

How would Max define "really bad stuff"? As opposed
to just ordinary bad stuff? Stuff bad enough to make her
swallow her pride and ask him to come help.

So they were talking pretty unimaginably bad.

"Okay, I got it," said Mike, sitting back. He had a
proud, satisfied smile on his face. "It'll work a little like a

virus, in that it'll access other addresses through people's e-mail programs, but it won't cause any damage." He frowned. "I think. Anyway, type your message and then hit this special Send box I created. Let's see what happens."

Fang swallowed. This was it. This was his chance to get kids to take this seriously, tell them what was going on. All over the planet, kids would read this message.

This was *his* chance to save the world.

He started writing.

94

To: undisclosed_recipients
From: Fang
Subject: URGENT! We want our planet back!

Hey. If you get this message, we might have a chance. I mean the world might have a chance. Long story short: The grown-ups have taken a nice clean planet and trashed it for money. Not every grown-up. But a bunch of them, over and over, choose money and profits over clean air and water. It's their way of telling us they don't give a rat's butt about us, the kids, who are going to inherit what's left of the Earth.

A group of scientists want to take back the planet before it's too late and stop the pollution. Good, right? Only problem is they think they need to get rid of half the world's population to do it. So it's like: Save the planet so the pollution doesn't kill people, or . . . just kill people to start with, save everyone time. For you kids at home, that's called "flawed logic." I mean, call me crazy, but that seems like a really bad plan.

The other thing about these scientists is that they've tried to create a new kind of human who might survive better, like if there's a nuclear winter or whatever. I won't go into the details, but let me just say that this idea is as boneheaded and dangerous as their "kill half the people" plan.

What I'm saying is: It's up to us. You and me. Me and my flock, you and your friends. The kids. We want — we *deserve* — to inherit a clean, unmessed-up planet, and still keep everyone who's already living on it.

We can do it. But we have to join together. We have to take chances. Take risks. We have to get active and really do something, instead of just sitting at home playing Xbox. This isn't a game. We can't defeat the enemy by hitting them with our superlaser guns.

We want our planet back.

Kids matter. We're important. Our future is important. ARE YOU WITH ME?

95

The Gasman finished reading over Fang's shoulder.

"I wish *I* had an Xbox," he said. Fang rolled his eyes.

"Cool message, dude," said Mike. "I feel like jumping up and starting a rally. Now what?"

"Now," said Fang, starting to type another message, "we go to Germany."

He ignored the way his heart thumped when he thought about seeing her — them — again. If she still had the cretin with her, he was going to be pissed. But cretin or no, splitting up the flock was wrong. If the world was coming to an end, they needed to be together.

To: Max
From: Fang
Subject: Yo

Yo, Max. We're on our way. This better not be a joke.
Fang.

He clicked the Send button.

96

You know that old saying "When life gives you lemons, make lemonade"? Well, we were chained in a dungeon in Germany, my mother was a power-hungry, psychotic *refrigerator,* and my best friend and half my flock were MIA.

These were definitely lemons, so I thought about that saying.

And you know what? Whoever coined the phrase ought to have been smacked senseless. I mean, how lamebrained was that? "Life totally messing you up? Just turn that frown upside down!" What a moron!

"Max? You're muttering again." Nudge sounded tired.

I looked at her. "Sorry." I sighed and got to my feet. We were each now chained to the wall by one ankle. Our chains were about eight feet long, so we could walk around. See? My mom had a soft heart after all! Instead of being chained by both wrists, we were only chained by one ankle!

I mean, if I'd been looking for proof that she really did love me, this was it, right?

Total reached out and very gently closed his teeth around my ankle as I went past. "Muttering," he said.

"Sorry." I moved as far away as my chain allowed.

I was making the kids crazy with my barely suppressed rage and disappointment. And here's the kicker: I had asked Fang for help. I had asked him to come back because I needed him. My stomach churned just thinking about it. That was me: Maximum Ride, Damsel in Distress.

I know this will surprise you, but I don't damsel well. Distress, I can do. Damseling? Not so much.

"I don't remember you muttering this much, before," Ari said, crouching next to me.

"I was a little saner then," I said.

"Oh." He traced a finger through the grime on the floor. Suddenly I remembered him saying, "I can't read."

Knowing he was watching me, I slowly drew the letter *A* on the floor, making little trails through the dirt. Then I drew an *R*. And an *I*.

"That spells Ari," I told him. I drew it again, slowly. *A . . . R . . . I.* "Now you do it."

He started the A, then stopped. "What's the point?" he asked, and I was stung because he was right. He didn't have much time left. Did it really matter if he knew how to read?

"You should know how to write your name," I said firmly, pushing his hand toward the floor again. "Come on. First *A*."

Concentrating, Ari dragged one ragged claw through the dirt. He made a rickety, asymmetrical *A*.

"A drunk monkey could do better, but you'll get there," I said. "Do the *R*."

He started on the *R*, first drawing it backward. I didn't know if this was normal for his age or whether his brain had been affected by all the experiments done on him. I rubbed it out and showed him how to do it correctly.

Jeb had taught me and Fang to read. I'd taught Gazzy and Nudge and Angel. We were a little shaky with spelling and grammar sometimes, but all of us could forge signatures like a pro. He hadn't taught his own son.

"How come you're doing this?" Ari's hesitant question caught me off guard.

"Uh — to make up for almost killing you in New York?"

Ari didn't look at me. "You did kill me," he said. "They brought me back. Fused some of the bones in my neck." He ran a meaty paw over his neck as if it still pained him.

"I'm sorry," I said. I can count on the fingers of one hand how many times those words have passed my lips. And three of them had been in the last five minutes. "You were trying to kill me first."

He nodded. "I hated you," he said calmly. "Dad gave you everything, he really loved you. I was his son, and I didn't mean anything to him. You were so strong and perfect and beautiful. I just hated you. Wanted you dead. And he used that. He used me as part of your testing."

I was rattled. Ari seemed so matter-of-fact. "He was proud of you," I said, dredging up memories of a long time ago, before Jeb had stolen me and the rest of the flock out of the lab. "He liked you following him around in the lab."

"You never even noticed me," Ari said, slowly tracing the *I* in his name.

"I did," I said, thinking back. "You were a cute little boy. I used to be so jealous of you because you *were* his son. You belonged to him in a way that I didn't belong to anyone. I wanted to be perfect so Jeb would love me."

Even as I said the words, I was just realizing them myself. Ari looked up at me, surprised. I rocked back on my heels, facing these painful truths. It was like Dr. Phil had apparated right into our dungeon.

"I knew I was a freak," I said softly. "I had wings. I lived in a dog crate. But you were a regular little boy. You were Jeb's real son. I kept thinking, If I'm strong enough, if I do everything he tells me, if I'm the best at everything, then maybe Jeb will love me too." I looked down at my new boots, already dull with dirt. "I was so, so happy when he stole us from the lab." My throat got tight, remembering. "I didn't think it could last. I was afraid. But I was happy that I was going to die away from the lab. Not in a dog crate. And then it went on. No one found us. Jeb took care of us, taught us stuff, how to survive. It was almost like a normal life, like normal kids. And you know, Ari," I said, "I was so happy to be gone, so happy to have Jeb, that I didn't even think about the little boy he'd left behind. I guess I just thought you were with your mom or something."

Ari nodded, and after a moment he swallowed and cleared his throat. "I don't have a mom."

"It's not what it's cracked up to be," I said, and he smiled.

"I understand now," he said. "It wasn't your fault. You were just a kid, like me. It wasn't either of our faults."

I pressed my lips together hard, determined not to make poignant tear streaks down my no doubt filthy face.

"I saw a Shakespeare movie on TV once," I said. "The guy said something like, 'Anyone who fights with me today is my brother.' So — if you fight with me today . . ."

He smiled again and nodded, understanding. Then we hugged, of course, because the Hallmark moment wouldn't be complete without it.

97

Not long after the Hallmark commercial, several Flyboys appeared in the dungeon and moved us — to somewhere even worse.

"This is *great*," I said, radiating sincerity. "I love what you've done with the place. Really."

The thing about sarcasm is that it's lost on robots, like Flyboys, for example. But I could always hope that they had voice-activated recorders on them and that later they'd be playing my snide message back to Crazy Old Mom.

The Flyboys turned, rotors humming, and stalked away. No sense of humor.

Nudge, Angel, Total, Ari, and I surveyed our change of scenery.

"Let's see," I said. "High stone walls, lifeless span of grit, mutants marching around . . . I don't know — I'm thinking it says 'prison yard.' How about you guys?"

"Prison yard sums it up," Total agreed, then trotted off to pee on the wall.

"Prison yard is too good for this," said Nudge. "Like,

cheerless, joy-sucking plain of despair would be more like it."

I looked at her in admiration. "Nice! You've been reading the dictionary again, haven't you?"

Nudge blushed happily.

"Look! There I go," Angel said, pointing. Twenty yards away, her clone rambled about with the others, looking more like Angel than Angel did. About two hundred beings were in what used to be the castle stable area, I guessed. No one was talking. Mostly they were shuffling in a large, clockwise circle, getting their "exercise." They seemed so much like a mindless school of fish, or perhaps a flock of sheep, that I wanted to run through them, shouting, to see if they'd scatter.

"Do you see me?" Nudge asked, peering through the crowd.

"I still can't believe I don't have a clone," Total huffed, trotting back.

"You're unduplicatable," I said.

"I doubt it," he said. "I mean, maybe it wouldn't talk, maybe it would just go arf, but still. Like, what, they couldn't bother?"

"Arf?" I said.

"Oh, there I am!" said Nudge, up on her tiptoes. "I see the other me has hair issues too."

"Why would they make clones of us?" I wondered out loud.

"You." The metallic voice had no inflection. We spun to see a Flyboy behind us.

"Yes, C-Threepio?" I said politely.

"Walk." The Flyboy pointed at the throng, then took a step toward us.

Well, you don't have to threaten me twice. We quickly headed into the crowd and started pacing along with the rest of them.

I was keeping my eye out for Max II, who, last time I'd had a close encounter with her, had been trying to kill me and had narrowly escaped being killed by me. In case she wasn't a 'let bygones be bygones' kind of gal, I was braced for the worst.

"So is this what prisons will be like after Re-Evolution?" Angel asked, holding my hand. "With the collars and everything?" She rubbed the one around her neck, its green LED blinking every two seconds.

"I guess so," I said, resisting the urge to tug at my own collar. "I guess they have these things rigged up to shock us if we try to escape. They probably have tracers in them too." Which was why we hadn't done an up-and-away as soon as we got out here.

"How come they'll still have prisons, after half of everyone is dead?" Nudge asked. "I thought people would quit fighting for stuff. I thought the future people would be perfect. If they're perfect, they won't go around committing crimes, will they?"

"There," I said. "Decades of psycho logic picked apart

in three seconds by an eleven-year-old. Take that, modern science!"

And speaking of modern science, I was about to be confronted by one of its marvels. Or disasters. All depends on your point of view.

"Max."

I turned quickly at the too-familiar voice. And there I was, pretty as heck, brown eyes, a few freckles, fashion challenged, and a bad attitude. Max II.

98

"Gosh," I said. "It's like looking in a mirror."

"Yeah," she said. "Except I've had a bath recently."

"Touché. So, me, how's tricks?"

"What are you doing here?"

"Selling Girl Scout cookies," I said. "Want some? The Samoas are terrific."

Max II started walking next to us, and we kept pace with the crowd, moving in a big oval around the barren yard. I stayed on guard, in case she suddenly attacked me.

"Baa," Nudge bleated. "Baaa."

I laughed, and Max II looked at me. "How can you *laugh?*" She gestured angrily at the walls, the guard towers, the armed Flyboys that stood around like remote-controlled puppets.

"Well, she baaed like a sheep," I said. "It was pretty funny." I patted Nudge's head. "Especially with her lamby hair. Maybe I should call her Lamby from now on."

Nudge grinned, and Max II got angrier. "Don't you realize what's going on? Where we are?"

"Uh, a honking big castle of evil in Germany?" I offered. "I've narrowed it down that far."

Max II glanced around, as if making sure we weren't overheard. Since we were shoulder to shoulder with a couple hundred other people, it was kind of a wasted gesture.

"This is the last stopping place," she said under her breath, not looking at me. "Look around. We're all rejects. They were trying to build an army out of us, but then they got the Flyboys to work. Now we're obsolete. And every day, a bunch of us disappear."

I studied her. "I'm sorry — did I miss something? Last time I saw you, you were trying to kill me. Are we friends now? Did I miss the memo? Now you're clueing me in on the sitch?"

"If you're against *them,* then we're on the same side," Max II said firmly.

She could have totally been lying, of course. In fact, it was safest to assume that she was. But her words were all too likely to be the truth.

"How long have you been here?" I asked her.

She looked away. "Since Florida. They . . . were really mad that I let you beat me."

"You didn't *let* me do squat," I said.

Sighing, she gave a brief nod. "I was supposed to win. I was supposed to finish you off. They never counted on you winning. And then you didn't kill me. It was awful."

"You're welcome," I said, feeling fresh anger ignite. "I'll try not to humiliate you by letting you live next time."

Max II looked at me sadly, and it really was creepy; so much like looking in a mirror that I felt my face try to assume the same expression, so we'd match.

"There won't be a next time," she said. "I'm telling you, this is the last stop. They brought us here to kill us."

"Yeah, I get that a lot," I said.

"You don't understand," Max II said, agitated. "We're all slated to die. Every day, more of us disappear. When I first came here, this yard was so full, we had to take shifts. There were thousands of us. Now this is all that's left."

"Hmm," I said.

"With this many of us, I guess we have until . . . maybe tomorrow," she said, looking around, mentally calculating.

Okay, this was not sounding good. I thought we'd have a couple days to regroup, find a way out of this. If Max II wasn't lying, then I needed to step up our time frame in a big way. If Max II was lying, I still had no reason to want to hang around.

We continued to shuffle in big circles, and now both Nudge and Total were baaing occasionally. I was deep in thought, trying to come up with one of my typically brilliant plans, when a mutant bumped into me for a split second, then moved away.

It left something in my hand.

A piece of paper.

Very, very surreptitiously, I unfolded it and glanced

down. It was a note, and it said: *Fang on his way with flock. Says it better not be a joke.*

Inside me, a hard knot of tension that I hadn't even known I had seemed to unravel. Oh, God. Fang was coming. I would have been more suspicious, but the "it had better not be a joke" thing could only have come from him.

Fang was on the way. With Iggy and Gazzy. We would all be together again.

"Max? What's wrong?" Nudge looked at me with concern. "You're crying."

I touched my cheek to find that I *was* crying, tears streaking down my face. I wiped them away on my sleeve and snuffled. I was too happy to speak for a moment.

"Fang's coming to help us," I said under my breath, looking straight ahead. "He's on his way."

99

We all exercised in the Yard of Despair for another half hour. My mind was spinning — knowing Fang was on his way had given me a jolt of adrenaline. I wondered when he had left. I wondered if I would be able to bear it if Fang's message was all another "test," if it wasn't real.

On the other hand, sometimes a happy delusion is better than grim reality.

In the meantime, I took baby steps behind the mutant in front of me, holding Angel's hand, feeling Total's little side brushing against my leg from time to time.

And I started watching and listening more intently. I'd thought the mutants were silent, but now I began to pick up on things they were saying so softly that the words almost got lost in the dry shuffling noise of their boots against the grit.

I tapped Nudge's hand and nodded my head at the crowd. Angel looked up at me, feeling my intention, and started paying attention also.

Like a prison, the mutants were murmuring, as softly as the wind. *Unfair. Lied to us. So many of us gone. Don't want to disappear. Don't want to be retired. What to do? There are so many of them. Too many of them. This is a prison. A prison of death. Unfair. I did nothing wrong. Except exist.*

I moved slowly through the crowd, listening to the murmurs, the messages. Angel was picking up on their thoughts. I saw her blue eyes become troubled with her new knowledge.

By the time a strident electronic buzzer told us to go back inside, I had formed a semiclear picture of the group's emotions. They didn't want this to happen to them — what had happened to their fellow inmates. They wished they could change things. Some of them were really angry and wanted to fight, but they didn't know how. I guessed their fighting instincts had been engineered out of them. Mostly, they were confused and disorganized.

Which is where a — ahem — leader would come in.

My plans were starting to percolate as I marched with the others back into the fantasy world of mad scientists, and that plus the knowledge that Fang was on his way made me almost cheerful.

Until three Flyboys stepped in front of me, Angel, Nudge, Ari, and Total, pointing guns at us.

I groaned. "What now?"

"You come with us," they intoned, as if one.

"Why?" I asked belligerently.

"Becuss I vant to talk to you," said our old pal ter Borcht, stepping out from behind them. "Vun *last* time."

100

We were prodded through long, winding stone corridors in the bowels of the castle, occasionally tripping on the uneven stone floor. I felt as though I'd been chilly for days and rubbed Angel's and Nudge's arms to help them keep warm in the dank chill.

"I hate this guy," Ari muttered, keeping his head down.

"There's a club," I told him. "The Haters of ter Borcht Club. Have you gotten your badge yet?"

Finally we were pushed into a — come on, you can guess — yes: a white, sterile-looking lablike room filled with tables holding schmancy, no doubt expensive science equipment that I longed to start whacking with a baseball bat.

Once we were in, the doors slammed shut behind us, and several Flyboys stood in front of them, guns ready.

"The meeting of the Haters of ter Borcht Club will now come to order," I murmured. Nudge swallowed a snort, and Angel projected a grin into my head. *Can you do anything with him?* I sent her in a directed thought.

No, came her regretful reply. *I get stuff from him — awful, scary, disgusting stuff, but I can't seem to send anything in.*

Which messed up Plan A.

"So!" said ter Borcht, coming toward us. "I vass verry disappointed dat you are not dead by now!"

"Vee feel de same vay about you!" I said, crossing my arms over my chest.

His eyes narrowed. Really, sometimes I impress even me.

"But I don't tink I vill haf to vait dat much longer," he said. "Maybe by dinner, yah? In de meantime, some people vant to talk to you."

"This oughtta be good," I whispered.

"Five bucks says they're *scientists,*" Total whispered back.

"No kidding."

The doors swung open behind us, and a team of five people walked in. They were Chinese? I wasn't sure.

"Tsk," said Total. "*Last season's* white lab coats. So tacky."

"How can you tell?" I asked, not bothering to lower my voice.

"This year's has smaller pockets and wider lapels. *Their* coats are so . . . I don't know. *Revenge of the Nerds*?"

The five Asian whitecoats looked confused, and ter Borcht practically had steam coming out his ears.

"Enuff!" he snapped, clapping his hands together hard. "Dey vill ask you qvestions. You vill answer. Are ve clear?"

"Clear as pea soup!" I said.

If ter Borcht could have hit me, he would have. I guess he didn't want to do it in front of the Clean Team.

Instead, purple in the face, he stalked behind his desk and sat down, angrily shuffling papers. The Clean Team came closer, looking at us curiously, as if we were a zoo exhibit. Gee, I haven't felt like *that* before.

We stayed quiet, but inside I was getting more and more tense. I could take all five of these yahoos out by myself, I thought. And ter Borcht too, as a bonus. Not to mention the Flyboy guards, guns and all. What stopped me? My collar. For all I knew, all he had to do was press a button, and I would drop to the ground, electrocuted.

The Asian scientists talked softly among themselves. I remembered hearing that some country had wanted to buy us, to use as weapons somehow. I know, I know, it sounds totally loony, a child wouldn't believe it, but you have no idea how incredibly stupid the war guys can be.

Slowly the whitecoats walked around me, Nudge, and Angel, seeming to marvel at how incredibly lifelike we were. Total they ignored completely. When they looked at Ari, they couldn't disguise their dismay. I'd gotten so used to his appearance that it didn't register on me anymore. Ari didn't look human, didn't look like an Eraser. He just looked like a mistake.

His face flushed as he caught their expressions, and I

felt really sorry for him. He'd gone from being a cute three-year-old kid to being a hulking patchwork monster within four short years. He knew what he looked like, knew he was dying, and he didn't understand why any of it had happened.

101

"Take a picture, it'll last longer," I told the whitecoats, and they almost jumped when I spoke, staring at me with new curiosity.

"Ah, hallo," one guy said in heavily accented English. "We will ask you some questions, okay?"

I rolled my eyes, and they murmured excitedly among themselves.

"You have a name, yes?" he said, pen ready over his clipboard.

"Yes," I said. "My name is seven-five-nine-nine-three-nine-ex-dash-one. Junior." I heard ter Borcht hiss over at his desk, but he stayed out of it.

The whitecoat looked at me in confusion, then turned to Nudge. "What is your name?"

Nudge thought. "Jessica," she decided. "Jessica Miranda Alicia Tangerine Butterfly." She looked pleased with her name, and smiled at me.

The whitecoats murmured among themselves again, and I heard one of them whisper, "Butterfly?"

They turned to Angel. "We will call you Little One," the

leader said, obviously deciding to dispense with the whole confusing name thing.

"Okay," Angel said agreeably. "I'll call you Guy in a White Lab Coat." He frowned.

"That can be his Indian name," I suggested.

One of the other ones spoke up. "Tell us about your sense of direction. How does it work?" They all looked at me expectantly.

"Well, it's like I have a GPS inside me," I told them. "One of the talking ones. I tell it where I want to go, and it tells me, Go twenty miles, turn left, take Exit Ninety-four, and so on. It can be pretty bossy, frankly."

Their eyes widened. "Really?" said one.

"No, you idiot," I said in disgust. "I don't know how it works. I just know it has an unfailing ability to point me in the opposite direction of a bunch of boneheads."

Now they looked a little irritated. I gave them another, say, five minutes before they cracked and this interview came to an exciting end.

"How high can you fly?" one asked abruptly.

"I'm not sure. Let me check my tummy altimeter." I looked down and pulled up my sweatshirt a couple inches. "That's funny. It was here this morning. . . ."

"As high as a plane?" Guy in a White Lab Coat snapped.

"Higher," said Nudge. They whirled on her.

"Higher than a plane?" one asked eagerly.

Nudge nodded confidently. "Yep. We can go so high

that we can't even hear the rubber band making the little propeller go around — *thwip, thwip, thwip.*" She made a circling motion with one finger. She frowned. "You meant a toy plane, right?"

Ter Borcht exploded to his feet. "Enuff! You vill get novere vis dese failures!"

"Now, now, Borchy," I said. "These nice people came all this way to talk to us. They know we can fly really high. They know we can always find our way, even in the dark. They know we can go faster than, like, a hundred miles an hour. I'm sure they want to know more about us." *Let's just dangle a carrot and see what they do,* I thought. It would be *my* little science experiment.

The five whitecoats were busy scribbling down these tidbits. Ter Borcht, looking furious, sat down heavily.

"You know, Borchy," I said in a loud whisper, "you might want to lay off the fried foods." I patted my stomach, then pointed to his much, much bigger one. I winked at him and then faced the questioners seriously. "I guess you guys also know that we need lots of fuel to keep going. Every two hours. Stuff like milkshakes, doughnuts, chicken nuggets, steak, french fries, uh . . ."

"Hamburgers," said Angel. "And carrot cake and pastrami and, um, French bread and —"

"Waffles," said Nudge. "And baked potatoes with cheese and bacon. And more bacon by itself. And peanut butter sandwiches and Snickers bars and root beer an' —"

"Hoagies," said Ari in his rusty voice. They looked at

him, startled, as if they hadn't figured him capable of speech.

Then the five whitecoats huddled and talked excitedly among themselves while I wiggled my eyebrows at my flock and got hopeful about a major snack headed our way.

"You don't need to eat," ter Borcht said more calmly. "You are dying soon anyvay."

The head whitecoat went over to him and talked, and ter Borcht started looking angry again. I heard him say, "No! It's too late."

"Why can't you get into their heads?" I whispered very softly to Angel. "Make 'em see ants everywhere or something."

"I don't know," Angel said, disappointed. "I just feel . . . shut out. It's like I start to get in and then I get pushed out again."

"Now I'm really hungry," Nudge whispered.

"Me too," said Ari.

"Me three," whispered Total. "I'm ready to eat one of *them*."

The rest of us made "eew" faces, but then the door to the lab opened, and everyone turned to look.

It was Mom. And frankly, she didn't look that happy to see me.

102

Mom — Marian Janssen — greeted the Chinese scientists warmly, so I figured they were offering her a big chunk of change to buy us as weapons.

"Are you finding out the information you need?" she asked. Ter Borcht snorted loudly over at his desk, and she cast him a glance.

"Are they cooperating?" Marian asked the room in general.

"What do you think?" I asked, just as Guy in a White Lab Coat said, "No."

Marian took out a PDA. "I told you I had much of this information, but I understood that you wanted to interview them yourselves. Now, what do you need to know?"

"How fast can they fly?" asked one.

Marian clicked her PDA. "Max, here," she said, gesturing to me, "has exceeded two hundred miles an hour, straight on, and upward of two hundred sixty miles an hour in a steep dive."

The scientists looked impressed. I started to feel an icy chill creep down my back.

"How high can they fly?" another one asked.

"Max has been documented at altitudes of approximately thirty-one thousand feet for short periods of time. Her oxygen consumption increased appropriately but created no hardship. Her normal cruising altitude is usually between fifteen thousand and twenty-two thousand feet."

Again the scientists looked impressed and made notes. One entered things into a calculator, then whispered results to the others.

I felt Nudge's and Angel's eyes on me, but I had a sinking feeling inside and didn't want to look at them. I was betting that Spy Mom had gotten all this information from my chip, the one I'd had Dr. Martinez take out.

The head guy looked at me speculatively. "How much weight can they carry?"

"We believe they can carry up to four-fifths of their own body weight for periods of up to an hour," said Marian. "And one-half of their body weight almost indefinitely."

Like our backpacks, for example.

"How much body fat do they have?" asked one of them. "Do they swim well?"

I decided to keep my mouth shut about Angel's ability to breathe under water.

"We believe they have normal swimming abilities but with greatly increased endurance," said Marian, cool as a polar bear's nose. "Their body fat is extremely low. Max is five-eight but weighs barely a hundred pounds. Of that weight, extremely little is fat or bone. Mostly she's made of muscle."

She's made of muscle. Like I was a kit that had been put together.

Okay, I get it. Shut up.

"But they can swim? They don't sink?" asked one.

Marian shook her head. "Their bones are extremely light and porous, filled with tiny air pockets. In addition to their lungs, they have peripheral air sacs along each side. They don't sink."

"Okay, this is stupid," I said in a bored tone. "There's no point in discussing this — except that it shows how clearly you need to get a life — because there's no way we're going to be weapons for anyone."

"That's right," said Nudge. "I'm not carrying bombs or assassinating anyone!"

That's right. We have *standards,* missy!

"You'll do what we tell you," said Marian chillingly. "I'm sure we can find some way to motivate you."

Instantly I thought that if they were hurting one of the others, I would do just about anything to stop it.

Again, information better kept to myself.

"I have to tell you, we don't work cheap," I told the Chinese scientists. "We'll need serious bling, big-screen TVs, vacations in Hawaii, and the best cheeseburgers that money can buy. For starters."

They nodded eagerly, thrilled at my giving in, which, frankly, was pathetic. I mean, don't they have cynics in China? Clearly these guys were not the brightest crayons in the box.

103

"Okay, enough!" the Director snapped. Turning to the scientists, she said, "We can get you any other information you need. In the meantime, we're going to work on a serious attitude adjustment."

"Basically, I have two speeds," I told them. "Hostile or smart-aleck. Your choice."

Ignoring me, Mom ushered the whitecoats out the door.

"That wasn't clever," she said, turning back to me. "Your survival depends on your *extreme* cooperation."

"Dere iss no survival!" ter Borcht said angrily, standing up. "Dey are dead!"

She ignored him too.

"You were designed to be very smart, Max," she told me. "We electrically stimulated your synaptic nerve endings while your brain was developing."

"And yet I still can't program my TiVo," I said.

I thought I heard Total stifle a snort, but I didn't look down.

"It's time to start using your smarts," the Director went on tightly. "Dr. ter Borcht is not the only one who wants you dead. Working for the Chinese is your one opportunity to continue living."

I stared at her in amazement. "How do you even live with yourself?" I said, genuinely dumbfounded. "You're willing to *sell children* to a foreign government so they can use us as *weapons,* possibly against other Americans. I don't get it. Were you hiding behind a door on morals and ethics day? Then you have the gall to call yourself my *mother?* You couldn't mother someone if they shot five gallons of estrogen into your veins! What about *their* mothers?" I waved at the flock. "Please tell me their mothers aren't half as lame as you!"

"Their mothers were nobodies," Marian said. "Donor eggs. Lab workers, techs, anyone we found. That was the point — that we could create a superrace out of anything. Out of *trash,*" she said meanly.

I heard blood rushing through the veins in my head. "Well, you're right there," I said. "Because we *are* a super-race. And I *did* come from *trash.*"

The Director clapped her hands, and the Flyboys at the door snapped to attention. I felt Ari and the others straighten up, go on higher alert, waiting to see how badly this situation would devolve. Which it was guaranteed to do.

"You're a child, Max," she said, obviously trying to control her anger. "Which makes it unsurprising that you can't see the big picture. You're still putting yourself at the center of the universe. It's time you found out you're just a small speck in the big scheme of things."

"Which means what?" I demanded. "That I'm nothing? That I'm not a person? That you can do anything you want to me and it's okay? You're so full of it! But you're wrong. I know that I *do* matter. I *am* important. And *you're* a pathetic, cold, pointless wastoid who's going to grow old *alone* and die, then roast in hell *forever*."

I have to say, that sounded dang good, considering I don't even know if I believe in hell. I *do* believe in hateful rhymes-with-witches, though, and I had one standing right here who was glaring sparks at me.

"This is what I mean," she said. "Your childish insults don't affect me. Your useless anger doesn't affect me. You'll end up doing what I say or you will die. It's that simple."

"That's one of the *many, many* differences between you and me," I snarled. "I have enough smarts to know that it's *never* that simple. And I can make this more complicated than you could possibly imagine." I put real menace into my voice, leaning forward threateningly and clenching my fists. Her eyes flickered.

"See, you don't know squat about me, *Mom*," I went on icily. "You have no idea what I'm capable of. Just because you made me doesn't mean you know what I can do, what I've done. And here's a news flash: My chip is gone. So you can take your spyware and shove it."

Her glance quickly shot to my wrist.

I dropped my voice and stared into her eyes. I could tell she was trying hard not to look away. I was so furious I could have cheerfully ripped her head off. "But you're going to *find out,* Mom," I said very softly. "And it's going to give you nightmares for the rest of your wasted life."

Oh, my God, I was so badass. It was all I could do to not give a *mwa ha ha ha!*

The Director clenched her teeth and visibly controlled some shallow breaths. Finally she spoke. "You're wasting your time, Max," she said. "You can't hurt me."

I grinned evilly, and she flinched for a split second, then made her face expressionless.

"Yes, Mom," I whispered. "I really can."

104

I'm sure some of you get sent to your rooms sometimes by your parents. All I have to say is, the next time it happens and you're lying there all mad thinking about how hard your life is, just picture me standing next to you, ready to smack you upside the head. When *I* get sent to my room, it's in a freaking *dungeon!* With rats!

Plus, how many of your parents chain you to the wall? I'm betting not that many. Okay, maybe some. I don't know how regular families work. But probably not many, am I right?

"Yeah, you showed her," Total muttered, licking his paw where his shackle was chafing it.

I made a face at him. "God, my mom's such a witch."

"We've been in worse places, in worse situations," Nudge said.

"For all we know a PetSmart truck is pulling up outside, unloading dog crates," I said gloomily, unwilling to be comforted.

The speakers wired to the walls crackled to life, and I

groaned as more multi-culti propaganda began to assault our ears.

I inched over toward Nudge and Angel. My chain let me sit between them, and I unfolded my wings and shook them out. Then I carefully wrapped my wings around Nudge and Angel, encasing them in a warm, feathery cocoon big enough to hold all of us. Total couldn't be left out, so he dragged his chain over and crawled beneath my wings too.

I looked over at Ari. He was asleep, or pretending to be asleep, so he wasn't part of the feathery fun fest.

It was quiet and dim here; the stones were cold under my jeans, and I could feel a chill starting to seep into my skin. Another hour or two and we would be miserable with cold. How long would it take Fang to get here? How could he even get here?

Total pricked his ears and raised his head slightly. Looking into the shadows, I saw a tall shape moving toward us. In an instant I had recognized the gait, the height, the body language. Jeb. He was like really spicy Mexican food — kept coming back on ya.

I didn't have the energy for more sparring.

When he was close enough, I said, "Please tell me that icebox was kidding about being my mother."

He knelt in front of us, and I gathered the younger ones more closely under my wings.

"The Director is a brilliant woman with a global vision," Jeb said.

"Yeah, a *deranged* global vision," I said sourly.

"She's a remarkable, gifted scientist."

"Why can't she use her powers for good instead of evil? Like, cure cancer or something. And no, killing everyone who *has* cancer does not count as a cure."

"Dr. Janssen is an ambitious, talented political strategist," Jeb said. "She could very well end up running the world. One day she might be the most powerful person on Earth. As her daughter, you would be in a position of unimaginable advantage."

"Except that I would have changed my name and dyed my hair and would be living incognito somewhere to avoid the embarrassment of having a ruthless, power-crazy Dr. Frankenstein for a mother," I pointed out.

"Even if she were the most powerful person in the world, and being her daughter would give you almost unlimited power too?" Jeb asked.

I made a face. "If I had that much power, the first thing I would do is slam her into jail."

Jeb just looked at me. "What else would you do?"

"Put her in jail," I repeated. "Plus all the others who lent a hand to this hateful Goldfinger plan of world domination. Plus, I would say that all wars would be fought only on foot with nothing more than swords. No guns, no missiles, no bombs. Only swords." I looked up, warming to the idea of World Emperor Max. "And I would seize all the offshore hidden bank accounts of companies and people who had contributed to ruining the environment.

With that money, I would make sure that health care and education were available to everyone for free."

I felt Nudge and Angel smile against my shoulders, and I sat up straighter. "Plus, housing and food for everyone. Companies that polluted would be shut down and banished. People in the government who ignored the environment and started wars would be booted out of office and made to work in the fields. And —"

Jeb held up his hand and stopped me. *"You just passed another test, Max."*

105

"Excellent," I said, irritated all over again. "Then get us out of this stinking dungeon."

"What test did she pass?" Nudge asked, raising her head a little.

Jeb turned to her. "She's incorruptible."

Bully for me. "At least by *power*," I said. "You haven't tried Snickers bars or cute shoes."

Jeb smiled at me. It still hurt my heart when he did that.

"You don't want the Director to be your mother no matter what kind of power you would get from it."

"I don't want the Director to be my mother because she's an insane *witch*," I said.

His smile widened, and I barely suppressed an urge to punch him.

"The Director isn't your mother."

Had I heard right? Was he just snowing me? I felt Nudge and Angel stiffen, and Ari clumsily sat up and rubbed his eyes. He blinked at seeing Jeb but didn't say anything.

"What do you mean?" I said suspiciously. "Is this one of your chain yanks? I mean, for God's sake, make up your mind!"

"The Director, Marian Janssen, engineered your design and development," Jeb explained. "She oversaw the whole project. To her, that must feel like motherhood."

"Oh, my God, and here I thought she couldn't get any more pathetic." Relief was flooding through me that such a horrible, crazy person truly had not passed on her DNA to me.

"She didn't donate an egg?" I needed to be sure.

Jeb shook his head. "She shares no genetic material with you."

I dropped my head. "I'm really, really glad," I muttered. Of course, it left me with my same old "mystery guest" for a mother, but I swear, *anyone* would have been better than that freak show. I couldn't believe Jeb had just waltzed in here and told me. He, more than anyone else, should have known how huge it was, finding out who my mother was. Or wasn't.

I looked up at him. "Well? Any other bombs you want to drop before you leave? Any more fake directions you want to steer me in?"

Jeb hesitated. "Do you remember in New York, when you killed Ari, and I yelled that you had killed your brother?"

I looked over warily and saw Ari tense, staring at Jeb.

"Yeah. Lucky for you he's hard to kill."

Ari shot me a brief smile.

"He *is* your brother, Max," said Jeb. "At least, your half brother."

I couldn't breathe. What did . . . what . . .

"I'm your father, Max," said Jeb simply.

106

Everything faded away except Jeb's face.

I couldn't even hear the propaganda blaring from the speakers anymore. I felt the damp heat of Nudge's hand tighten in mine, felt my feathers brushing the cold stone floor, but all I could do was stare at Jeb while his words rattled senselessly inside my brain.

My eyes flicked back to Ari. He didn't look upset — just stunned.

"What are you talking about?" I said, unwilling to have the rug pulled out from under me, which, face it, seems to be these guys' main source of yuks.

"I'm your father, Max," Jeb repeated. "I wasn't married to your mother, but we decided together to create you."

I couldn't even look at him. For years and years I had wished that he was my dad. In my mind, without telling anyone, I'd pretended he was. It was what I'd wanted more than anything in the world. Then he'd disappeared and I'd grieved for him with a broken heart.

Then he'd turned up again — surprise! — evil. Which had broken my heart even worse than the first time.

Now Jeb was saying that he really was my dad. That my wishes had come true. Except I no longer trusted him, no longer admired him, no longer loved him.

"Hmm," I said.

He reached out and patted my knee briefly. "I know it's an awful lot to take in, especially given the past six months. All I can say is that one day I hope to be able to explain it all to you, Max. You deserve that, and so much more. But know that I'm your father. And I know this sounds impossible, but I'm asking you to trust me as your dad."

"That really can't happen at this point," I said slowly.

He nodded. "I understand. But I'm asking you to try."

"Hmm."

"Half brother?" Ari asked.

Jeb turned to him. "Yes. You had different mothers. Your mother was my wife, who died shortly after you were born."

Ari was absorbing this when I asked, "But I was born before Ari. Who was *my* mother?"

"Your mother and I had no personal relationship," said Jeb slowly. "But we agreed on what to do; we agreed that we wanted to be part of your beginning, part of your heritage. It was a monumental, stunning idea, that we —"

"I don't want to hear this!" I cried, folding in my wings. I was ready to kill him, drawing out this moment like torture. "I don't *care* about all the 'beautiful science,' la la la! You tell me who my *mother* is before I yank your eyes out!"

Jeb looked at me, unperturbed. "She's a good woman, and you remind me of her."

I stood up, trembling with rage and tension. *"You . . . better . . . tell . . . me."*

My hands were clenched into fists. Angel and Nudge stood up too, behind me. Total was growling low in his throat. For such a small dog, he could sound like a rottweiler when he wanted to.

"Your mother is Dr. Martinez. Valencia Martinez. You met her in Arizona."

107

I almost fell over backward. For a second I thought I was going to faint — I got tunnel vision and my skin felt icy. There was no sound in the empty, echoing dungeon.

A dozen images flashed through my mind: her smiling face, her warm brown eyes, the smell of homemade chocolate-chip cookies. Her and Ella watching me, hands shading their eyes, as I took off. Eating meals together. She was the most real momlike mom I'd ever imagined.

"Dr. Martinez . . . is my . . . mother?" I whispered hoarsely.

He nodded seriously. "She was an incredibly important research scientist, specializing in avian genetics. But once you were a viable embryo, she was locked out of the process. Not by me, I might add. She went back to Arizona, brokenhearted. But she donated the egg that became you."

I frowned, my mind racing, looking for loopholes. I had to make absolutely sure, because if I got my hopes up and then was wrong, I didn't think I'd ever recover. "Dr.

Martinez is Hispanic," I said. "I don't look anything like her."

"You have her eyes," said Jeb.

Well, I did have brown eyes.

"And I was blond as a little boy, like you are. So was Ari, if you remember."

I glanced at Ari, who was now, you know, wolf colored. He *had* been blond.

I focused my laser gaze on Jeb and made my voice as hard as an ice pick. "If this is an elaborate test, something else I'm supposed to pass somehow, you will never see the light of day again."

Jeb's mouth quirked on one side. "This, I'm happy to say, is not a test. Out of everything I've ever told you, it is the most true. Valencia Martinez is your mother. And I'm your father."

I looked at him, still furious about everything that had happened since he'd disappeared on us more than two years ago. I wanted to hurt him one-tenth as much as he'd hurt me and the rest of the flock.

"I don't have a father," I said coldly, and was both rewarded by and guilty about the flare of pain I saw in his eyes. I looked away and, still trembling with emotion, turned and went as far as my chain would let me.

When Jeb spoke, he used the Voice, the one I'd gotten so used to hearing inside my head, the one I hadn't heard since he'd told me it was him.

"Max — you're still here to save the world. That's what

you were born for, that's the point of everything, all of this. No one else can do it. I believe that with all my heart. This isn't a test, and I'm not snowing you. You have to do this. Nothing in the history of mankind has ever been more important. *Nothing*. Ever. *Ever*."

108

There was silence for a few moments. It was all too much for me to take in — like getting the most amazing, fabulous, unbelievable Christmas presents ever, and yet having them cause you an incredible amount of rage and pain.

"What about *our* parents?" Angel asked. "Me and the Gasman. Nudge, Fang. Where are they?"

"I don't know," Jeb said, standing up. "Some of them were never identified by name — only number. And we've lost track of others. Their roles were over so quickly."

"What about that information we found," Nudge asked, "where we saw some names and addresses and stuff?"

Jeb shook his head. "I don't know what you found, but I'd guess you misinterpreted it, or maybe it was planted by the Director. I've been finding out about many things she's done that I didn't know about."

Oh, I'm so sure, I thought.

Looking over at Nudge and Angel, I saw their faces fall, the light of hope fading in their eyes. I put my arms around them, and Total wedged himself among our feet.

"I'm sorry, guys," I said, holding them close. "But parents are totally overrated. We're all the family we need. Right?"

"We've just . . . spent so much time trying to find out," Nudge said softly.

Angel nodded. "I want to *know*, for *sure*."

"Someday we'll know the whole truth," I said. "But for right now, I'm just glad I have you guys. You're my family."

They gave me sad smiles and nodded.

I looked over my shoulder at Jeb. "You can go now. Unless you have any more heartbreaking news you'd like to deliver."

He looked regretful, and I automatically tensed up.

"You're supposed to come see the rally," he said. "And then there's a final test."

He sounded weird and didn't meet my eyes. I'm sure all of you will join me in leaping to the conclusion that something bad was about to happen.

And you would be right.

109

You are reading Fang's Blog. Welcome!
Date: Already Too Late!
You are visitor number: Our stat thing quit working. Got overloaded. But you're way up there, believe me.

Let's Stick Together, People!

Okay, folks, we're on the East Coast somewhere between Miami and Eastport, Maine. Don't want to be more specific than that. We're on our way to rejoin Max. Don't have time to rehash all the details, but let's just say that I've decided a flock ought to stick together while they can.

We've gotten more mail than we can handle, so thanks to everyone who's supporting us. I can only reply to a few people, so I'll do that here, and then we have to split.

To Advon777 in Utah: I don't know where you got a missile launcher, and I don't want to know. But even though it might come in handy, it still seems like a really bad idea for you to be messing with it. Maybe you should just put it back where you got it.

To Felicite StarLight in Milan, Italy: Thanks for the offer, but I really don't have time for a girlfriend right now. I found your ideas . . . creative, but this is not a good time.

To JamesL in Ontario: Thanks, man. I appreciate your support. We need all the help we can get, but waiting till you get out of second grade is fine.

To PDM1223: Excellent! That's exactly what I'm talking about! Tell people what's going on, spread the message, organize protests and stuff. Picket the gargantuan pharmco companies like Itex. I hacked into their files and found that the companies Stellah Corp, Dywestra, Mofongo Research, DelaneyMinkerPrince, and a bunch of others are all Itex under different names in different countries. Stellah Corp is in England, not far from you. See the whole list under Appendix F, for Fatheads. Everyone, read this guy's mail! He totally has a handle on what I mean, what needs to happen.

To everyone in the Seattle area: There's a protest organized for Saturday. Check the schedule that BigBoy-Blue has made (thanks, BBB!), attached as Appendix G, for the time and place. Folks in other cities, check the schedule. There's a tidal wave of stuff going on. Thanks to everyone who's making this happen! *We're gonna save the world!* We're the last hope!

— Fang

Fang typed the last words, then sat back and rubbed his eyes. It was two in the morning.

He, Iggy, and the Gasman were set up to sneak onto a freight plane at 6:10 a.m. The two other boys were asleep, curled up on sacks of seed corn in the corner of this cavernous hangar. Fang had offered to take the whole watch. He had to get caught up with his blog, and also, they seemed much more wiped than he was. They'd flown across the whole United States, with stops only for quick rests and meals on the run.

He shut down the computer, wanting to save the battery. He felt safer without its soft blue glow, with the middle-of-the-night blackness settling around him.

It was hard to believe what he was reading on the blog, the swelling underground movement that kids were organizing all around the world. Even in places like Kazakhstan and Taiwan, kids were getting mad, getting determined. Fang had heard from kids who seemed willing to die for what they believed in. He hoped that wouldn't be necessary.

He leaned back against a sack of corn, listening to the others' breathing. It was torture to wait until six like this, and then the whole flight across the ocean, and then look for Max somewhere in Germany. He'd give anything to be able to snap his fingers and be there. Unfortunately, that was one skill the mad scientists had forgotten to program in.

In the meantime, he was totally stoked about his blog, the one that Max hadn't taken seriously. He really thought these kids could make a difference. More important, they thought so too.

He put his hands behind his neck and stretched, then

permitted himself a small grin. Max had always teased that the flock had voted Fang "Most Likely to Become a Cult Leader."

Well, maybe he had. And maybe that was the only thing that could save everybody.

110

"Is this a pep rally?" Total asked in a low voice as we slogged our way up countless stone steps. "With cheerleaders? I love cheerleaders."

"I don't think it's a *pep* rally," I said under my breath. "Somehow I don't think the Mad Whitecoat team is squaring off against the Fightin' Freedom Lovers."

"What kind of final test?" Nudge asked, sounding apprehensive.

I sighed. "Something asinine, probably life threatening, and guaranteed to make me angry every time I remember it for the rest of my life."

Angel looked up at me, worried. "Do you think Fang will get here soon?"

I nodded. "I'm sure he's on his way."

But he probably wouldn't make it in time to spare me this idiocy. Instinctively I began taking deep breaths, superoxygenating my blood. My knuckles were scarred from the last little skirmish I'd had with the flying can openers, and I cracked them loudly, already bracing myself to feel pain and to ignore it.

The rally was taking place out in the wimpy winter sunlight of the prison yard. The sky and air felt as gray as the lifeless dirt beneath our boots. I thought about Dr. Martinez and how she might actually be my mom. Outside of the flock, she and Ella — Ella was my half sister! — were my favorite people in the world. I wished I could take several hours to just enjoy thinking about it. Now I might die before I ever saw them again.

The remaining ranks of mutants and wannabes were lined up neatly in the yard. There were fewer of them than before, and I remembered what Max II had said about how they disappeared every day.

Was this going to be another fight with Max II? Did they really want me to kill her this time? I prayed no one was sick enough to make me fight Ari again, but I wouldn't put it past them.

"Wait here," commanded a Flyboy in a metallic voice.

Sure, I thought, *because telling me what to do always works so well.*

Several Flyboys surrounded us, pointing guns. The guns seemed to be welded to their arms, part of them. An improvement over the last ones — now they couldn't drop their weapons or have them taken away. Those guys just kept innovating! That's progress, people!

"Welcome, everyone," said my ex-mom, walking out onto a platform. Her image immediately popped up on half a dozen movie theater–sized screens positioned all around the yard.

She opened her arms in greeting, and then I noticed the viewing stands full of people over to one side. Everything about them said "government wanks," and I figured they were here to be impressed, flattered, and bribed, not necessarily in that order.

"Welcome, honored representatives of . . ." Then she launched into a geographical who's who of countries all around the world. Pretty much every country I'd heard of, and a bunch I hadn't, seemed to be thinking about jumping on the Insane Apocalypse bandwagon.

"And now, prepare yourselves to view many of our most stunning achievements," said the Director, pressing a button that opened an eight-foot metal-clad door.

Great, I thought. *My day's about to get worse.*

Which, come to think of it, was the first of their stunning achievements, actually.

111

"Okay, they got me," Total whispered. "I am one stunned little dog."

Angel, Nudge, and I nodded silently, our eyes wide at what was happening in front of us.

I won't describe the scariest things we saw that morning, 'cause it would depress the heck out of you. Let's just say that if these scientists had been using their brilliance for good instead of evil, cars would run off water vapor and leave fresh compost behind them; no one would be hungry; no one would be ill; all buildings would be earthquake-, bomb-, and flood-proof; and the world's entire economy would have collapsed and been replaced by one based on the value of chocolate.

However, since they *were* evil, basically we saw stuff that would fuel the world's nightmares for the next five hundred years.

"Max, if you survive your final test, can you steal one of those magic outfits for me?" Angel asked, leaning against me.

"I'll try to get one for each of us," I replied, and then I realized what she'd said. "Hey! 'If'?"

She looked at me seriously, and I hoped she hadn't developed a way to predict the future. "We're way outnumbered, and I don't think they're gonna fight fair."

I held her hand tightly. "They never do. But I will survive, and I will steal you one of those magic suits."

She smiled.

"Here you see our patented process for growing replacement limbs," said the Director. A man walked out, reached over, and detached his arm from the shoulder. He showed that it was made of flesh and bone, and was attached to him by an electronic interface that looked suspiciously like an iPod data port.

"Way gross," said Nudge, and we all nodded.

"We made the replica arm out of biogenetic matrix," the Director explained.

"Is that from Duncan Hines?" I whispered.

"It functions exactly like the limb he lost — and even better," the Director went on. "We laced titanium cells into the bone material, strengthening its stress resistance by four hundred percent."

"And guaranteeing him hassles at airport security stations all over the world," I murmured.

"Next we have one of our most successful human hybrids," said Dr. Janssen.

A woman walked out, totally normal looking. Did she have wings? Was she an Eraser?

"Mara here had *Panthera pardus* genetic material grafted into her human DNA. It's given her some unique qualities."

"What's that?" Angel whispered.

"I don't know," I said.

"Something feline," said Ari.

He was right. Up on the platform, the woman opened her mouth to reveal humongous razor-sharp fangs, which looked even more lethal than the typical Eraser's. Then she crouched down, sprang up as if made of rubber, and landed fifteen feet above the platform, clinging to a tall light stand.

Everyone who hadn't gasped when they saw her fangs quit trying to be suave and went ahead and gasped.

The Director smiled and motioned her down. "As usual, the leopard genes were expressed in some unexpected ways."

Meaning they still didn't know what the heck they were doing.

Mara turned around. The Director unzipped her jumpsuit at the back, and an excited murmur raced through the crowd. Ol' Mara had leopard spots trailing down her spine.

"Guess she can't change *that*," I said, and Total snickered.

"And Mara is just the beginning," said the Director.

112

Growing up in the lab at the School, where we were surrounded by dog crates filled with mix 'n' match genetic experiments, we'd seen pretty much any combination of two living things that you could imagine, and probably a thousand that you couldn't. Virtually all of them had been unsuccessful, or "nonviable," as the whitecoats said. A tiny percentage made it past the embryo stage, and a few struggled along for a year or two before their horrific deficits caught up with them. As far as I knew, we, the flock, had been by far the most successful hybrid. Us and the Erasers. Even the Erasers only lived about six years or so. We were ancient compared with them.

Today we were seeing some successful hybrids, like Mara. After SpotGirl, the Director trotted out two people who could control the color of their skin just by thinking about it.

"Can they turn blue?" Nudge asked, fascinated. "Or purple?"

"Who knows?" I said, and then my stomach twisted as the people onstage literally turned camouflage right in front of us. I thought about what the military people of various countries could do with that and felt ill.

We saw people who could increase their height by about four inches, just by controlling their muscles and skeletal structures with their minds.

"Combine that with the skin-changing types, and you've got a recipe for a bank robber deluxe," I said. "They'd never be recognized."

We saw people with hard, scaly, bulletproof skin, or GatorGuys, as we called them. We saw a woman who could scream at pitches too high for any of us to hear but had Total writhing in pain on the ground, biting his lip to keep from shrieking swear words. Her voice could break glass, which isn't totally unusual, but it could also shatter metal, which seemed new and different — and completely horrifying.

"Think of what a successful nag she would be," I said to Ari, and he tried to smile but couldn't. His skin seemed to have a grayish cast, and he'd been unusually quiet for several hours. I wondered if he was near his end.

"These things all look like soldiers," said Nudge. "Like they'd be good in a war, you know?"

"They look all warry because they were built to be an army," I told her.

"Well, that would do it," she said.

"Don't these people ever think about anything else?" Total muttered in disgust. "There's more to life than world domination, you know."

"Max? What's that?" Angel asked, pointing.

I looked. Up on the stage the Director seemed to have a remote control in her hand. Then I saw a small swarm of glittery copper-colored things circling around her. Were they bugs? Had they started engineering bugs? Oh, great. Just what the world needed.

The Director motioned to someone. He opened a large plastic box, and hundreds of beautiful butterflies flew out. It was a weird jolt of color in this gray landscape. Well, besides the camo people, that is.

The glittery things weren't bugs.

They were nano-bullets, with their own internal guidance systems.

Within seconds they had locked on to the butterflies, and moments after that, all that was left were bits of shimmery wings, floating to the ground.

Nudge, Angel, Ari, Total, and I stared at one another in horror.

113

"What do they have against *butterflies?*" Nudge demanded, outraged.

"I think the butterflies were just an example," I said. "I think the point is that those things are tiny and deadly and can find the proverbial needle in the biogenetically modified haystack."

Total shook his head, then lay down and covered his eyes with his paws. "It's all too much," he moaned. "I'm too sensitive for this."

"And now, we have saved the best for last," the Director boomed over the loudspeakers. "I give you . . . Generation Omega!"

A boy came out. He looked about my age but was maybe a couple inches shorter than I was, and heavier by about forty pounds. He had pale brown hair and silvery blue eyes, and was wearing one of the magic suits, which could change color and form at a verbal command.

"Oh, they gave him the cute gene," said Nudge, and Angel giggled.

The Director beamed at the boy. He looked out at the crowd without expression.

"Omega here is our pinnacle achievement," said the Director, "the result of more than six decades of research. He is an unqualified success and far surpasses any hybrid made before."

"Ouch," said Total.

"In Omega lie our hopes and dreams for the utopia of the future," the Director gushed. "He is the key to the hyperevolved human of tomorrow. He's immune to virtually every disease known and has superacute reflexes and greatly increased strength. He tests off the charts of every intelligence scale devised. In addition, he has superior memory retention and reaction time. He's truly a superman."

"Plus, he cooks like a dream and makes darling floral arrangements in his spare time," I muttered.

"And he's here to demonstrate just how tough he is, how supremely suited he is to forge a new human existence in our brand-new world."

"Brand-new but full of dead people and empty buildings," I said.

"To begin, Omega will vanquish an obsolete but somewhat successful human-avian hybrid," said the Director. "And that will be a symbol for how everything will go from here on."

I stiffened and stared at her.

The Director looked back at me.

"Right, Max?" she said.

114

Have I mentioned how much I can't stand despotic psychopaths? Why, yes, Max, you have. Like, a couple hundred times.

Well, it's for reasons like *this*.

"Maximum Ride and Omega will fight to the death," said the Director merrily, as if announcing the next croquet competition.

"Max?" Nudge whispered, appalled.

Ari grabbed my arm and stepped halfway in front of me, to protect me. I smiled at him and shook my head slightly, and he stepped back with an angry frown.

"That guy wants to kill you, Max," said Angel, sounding scared. "His whole life, he's been trained to kill you."

Of course. Because God forbid he should have any kind of normal existence, watching TV, eating Twinkies, and so on.

Like a school of washed-out-gray fish, the mutants all turned to stare at me. They parted, as if Moses were waving his staff over them, and then Omega did a high double somersault off the stage, landing perfectly on the gray grit with a barely heard crunch.

"Angel, if you can, this would be a good time to mess with his mind," I murmured.

"On it," she said, but she didn't sound hopeful.

My heart had kicked into high gear, my fists were clenched, and adrenaline was whipping like white lightning through my veins.

From the end of the mutant corridor, Omega started coming at me, doing one handspring after another, leaping forward onto his hands, flipping over, then landing lightly, a human circle. He could move incredibly fast, and within seconds his booted feet landed crisply right in front of me.

Omega snapped upright, and for a second, those silvery eyes looked coldly into mine.

Before he knew what was happening, I had cocked my arm back and slammed my fist into his left eye as hard as I could.

I can move pretty fast too, when I want.

He staggered back but used the energy from my punch to fuel a spinning snap kick that would have caught me right in the neck if I weren't a great fighter and the fastest bird kid around.

Instead, I was ready, and I grabbed the heel of his boot and whipped it to the left, yanking him off balance so that he landed hard on his back in the dirt. *Hoo-yah*.

In a split second he sprang up again. I blocked his hard

elbow jab to my head, but his other hand knifed into my side, right over my kidney. The pain was immediate and stunning; it hurt so much that I wanted to sink to my knees and throw up.

But I hadn't been raised that way.

It's just pain, I told myself. *Pain is merely a message, and you can ignore the message.*

So I stayed on my feet, sucked in a breath, and smacked my open palm against his ear with all my force. His face crumpled, and his mouth opened in a brief, silent scream. I hoped I'd ruptured his eardrum. But all too quickly, his face straightened out and he lunged at me again, elbowing me in the ribs and then chopping the back of my neck with the edge of his hand.

Pain is merely a message. Right now I was holding all calls.

I managed to spin and kick him hard in the side, then followed with a snap kick right into his spine. If he'd been an ordinary human, it would have broken his back. But Omega just staggered, instantly righted himself, and came roaring back full force.

Usually I try not to kill people, 'cause I'm just a softie that way. Even Ari — I only killed him by accident. But I decided that since my ex-mom had said this was a fight to the death, in a way I kind of had permission to kill this weiner. And yes, I'm worried about the state of my soul and karma and blah blah blah, but right now I wanted to *live,* to come out of this battle alive. So I would deal with my karma later. And if I came back as a roach in the next life, well, at least I'd survive the nuclear holocaust.

I did a spinning kick where I literally looked like a propeller, both feet off the ground, scissoring at Omega with my powerful legs. One kick caught him hard in his back, and he lurched forward. As he tried to block the next one and grab my boot, I slammed right into the back of his perfect little head and knocked him to the ground.

In seconds I had sprung onto his back, grabbed one arm behind him, and yanked hard, up and to the left.

His arm popped out of its socket with a stomach-churning *thunk* sound.

"Maybe you should change your name to Theta," I hissed into his ear as he gasped, facedown in the dirt. "Or Epsilon."

Okay, now, the shoulder dislocation, I have to tell you, stopped most people cold.

"My . . . name . . . is . . . Omega," he ground out.

Then he jerked upward, throwing me off as his shoulder joint popped loudly back into place. He grimaced, then came after me again, murder in his bloodshot, silvery eyes.

115

You are reading Fang's Blog. Welcome!
Date: Already Too Late!
You are visitor number: Thing is still broken.

Watch Out, Guys, Here We Come

It's about five a.m. We should be sneaking on board the cargo plane soon. I've let the others sleep as much as they can — and of course now I'm so wiped I can't think straight. I'll try to grab some zzz's on the plane. Once it's up in the air, we're golden. We're probably the only people in the world who don't worry about plane crashes. If something happens to this plane and we start going down, I'll be like, later!

I hope Max is okay. Any of you guys — if you're around Lendeheim, Germany, go to the castle there and raise heck, okay?

— Fang

A slight sound made Fang quit typing. He listened. It wasn't dawn yet — through the hangar windows he could see the glow of the amber safety lights outside. Maybe the loading guys had shown up early.

And maybe Fang had been born yesterday and was a gullible numskull.

Silently he closed his laptop and stashed it in his backpack. Then he slid over to the others and touched their legs. They woke instantly, with no sound, the way they'd been trained.

The Gasman looked at Fang. Fang put a finger to his lips, and the Gasman nodded.

Fang reached over and tapped the back of Iggy's hand twice.

Iggy sat up carefully and nodded also.

Then their world imploded: The enormous metal doors at the hangar entrance opened with earsplitting creaks; the glass door by the hangar office shattered inward; and two high windows on the other side broke as Flyboys began crawling through like angry, angry wasps.

"Get outside!" Fang ordered the boys. "Iggy, open doors right in front, twelve o'clock!"

The trick to having obedient, unquestioning children was to have death be the other option, Fang thought as he raced toward the oncoming Flyboys.

There were dozens of them, some running in, weapons ready; some airborne, swooping down like big butt-ugly insects. They opened fire: Bullets began ricocheting off the metal hangar walls, off the pallet movers and Bobcats.

Fang flew straight through the crowd of Flyboys. Several of them landed blows on him, making him suck in his breath, but he stayed aloft and made it outside. Instantly a bullet grazed his shoulder. Hissing, he glanced down, saw it was just a surface wound, and raced upward. There! He saw the Gasman and Iggy also outside. Excellent. Now, if they could all meet up and somehow lose these suckers . . . *somehow?*

Fang darted here and there, keeping his wings in close, the way the hawks had. He banked and maneuvered tightly, able to move much faster and more nimbly than the Flyboys.

He could still hear shots from inside the hangar, and he had a moment to think, *They might not want to be shooting so close to that plane's gas tank,* then *boom!* As in — *BOOM!* The metal roof of the hangar blew upward, and a massive fireball boiled out. Jagged chunks of metal flew everywhere, and Fang saw the Gasman take a hot shard across his face. The Gasman gasped and put one hand to his cheek but still managed to punch both of his feet into a Flyboy's chest, knocking it sideways.

The Flyboys weren't great at flying sideways, and before that one could right itself, it crashed to the ground.

Bits of other exploded Flyboys rained around them. Fang swooped down, grabbed a fallen weapon, then rocketed back into the air. He tried to fire the gun, took a second to find the safety, then let rip a hail of bullets at a line of maybe ten Flyboys. It effectively mowed them down, and Fang seriously questioned Max's "no guns" rule.

"You will die today," several Flyboys promised in their weird metallic voices. "We are here to kill you and the others. Max and the rest of your flock are already dead. Now it is your turn."

116

Fang felt a cold jolt, then dismissed it. Max wasn't dead. He would *know,* somehow. He would have felt it. The world still felt the same to him; therefore, Max was still in it.

"We are here to kill you," the Flyboys intoned all together.

"Then you're out of luck," Fang snarled, and opened fire again. Another ten Flyboys dropped, hitting the ground with somewhat sickening crunching and splatting sounds.

"You will not die easily," yet another Flyboy droned.

"You got *that* right." Fang had never seen so many Flyboys before — there must have been three hundred? More? The Gasman and Iggy were still holding their own — the Flyboys seemed to be trying to capture them instead of kill them outright. *Because what would be the fun of that?* Fang thought.

"First we will dismember you," said a Flyboy. "We will post the pictures on your blog. To show what happens when you resist. Then we will make you recant everything you have said on your blog."

Fang grinned, continuing to bob and weave up and down by fifteen-foot drops. "*After* you dismember me? Did you fail basic human biology?"

"We will torture you," the Flyboys pressed on.

"I don't think so," said Fang, and mowed them down. God! The whole firing-a-weapon thing was *amazing!* It just worked so incredibly well! It was so *efficient!* What did Max have against guns, anyway?

"We will show the world how you take back everything you said." A new, unmowed-down crop of Flyboys continued the same old song.

"Here's a tip," Fang advised them. "If you *show* me being tortured and then taking everything back, people might catch on. They might actually guess that I didn't do it *voluntarily*."

"We will torture you," the Flyboys insisted.

"Okay, bored now," Fang said, and pulled the trigger. Only to have nothing happen. Maybe the gun was empty. In an instant he'd swooped and tried to pluck another gun from a crumpled Flyboy body. That gun was attached to its Flyboy, though, so Fang ended up being yanked to the ground. He dropped it, ran a bit to get away from ground-based Flyboys, then finally found an unattached gun.

Spinning, he fired, catching all the Flyboys directly behind him. Then he changed angles and shot up into the sky, watching with satisfaction as several Flyboys started flying lopsidedly, smoke streaming off them.

"Hey!" shouted the Gasman from above. "Watch that

thing!" Fang looked up to see the Gasman pointing to two holes in his jeans — Fang had shot right through his pants, but amazingly hadn't hit him.

"My bad!" Fang yelled. The drawback with guns, besides the fact that you might hit members of your own flock, was that they didn't take out hundreds of bad guys all at once. He needed something more massive. If Iggy or the Gasman had had any bombs, they would have used them by now. It was up to Fang.

He leaped into the chilly air again, shooting more carefully at Flyboys. When he was about five hundred feet up, he saw a broad expanse of gray with a rim of fire at its far edge.

The ocean. With the sun breaking at the horizon.

"It is your time to die," droned a full squadron of Flyboys, following him.

"I am one of many!" Fang shouted, heading east, away from the hangar. "I am one of many! *You have no idea!*"

117

I was braced and ready to launch into my next move against Omega when I heard the Director's voice boom, "Wait!"

I wasn't about to start listening to her *now,* and I sprang forward, fingers stiff to shatter his trachea —

But the metal collar around my neck zapped me with a nerve-shattering dose of electricity, and I dropped to the ground like a chunk of cement.

A while back, I'd been hit with a bunch of skull-exploding headaches that had left me weak and nauseated; this was a lot like that. When my scrambled brain finally cleared and my synapses began firing again, I was on my back with my worried miniflock peering down at me.

I shot to my feet as fast as I could, a little off balance, to see Omega standing to one side, ramrod straight like a soldier, not looking at me.

I shot Nudge a questioning glance, and she shrugged.

"You have anticipated my commands," said the Director, sounding unthrilled.

I didn't start it, lady, I was going to say, but then I remembered that, technically, I had, so I kept my mouth shut.

"The first part of the battle will be a test of speed," said the Director.

The crowd of lemmings parted in anticipation of a race.

"Begin where you are," intoned the Director. "Run to the opposite castle wall and back, four times. May the better man win."

I gritted my teeth. The Director was a sexist pig on top of all her other faults.

The wall was about six hundred yards away. There and back, four times.

Someone scraped a line in the dirt with his boot, and Omega and I stood on it. What else could I do? I was shook up and barfy from the electric shock. I didn't think being a conscientious objector would go over well at this point.

Omega seemed unruffled, cool, and not like he'd just popped his shoulder back into place.

"You can't win," he said calmly, not looking at me. "No human can run faster than I can."

"Bite me," I replied, and leaned over to get a good start. "Also, watch my dust!"

"Go!" the Director cried, and we were off.

Well. I must say, Omega was a speedy little sucker, I'll give him that. He hit the opposite wall several seconds ahead of me, and I was dang fast, and taller than he was. By our third lap, he had about a quarter length on me.

Neither one of us was breathing that hard — he was Superboy, and I was designed to be able to breathe in very thin air, way up high.

But he had no emotion — he wasn't angry, didn't seem determined to win at all costs, didn't seem invested in beating me.

Which made three *more* differences between us.

Finally we were on the last lap. He had almost a three-quarter-length lead on me. The crowd was silent — no one dared cheer. The only sounds were our breathing and the pounding of our boots on the ground.

When Omega was about thirty yards away from whipping my butt, I suddenly dove forward, pulled out my wings, and went airborne. I thought I heard the crowd gasp.

Keeping very low to avoid the electrified net at the top of the castle walls, which Max II had warned us about, I streaked toward the finish, my wings working smoothly. I tilted as I passed Superboy, so I wouldn't whap the back of his head with a wing — tempting though it was.

Then I shot across the finish line, ten feet ahead of him, and ran to a somewhat clumsy halt, trying not to careen into the gray sea of spectators.

I stood up, breathing hard, and punched my fist in the air. "Max, one!"

118

"Cheating disqualifies you!" The Director said, looking mad.

"I didn't cheat! Did you say 'no flying'? Did *anyone* say 'no flying'? No."

"It was a race on the *ground!*"

"Again, said who? Just because Wonderlad is stuck to the ground doesn't mean I have to be. I've evolved past being stuck to the ground."

Now the Director looked *really* mad. The sea of indistinct faces murmured; feet shifted on the ground. I folded my wings in, aware of dozens of eyes watching me.

"You are disqualified," the Director said shortly. "Omega is the winner."

"Whatever," I said, pushing down my disgust. I shot Omega a sideways glance. "Does she tie your shoes for you too?"

His perfect eyebrows drew together, but he didn't speak.

Nudge and Angel took my hands and stood close, and Ari came up behind me, as if to protect my back. I felt very comforted by their being there. I would have felt even better if I had seen Fang standing with me, ready to back me up.

"Next will be a contest of strength," said the Director. "Omega's muscles are approximately four hundred percent stronger and denser than a regular boy's. Bring out the weights!"

I am weirdly, wickedly strong, and not just for a girl, not just for my age. I'm stronger than just about any grown-up, man or woman. We all are. But I didn't have the bulk that Superboy did, and in general I was designed to be smart and fast, and to fly well. Not to be able to compete in a tractor pull.

It really was a tractor pull, in a way. Heavy weights were loaded onto a wooden platform. We were each given a thick chain. The idea was literally to pull the platform across the dirt. We were even until about five hundred pounds, then Superboy started to edge past me. I could barely budge six hundred and fifty pounds — he pulled it three feet.

They piled on more weight — eight hundred pounds. I couldn't believe I was going to lose a strength contest to a *boy*. There was no way.

I gritted my teeth, cracked my knuckles, and put the chain over my already bruised shoulder. Omega and I looked at each other, side by side. When the Director blew sharply on her whistle, I put my head down, planted my feet in the dirt, and pulled with all my might. Sweat broke out on my forehead. It felt as though the chain were wearing a furrow in my shoulder. Breath hissed through my clenched teeth.

I made the platform tremble a little, moved it maybe a quarter of an inch.

Omega hauled it almost a foot.

When he was pronounced the winner, he looked at me with those weird, expressionless eyes. I didn't think he was a robot, like the Flyboys, but I did wonder if his emotions had been designed out of him. Of course, with a guy, how could I tell? Ha ha!

Anyway.

You might not know this about me, but I hate losing. I'm not a good sport, I'm not gracious in defeat, and I hated Omega for making me lose. I was gonna get him. I didn't know how, I didn't know when, but I knew I would.

"The next contest will be intelligence." The Director looked smug.

I almost groaned. Of course I'm really sharp, really bright. But I'd had almost no schooling. What I knew I'd learned either from television or from Jeb. I knew a lot about how to fight, how to survive. I knew a bit about some places, like Egypt and Mongolia, from *National Geographic*. But I didn't have much book learning at all. The couple of months I'd spent at that hellhole of a school in Virginia had shown me that compared with most kids my age, I was a village idiot. Just in terms of book learning. Not about stuff that mattered.

"First question," said the Director. The crowd turned to

watch me and Omega in our duel of wits. "The castle walls are eighteen feet high, seven feet thick, and one thousand, twenty-seven feet long. One cubic yard of stone and mortar weighs one thousand, one hundred twenty pounds, or exactly half a ton. How many tons of stone and mortar are contained within the walls?"

Omega looked off into the distance, obviously starting to calculate.

"You are kidding me," I said. "Why would I ever need to know that?"

"Like, if you had to make repairs?" Nudge guessed.

"Couldn't I just hire a wall repair company?" I asked.

"It's a simple calculation," said the Director, still smug.

"Yeah? Let's see *you* do it."

Her cheeks flushed, but she stood tall. "Are you conceding?"

"I'm not conceding anything," I said. "I'm just saying it's completely pointless. How about I just pick a lock instead? Me and Omega. Let's see who can do it faster."

"Two thousand, three hundred ninety-six point three three tons," said Omega.

"Okay, smartyboots, how about if you're flying at eighteen thousand feet at, say, a hundred and forty miles an hour," I said. "You're facing a southwest wind of about seven knots. How long would it take you to fly from Philadelphia to Billings, Montana?"

Omega frowned as he started to work the math.

"Are you saying you know how to make that calculation?" the Director asked.

"I'm saying I'm smart enough to know that I'll get there when I get there!" I almost shouted. "The questions themselves are dumb: They don't have anything to do with being able to survive."

"In the new world they do, Max," said the Director. "Maybe not in your world. But your world is over."

119

I was having a really bad day. These tests were a waste of time. I was expecting to get jolted with a lightning bolt of electricity at any moment. I was losing to a *boy*. Still remaining in this contest was a fight to the death.

And Fang still wasn't here.

I knew he hadn't had enough time to get here. There was a reasonable hope that he could be here within the next six hours or so. But he wasn't here now, and I was reaching my breaking point.

I looked at Nudge and Angel. Nudge seemed very tense, and her fingers were curling at her sides. Angel had that scary intent expression she got right before she convinced a stranger to do something. All of a sudden, I remembered that Dr. Martinez was my real mom. Probably. I'd been lied to so many times that it was hard for me to accept anything as fact. But she might have been my real mom.

I wanted to see her. And my sister, Ella.

I needed to get out of here.

Next to Angel, one of the mutants frowned, looking confused. She blinked. I saw Angel stare at her, concentrating. *Uh-oh*. Then the mutant leaned to the one next to her and whispered something so softly I couldn't hear it.

Angel looked pleased, and my stomach knotted up.

"What's going on, sweetie?" I whispered through clenched teeth.

"Things are going to get exciting," Angel said with satisfaction.

"Define 'exciting,'" I said cautiously.

Angel thought. "Everyone freaking out?" she offered.

"Uh . . . in a good way?"

"In an *exciting* way," she said, watching the crowd.

"Now we come to the definitive battle," the Director said into the loudspeaker.

Right then, all heck broke loose. The best way to describe it would be to say that suddenly everyone drank crazy juice and went haywire. Mutants spontaneously began fighting with one another. Some of them had clearly been trained to be soldiers, but there was quite a bit of cat-fight face-slapping and shoving going on too.

"People!" the Director yelled into her loudspeaker. "People! What is going on?"

"They don't want to be here anymore," Angel said, watching them.

"We don't want to be here anymore!" the crowd yelled.

"They're tired of being treated like numbers and experiments," Angel explained.

"We're not numbers!" I heard angry voices cry. "We're not experiments!"

"Hmm," I said, scanning the area, looking for ways to escape.

"They feel like pawns," Angel went on.

"We're not just pawns!" the mutants yelled.

"They're people too, even if they were just cloned and created," Angel said, stepping closer to me and taking my hand.

"We're people too!" voices shouted. "We're people too!"

"O-kaaay," I said, and quickly gathered Nudge, Angel, Ari, and Total. "Let's get out of here. We'll make our way to the wall and go along it till we see a way to break out." They nodded and we began to move through the crowd, dodging flying fists and angry shoving.

"Robots!" yelled the Director, and everywhere, the robots stood at attention and armed their weapons. "Get this crowd under control!"

120

Yeah, because it wasn't bad enough, with everyone fighting. Now we had to get the bloodthirsty robots involved. And they had *guns*.

We continued to push through the crowd, trying to reach a castle wall. I saw Flyboys starting to wade into the crowd of angry, fighting people.

"Why are they fighting each other?" Nudge asked, close to my shoulder. "They should all gang up on the Flyboys."

Angel looked around. "Oh. Yeah."

She stood still for a minute, her brow furrowed with mighty concentration. Then, one by one, all around us, mutants slowed down in their fight, looked around, then turned to attack the Flyboys.

I grabbed Angel's hand and started to push through the crowd again, keeping low. "You are a scary, scary child, you know that?" I asked her.

She smiled.

I almost walked right into a thick line of Flyboys. Looking up, I saw solemn Eraser faces with glowing red robot eyes.

"You must stop," intoned one.

"I disagree." In an instant I launched myself at it, trying to knock it off balance. It was the second-to-last model, and I knocked its weapon out of its hands.

But not fast enough to avoid another Flyboy clocking me in the head with the butt of its gun. I staggered as a starburst of pain exploded behind my ear. A second later, warm blood started running down into my collar.

My flock sprang into action. Nudge jumped high in the air, whipping out her wings to hover below the electrified net but above the fray. Total chomped down hard on a Flyboy's ankle, and I could hear his fangs hit the metal below the thin layer of skin.

"The base of their spines!" I heard a voice call from behind.

I spun to see Jeb wading through the crowd toward us, dodging punches and kicks. "Hit the Flyboys at the base of their spines," he said. "It's a design flaw."

I had zero reason to trust him, despite all his yapping about being my dad, blah blah blah. Still, I had nothing to lose. Wheeling, I escaped my Flyboy and whipped around in back of another one. As hard as I could, I aimed a flying sideways kick with both feet right at its tailbone area.

Crack! Its legs crumpled, and it snapped forward from the hips, unable to move. A couple seconds later, the red glow in its eyes faded.

Huh. Whadaya know.

121

Then it was like a flashback to when I was eleven years old, fighting side by side with Jeb. He was the one who'd taught us to fight so well, to win at any cost. It was Jeb who'd taught us to never play fair, never telegraph our punches, always use any means to win a battle. Now, with him taking out Flyboys right next to me, it was just like those training days, like I was a little kid again, pretending he was my dad.

"Block it!" Jeb yelled, yanking me off memory lane. Instinctively I threw my arm up in time to block a Flyboy's overhand punch.

"Nudge! Angel! Attack the base of their spines!" I shouted. "Snap them!"

The fight began to turn in our favor then. As long as we could get behind a Flyboy, we could take it out about 80 percent of the time, which was all we needed.

Some of the mutants, however, didn't seem to have gotten Angel's latest memo and were still fighting one another, and us too.

Behind me, Ari was using his enormous strength to literally toss smaller mutants over his head into the mosh pit of death that made up the castle courtyard. He saw me snap a Flyboy's back, and he spun to do the same. The Flyboy managed to catch Ari with a hard punch under his jaw, and I saw his head jerk upward.

Roaring with fury, Ari righted himself and lunged at his attacker . . . only to sink to his knees slowly, a puzzled look on his face.

"Cover me!" I shouted at Nudge, Angel, and Total, and sprang to Ari's side.

I grabbed him under one arm and tried to help him stand. I couldn't get him up.

"Max?" he said, sounding confused.

"You hurt? You get shot? Where?" I demanded.

He looked down at his shirt and jacket. There were no spreading rosettes of blood. He shook his head. "I just . . ."

He glanced up at me, and there he was — seven-year-old Ari, the little kid who used to follow me around. I saw him there clearly in those eyes.

"I just . . . Oh, Max," Ari said, and then he slumped against me, eyes still open, weight so heavy on me that I fell to my knees next to him. I stared at his face, shook his shoulder.

"Ari!" I said. "Ari! Come on, snap out of it! *Please*, Ari?"

All around us, the battle thrashed on, but Ari was silent.

"Ari?" Horrified, I pressed two fingers against his neck, feeling for a pulse.

Ari's time had come. He had expired.

Right here, right now, in my arms.

122

Oh, God. I felt as if my breath, my spirit, had been knocked out of me. For several seconds I just stared numbly at Ari's ruined face, his unseeing eyes. My throat was gripped tight with emotion, and I brushed my fingers over his eyelids, closing them.

This poor, poor kid. I hoped wherever he was, he was no longer in pain, no longer ugly, no longer unloved and unwanted. Hot tears sprang to my eyes, and I wanted to sob.

Swallowing hard a bunch of times, I looked up and saw that everyone around me was still engaged in a life-or-death battle. They had no time to help me, no time to acknowledge Ari's death. A whistling noise next to my ear made me realize that I was still under attack myself — a Flyboy had just swung its weapon at me, trying to crush my skull.

Feeling helpless and furious, I gently lay Ari down in the dirt. "I'll come get you," I promised in a whisper. Then, enraged, I leaped up, grabbing the first Flyboy in my way. I twisted its neck as hard as I could. The Flyboy fell, and I moved on, smashing another in the back, dropping it like a sack of rotten groceries. Roaring with fury, I ripped the weapon from a downed Flyboy and swung it around my head, cracking it against three more robots, knocking them off balance, slowing them down so that Jeb and Nudge could take them out from behind.

Ari was dead, and *for what?* Why had this happened to him? Why had his life been seven years of pain and confusion and loneliness?

"Ari!" Jeb had finally seen his son. He rushed to Ari's side and knelt next to him. Looking stunned, he gathered Ari's hulking form and held him to his chest. "I'm so sorry." I saw his mouth shape the words, though I couldn't hear them. "I'm so sorry." He bent over Ari's form, mindless of his vulnerable position.

Then he looked up and caught my eye. His eyes were shiny with tears, which shocked me. He pitched his voice so I could hear him. "Omega can't track things fast with his eyes."

I waited for more, but that was it. I turned and whaled back into the fight, trying to accomplish the universal goal of every warrior everywhere: Get the other guy. Do not let him get you.

So big whoop: Omega couldn't track things well. Thanks, Jeb! Any other tidbits of wisdom for me? Like "Omega has an off switch"?

Who knew where the heck Omega was, anyway? For all I knew he was up on the stage, getting a manicure.

Swinging my weapon like a baseball bat, I felt the satisfying but bone-jolting *thwack!* as it slammed into a Flyboy's shoulder. It turned, and I swung at the base of its spine. *Crack!* Another Flyboy shortened to the height of a coffee table.

"She says we must fight."

The quiet words spoken near my nonbloody ear made me wheel to face . . . Omega. He looked spick-and-span, as if he'd managed to sit this one out.

"You don't have to do everything she tells you," I said, still lunging and fending off Flyboys. The gun flew out of my hand.

Omega spoke to the Flyboys around us: "Stop. She is mine."

Which made me even madder, if possible. "I'm . . . not . . . *anyone's!*"

The fact that the Flyboys listened to him and moved on to other targets made me see red, and it wasn't just the blood running into my eyes. Though of course that didn't help.

"We must fight," said Omega.

I was so tired of all the puppet masters pulling our strings.

"You can decide not to," I told him firmly.

He frowned. "I don't know how . . . to not."

"Oh, for crying out loud," I muttered, then swung back and walloped him in the side of his head as hard as I could.

123

Ow ow ow! Something in my hand went *crunch,* as if I'd broken a small bone. *Oh, my God, it hurt!* I sucked in my breath and tried not to scream. Like a boy!

Omega staggered but caught himself and immediately spun into a snap kick at my knee. I dodged it and wheeled into a spinning side kick, which connected solidly with the top of Omega's leg. Tucking my hurt hand against my body, I focused on kicks, aiming high at his head, bobbing and weaving to avoid his blows. He managed to block almost everything I threw at him, his silvery eyes following my movements calmly and precisely.

He can't track things fast.

What did that mean?

As an experiment, I took my hurt hand and waved it quickly in front of his face, as if I were about to hit him from a bunch of different directions. Sure enough, his eyes couldn't follow it, and he paused, as if to concentrate on it.

So I punched him with my other fist, a really hard blow right at his nose.

Apparently his perfect schnoz was not 400 percent stronger than the average nose, because it broke. Omega blinked and stepped back, looking startled, then blood started gushing from his nose. He touched it, alarmed.

"Head wounds always bleed a lot," I told him.

Then I whipped my hand all around him, up and down, side to side, and again he tried hard to track it, as if he couldn't help himself.

I jumped and landed a scissors kick against his neck, and he went down on his knees, coughing. Once more with the hand waving. It was like hypnotizing a cat. Then I clasped my hands together, wincing from the pain in my broken one, and gave Omega a powerful two-handed punch that sent him facedown into the dirt. Of course, hitting him with my injured hand hurt so much I almost shrieked and passed out right next to him.

But I held tough. Just barely. But enough.

I looked down at Omega, the superboy, the pinnacle of Itex's achievement. I'd bested him because he couldn't track things well with his eyes. I'd won because Jeb had told me about it. I looked up at the Director. She was staring at me with the pure, cold hatred of someone who's been defeated by something she thought was inferior.

Well, that's the breaks.

Omega was out cold but not dead. We were supposed to fight to the finish. If he'd gotten me on the ground, he would have killed me, poor sap. He didn't know any better.

But I did. I could have given him a quick sideways kick at the base of his neck, which would have snapped his spine. Instead I walked away, heading back to where my half brother's body lay.

Who's the better man now, you idiot? I thought at the Director.

124

The electric net topping the castle walls could keep stuff in but not out, interestingly. I was pushing through the crowd, tossing off a quick punch or kick here and there, trying to get to Ari, when suddenly a large rock flew over the castle wall. It hit a mutant on the head, and she sat down abruptly.

I looked up. An actual arrow, flaming like in the movies, was flying overhead. It streaked right through the net and buried itself in the back of a Flyboy, who promptly caught fire. What else?

When humans catch fire, they run around screaming, or possibly remember to stop, drop, and roll. When a Flyboy catches fire, it just stands there looking stupid until it turns into a tall, flaming statue. Apparently, once a Flyboy is really aflame, its joints and pulleys quit working and it can't move. Useful info I tucked away for future use.

More rocks began flying overhead.

Getting Ari would have to wait. I had the living ones to take care of now.

"Angel!" I shouted. "Nudge! Total! Stand next to the

wall!" I hadn't noticed Total in a while, and I was glad to see him bound out of the crowd toward me. He was limping, holding one paw up, but leaped into my arms and licked my face.

"Bleah. Blood," he said, and quit licking. *Bleah right back atcha,* I thought.

"Who's throwing the rocks?" Nudge asked, as we pressed against the wall.

"I don't know," I started to say, just as Angel said, "Kids."

"What do you mean 'kids'?" I asked. More rocks flew overhead, and several more flaming arrows.

"I think it's kids out there," Angel said. "It feels like kids."

I watched as another large rock hit a Flyboy in the knees. The robot buckled, and then two mutants fell on it, punching it and pulling its hair.

"Kids or, like, cavemen?"

"Kids," said Angel.

"Save the flock! Kill the Flyboys! Destroy Itex!"

My eyebrows lifted as the growing roar outside became more distinct. Slowly, the noise in the courtyard stilled, and the roar outside grew louder. More and more rocks, some as big as melons, and flaming arrows streaked over the walls.

"Save the flock! Kill the Flyboys! Destroy Itex!"

I looked at Nudge and Angel. "Wonder if they're blog readers?"

"Chase them away!" the Director's voice boomed over the loudspeaker. Her angry face appeared eight feet tall on the screens around the courtyard. Some of the screens were now broken, and all had dirt and blood splashed on them. They had probably cost a lot too.

"Chase them away!" the Director shouted again. "They are vermin! They are here to destroy you! Chase them away!"

As always, the Flyboys jumped to do her bidding without question. There were maybe sixty left, and as one they shot out their wings and took to the air.

"Uh," said Nudge, watching.

Yes. Oops. No one had turned off the electric net. Sixty Flyboys rose quickly upward, and sixty Flyboys instantly shorted out when they hit the net. They fell to the ground in perfect unison.

"That was poor planning on her part," Total observed, and I nodded.

Bam! Bam! Bam! I heard the squeal of an engine outside, and then bone-rattling thumps against the tall gates. The people outside were trying to drive a vehicle through, trying to break down the gates.

125

Westfield, England

The regional director of this School looked over the tops of his glasses. "Holloway? What's that noise outside?"

His assistant moved to a window. A look of alarm passed over his face. "It seems to be some kind of demonstration, sir," he said.

"Demonstration? What the devil do you mean?" The regional director moved to the window. What he saw made his mouth open in astonishment. Hundreds, maybe thousands of people were protesting outside the School's gates. They were . . . they looked almost like *children*. But that didn't make sense.

"Is this some antinuclear demonstration?" he asked Holloway. "Do they have signs? Perhaps we should call security."

Holloway listened at the window. The roars outside became more distinct. "Save the flock! Destroy Itex! Save the world! Destroy Itex!"

The two men stared at each other. "How could they

possibly know we're an arm of Itex?" the regional director asked.

Crash! A softball-sized rock flew through their window, showering them with glass shards.

Now they could hear the chanting clearly:

"We want . . . what's ours!

"You belong . . . behind bars!

"Itex is an evil giant!

"Us kids ain't buyin' it!"

The regional director looked at Holloway, who had several scratches from flying glass. "Call security."

Martinslijn, Netherlands

Edda Engels looked up from her lab bench and listened. Odd sounds were coming in the window. She went to investigate, only to dodge a heavy glass bottle, tipped with a burning rag. Wha? Was that a Molotov cocktail?

Boom! It exploded just as Edda dove beneath her desk. What was going on? Outside, it sounded like hundreds, maybe more, were surrounding her lab. What were they saying?

"You've ruined our water and our air!

"You're evil and you just don't care!

"Fang is right: the time has come

"For us kids to claim our home!"

Who was Fang? Edda wondered. And more important, how could she get out of here? The fire was spreading.

Woetens, Australia

"What's all that dust, then?" The chief operating officer of the Australian branch of DelaneyMinker peered out the window. Miles and miles of desert stretched away as far as she could see. On the horizon, a wide, low dust storm was coming at them.

"Hand me those binoculars, would you, Sam?" she asked her assistant.

Sam handed her the binoculars.

"Is it . . . School Day?" asked the COO. "Are we expecting field trips?"

Sam looked at her. "We don't get field trips here. It's a top-secret facility. Why?"

"Well, it looks like . . . children! On motorscooters, apparently. And some of those four-wheel thingies."

"ATVs?" asked Sam. He took the binoculars and looked.

A line of small vehicles stretched for at least a mile. It *did* look like children. Was this some sort of nature club? He squinted and adjusted the focus slightly. They were carrying signs. He could almost make one out . . .

DELANEYMINKER = POLLUTING STINKER

And another one:

THE PLANET IS OURS! GET OUT!

"You may want to go into lockdown," said Sam, sounding far calmer than he felt.

126

"Iggy!" Fang yelled. "Gasman! Follow me!" Wheeling through the sky, Fang worked his wings powerfully, racing across the gray ocean toward the horizon.

Risking a backward glance, he saw that Iggy and the Gasman were behind him and closing fast.

"Dive-bomb," Fang said. "On my count."

The Gasman looked down, frowned, then drew in a deep breath and nodded.

"Oh, God," said Iggy. "Talk about cold . . ."

"We are here to destroy you," said the Flyboys, sounding like an angry swarm of mechanized bees.

"One!" Fang called, heading away from shore as fast as he could. He hoped there was a steep drop-off along this part of the coast. "Two!"

"You will recant!" the Flyboys droned. "You will recant!"

"Three!" said Fang, and tucked his wings in tight against his body. He aimed himself downward, right at the water. From this high, going this fast, hitting the water was going to feel like hitting concrete. But it couldn't be helped.

He heard the Gasman's and Iggy's jackets flapping as they accelerated downward.

"This is going to be bad!" Iggy called.

"Yep," Fang agreed, his voice snatched away by the streaming wind.

"There is no escape!" droned the Flyboys, who were, of course, following them fast.

Yeah? thought Fang. *This is true.*

Smash!

Hitting the cold ocean was in fact a whole lot like hitting concrete, Fang decided, but he was so streamlined that he shot straight down like an arrow, spearing the water. It felt as if God had punched his face, but he was still alive and conscious.

He heard the impact of the Gasman and Iggy hitting the water but could barely see anything when he opened his eyes.

As the boys started to make their way up to the surface, their ears popping, they saw and felt hundreds and hundreds of Flyboys smashing into the water.

It turned out they could not swim.

It also turned out that water was not a good environment for their systems to function properly in. The electrical charges of the Flyboys shorting out actually made Fang's skin tingle, and he motioned to the Gasman to get away, now! The Gasman grabbed Iggy, and they swam hard after Fang.

They bobbed to the surface about eighty feet away from

where a showstopping lights-and-sparks display was taking place. The Flyboys couldn't help themselves, even as they saw dozens of their colleagues exploding and shorting out in the water.

Some of them tried to backpedal, but their wings weren't designed that way — and the Flyboys behind them just hit them and dragged them all down anyway.

"Awesome!" shouted the Gasman, punching his fist in the air. "Oh, Iggy, man, if you could only see this!"

"I hear it," said Iggy happily. "I feel it. There's nothing like the smell of the shorted closed-circuit system of an electric Frankenstein."

"So, guys," said Fang, treading water. "Good plan?"

"Excellent plan, dude," said the Gasman, and Iggy held up his hand for a high five.

Fang slapped it, then they swam toward shore.

127

With a gigantic splintering, grinding noise, the enormous castle gates burst inward. What was left of the mutants hurried out of the way.

A giant yellow Humvee careened in through the gates, its front end considerably smashed.

The driver's door popped open, and a teenage girl leaned out. "I just got my license!" she said excitedly in a heavy German accent.

Then hundreds of kids started pouring through the broken gates, only to stop and stare at the courtyard, littered with bodies and busted Flyboys.

Onstage, the Director was white-faced. Her order had effectively finished off the last of this batch of Flyboys. Maybe she had more stashed inside. At any rate, she turned and started hurrying toward the metal door that led back into the castle.

I tumbled Total into Angel's arms and grabbed Nudge's hand. "Come on!"

The two of us took off into the air — the Flyboys had shorted out the electric grid as well as themselves.

"Help me get her!" I told Nudge.

Just as the Director reached the metal door and was grabbing hold of the lever, Nudge and I dropped down on either side of her.

"Not so fast, *Mom,*" I snarled.

128

Nudge and I each grabbed the Director under an arm and took to the air.

She was no lightweight, but together we took her high, way over the castle. She was screaming in terror, looking down, kicking her feet, losing both of her sensible shoes.

"Put me down this instant!" she shouted.

I looked at her. "Or what? You'll send me to my dungeon?"

She stared at me with contempt.

"Oh, did you see?" I said. "I defeated Superboy. But who knows? Maybe someday you can turn him into a real boy."

"Omega was far superior to you," the Director spat.

"And yet here *I* am, dragging your stupid butt across the sky, and there *he* is, doing a face-plant in the dirt," I pointed out. "If by 'superior,' you mean totally inadequate in every way, then, yes, Omega is far superior."

"What do you want?" the Director snapped. "Where are you taking me?"

"Mostly just *up*," I said. "I do want some answers, though,"

"I'll tell you nothing!"

I looked at her seriously, her stiff blond hair streaming out in back of her. "In that case, I'm going to drop you from way, way up here, and watch you go two dimensional. We call it 'flock splatter art.'"

A look of genuine fear entered her cold eyes, which cheered me a little.

"What do you want to know?" she asked cautiously, trying not to look down.

"Who's my real mom? And no, designing me doesn't make you a mom." I knew what Jeb had told me; I wanted confirmation.

"I. Don't. Know."

"Oops!" I let go of her, and she shrieked as she and Nudge started plummeting.

"I'll tell you!" she screamed, looking up at me.

I swooped down and grabbed her again. "Now, you were saying . . . ?"

White-faced, she swallowed and took some deep breaths. "A researcher. She studied birds. She offered to donate an egg. It isn't important who she was."

My heart leaped. "Her name?"

"I don't remember. *Wait!*" she said, as my fingers loosened. "Something Hispanic. Hernandez? Martinez? Something like that."

I could hardly breathe, and it wasn't because we were at

five thousand feet. Dr. Martinez really was my mother. I hugged the knowledge to me like a life jacket.

"You're not the only successful hybrid, you know," the Director said.

"Well, there's darling Omega," I admitted. "And Spot, the cat girl."

"And me," the Director said.

I whistled. "Don't tell me, let me guess. You're half . . . vulture? Hyena? Some kind of marine bottom-feeder?"

"Galapagos tortoise," she said. "I'm one hundred and seven years old."

"Huh. And you don't look a day over a hundred and five," I said.

She glared at me.

I looked down and saw that the castle was surrounded by German *polizei* cars. Today was over. Today had been saved. Maybe even the world?

"Bye," I told her, and let go.

Nudge couldn't hold her, and the Director spun downward, screaming in terror and surprise.

That isn't you, Max, said the Voice.

The Voice! I hadn't heard it in a while.

Why's that, Jeb? I asked inside my head. *Because you didn't* design *me that way?*

No, said the Voice. *Because that's not who you are as a person. No one designed it. It's all you. You're just not a killer. You've shown that again and again. And it makes me prouder than anything else about you.*

I sighed. *Yes, it's true, I am pretty wonderful,* I thought to the Voice. But deep down, where I hoped the Voice couldn't hear me, I did feel a little proud, a little heart-warmed.

Talk about manipulation.

"Okay, let's go get her," I told Nudge, and we swooped down and caught the Director with a good two hundred feet to spare.

129

After it was all over but the shouting, my only desire was to streak toward home. But of course I was outvoted, three to one. Even when I claimed that each of their votes counted for only half a vote, they still outvoted me.

Within hours we were at *their* chosen destination,

"Let me see the screen," Angel asked, leaning closer.

Yes, we were at a cyber café in France. Why France? The food! The cute shoes! The fact that Total could go into restaurants and grocery stores!

"Now I can't see," Total complained. He leaned forward on his paws on the table.

"Coffee!" said Nudge happily, slurping from her mug. "Looove it!"

"Please tell me that's decaf," I said.

The screen dinged, and there was Fang's face. And Gazzy. And Iggy, all crowding around their computer back in the States.

Fang! It felt like years since I'd seen him, talked to him. In the past three days, every memory I'd ever had of him had played through my brain. In the dungeon, it was thinking about him that had kept me going. Then getting that note from the mutant in Lendeheim, saying he was coming — it had been one of the best moments of my life.

"Where the heck were *you?*" I demanded. "I thought you were on your way!"

"Little Flyboy complication," he said, his voice sounding funny through the computer. "Did you know they can't swim? They sink like rocks. They don't like water at all."

His solemn face, his eyes as familiar to me as my own, seemed to make my world straighten out again. I laughed, and everything in me felt whole and complete. I knew the flock would stay together now, no matter what.

"You guys stay put," I said. "We'll come to *you.*"

"You got it," he said, and my heart melted.

"Bring me something from France!" Gazzy cried in the background.

"Okay," I promised him.

"Me too!" Iggy put in. "Like, a French *girl!*"

I groaned. Can we say 'sexist pig' one more time?

But he was *my* sexist pig, and I would see them all soon. I couldn't wait.

EPILOGUE

WE ARE THE CHAMPIONS — FOR THE MOMENT, ANYWAY

130

When I saw them at last, on a barrier island off the coast of North Carolina, I almost couldn't speak. Nudge, Total, Angel, and I coasted to a landing on the beach, feeling the sand squeak under our shoes.

There was a line of gnarled oaks at the top edge of the beach, and I looked through them, then checked my watch.

"You're late."

Fang stepped out of the shadows, eating an apple. He was dressed in black, as usual, and his face looked like a lumpy plum pie. But his eyes shone as he came toward me, and then I was running to him over the sand, my wings out in back of me.

We smashed together awkwardly, with Fang standing stiffly for a moment, but then his arms slowly came around me, and he hugged me back. I held him tight, trying to swallow the lump of cotton in my throat, my head on his shoulder, my eyes squeezed shut.

"Don't ever leave me again," I said in a tiny voice.

"I won't," he promised into my hair, sounding most un-Fang-like. "I won't. Not ever."

And just like that, a cold shard of ice that had been inside my chest ever since we'd split up — well, it just disappeared. I felt myself relax for the first time in I don't known how long. The wind was chilly, but the sun was bright, and my whole flock was together. Fang and I were together.

"Excuse me? I'm alive too." Iggy's plaintive voice made me pull back. I wiped my sleeve across my eyes, then turned and hugged Iggy hard, and Gazzy, and then we were all hugging one another and promising never to split up again. Basically we just got caught up, and ate doughnuts and apples, which the boys had thoughtfully provided.

"Well, what now?" Gazzy asked, as I tried to smooth his sticking-up hair.

I let out a deep breath and looked at my flock.

"I need to go to Arizona," I said.

131

Jeb was already there, at Dr. Martinez's house. I had half expected it.

The flock and I landed in the woods close to the house, and after looking carefully around, we stepped into the yard. Immediately, Magnolia, the basset hound, lumbered out from under the porch, baying. She ran over, saw Total, and started barking harder.

"Oh, *please*," said Total.

The front door opened, and Ella burst out, her face alight. Then she saw I wasn't alone, and she stopped, staring at the rest of the flock.

"Oh, gosh," she breathed. "All of you . . ." Her face split into a humongo smile, and she raced to me, catching me in a skinny, wiry hug. "You're my sister!" she cried. "I had wished you could be. Now you are."

She pulled back, and we just smiled at each other. I mean, I felt much closer to Nudge, sisterwise, but knowing that Ella and I shared nonbird blood meant a lot to me. It made me feel more solid, somehow. That sounds stupid, but that's how it felt.

"Max." Dr. Martinez stood on the porch, her hand to her mouth. Jeb came out after her, his face drawn and sad. He looked glad to see us all, though. I remembered how he'd looked when Ari died. I was so confused about him it made my head hurt.

"Hi," I said lamely. Unfortunately, finding out who my parents actually were had not improved my social graces by leaps and bounds. Oh, well.

Dr. Martinez — it felt too weird to call her anything else — came down the steps, and then she was hurrying to me. I stood stiffly for a moment while she wrapped me in a warm, momlike embrace that felt like the best, softest blanket in the whole world.

"Oh, Max," she breathed, stroking my tangled hair. "I couldn't believe it when I saw you before. I wasn't sure. But it was you! It was you all along."

I nodded, slightly horrified to see tears running down her cheeks. "Yep," I said, then cursed myself for being so awkward and tongue-tied. This was my mother! This was who I'd dreamed of my whole life! Not only that, but she was the best mother in the whole world, the one person I would have picked! And I was standing here like a scarecrow.

I cleared my throat, looking down at my feet. "I'm glad it was you," I managed to get out, and then, total nightmare, I started bawling into her sweater.

132

After my fourth chocolate-chip cookie, I started calling her Mom. All of us, the whole flock, plus Ella, Mom, and Jeb, rested up. The flock and I took fabulous hot showers, and Mom came up with some clothes for all of us. Everyone seemed to adore her and gave me envious but happy looks. I felt so proud of her.

It was weird to see her trusting Jeb. He seemed normal, like he used to when we lived with him. We all kept our distance, though, even when he tried to reach out to us. Maybe in the future we could get over everything that had happened. He did his best to explain the stuff he'd done. Part of it was because he truly believed it was the best way to train me to save the world. Part of it had been designed to seem much worse than it was. And basically, he'd helped me escape any number of times. And part of it had been stuff he'd been forced to do — playing along with the Director so he could stay in a position to help me and know what was coming.

I was like, whatever. Deep down, I was glad to learn all that, but I wasn't going to make it easy for him.

"Okay, everyone," Mom said, coming in from the small kitchen. "Food's up!"

We all crammed in around her tiny dining table. She had made real Mexican food *herself*. We're not talking Taco Bell here. It was incredible, and she'd made enough for a big crowd because she knew how hard it was for us to get enough calories.

"Oh, man, this smells so good," Iggy moaned.

Ella watched him as he started eating, not spilling a drop. "It's so amazing, how you can do that," she told him.

Iggy seemed taken aback. "I've had a lot of practice."

"Well, I think you're amazing," said Ella, and Iggy blushed.

I glanced across the table and saw Gazzy and Angel sitting next to each other, looking calmer and safer than they had in so long.

"And Max, I've put some scraps in a bowl for your dog," Mom said. "It's on the floor, by the back door."

The flock and I went still.

Uh-oh, I thought.

Total stomped up to me, his glare accusing. "A *bowl* on the *floor!*" he seethed. "Why don't you just chain me to a stake in the yard and throw me a *bone!*"

Mom stared at him, and Ella looked like her eyes were going to pop out.

"Uh, well, they didn't expect —," I began.

"No, no, it's *fine!*" Total snapped. "Just put an old towel on the floor for me to sleep on! Listen, I've been practicing my barking! Arf! Or is it bowwow? I can never remember."

I looked at Mom. "Uh, do you think Total could maybe have a plate here?" I pointed to a tiny space next to me. "He, uh, likes to eat at the table."

"Because I'm not a complete *barbarian!*" Total said.

"Certainly," Mom said smoothly. "I'm sorry, Total."

I looked at Fang, and he rolled his eyes and reached for seconds. Everyone started talking again, and it was like a Norman Rockwell painting, all of us sitting there, eating together. Well, maybe Norman Rockwell with, you know, mutants and a talking dog. But still.

133

"You just got here," Mom said, teary eyed again.

"I know," I told her. "But we'll be back. Promise."

"Why do you have to go?" Ella wailed.

"I have . . . responsibilities," I said. "You know, a world to keep saving and all that."

We each hugged Mom and Ella about a hundred times. Total peed on their sage bushes and gave Magnolia a dirty look.

Then it was just me and Jeb, facing each other. I knew he wanted a hug. I also knew that my hugs didn't come cheap.

"So, why me, Jeb?" I asked. "How come *I'm* supposed to save the world, when I'm not even the most evolved experiment?"

"You're evolved enough," he said. He swallowed. "Max, you're the last of the hybrids who still has . . . a soul."

I thought about how empty and expressionless Omega had been. Hmm.

"She doesn't have soul," Gazzy scoffed. "Have you ever seen her dance?"

"Not *soul,* Gazzy," I said. "*A* soul."

"Oh."

One last good-bye, and then Fang and I looked at each other.

"Okay, let's hit it," I said, just as he said, "Up and away, guys."

I gave him a little smile. I turned to the others. "You heard 'im. Up and away!"

Then we were flying again, rising above the confusing and troubled Earth, into the simple, perfect, clear blue sky, where everything was peaceful and made sense.

"You know what?" Total said conversationally. Iggy had him in a carrier thing on his back that Mom had found in her attic. It made flying with Total much easier. Okay, basically it was a baby carrier, but for God's sake don't tell Total.

"What?" I asked.

"Your mom isn't so bad."

"Gee, thanks," I said dryly, and the others laughed.

And finally, as we fly off into the sunset, so to speak, there's only one thing for me to add:

Hopefully, we'll be back.

And if we are, it won't be pretty.

www.maximumride.com

They can save themselves,
but can they save the planet?

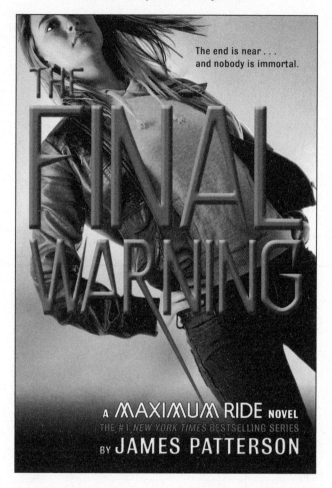

The end is near . . .
and nobody is immortal.

THE **FINAL WARNING**

A MAXIMUM RIDE NOVEL

THE #1 *NEW YORK TIMES* BESTSELLING SERIES

BY JAMES PATTERSON

the next thrilling chapter in the blockbuster series

by James Patterson

Turn the page for a sneak preview!

A Poem

By Max

> White is the color of little bunnies with pink noses.
> White is the color of fluffy clouds fluffing their way across the sky.
> White is the color of soft-serve ice cream in a cone.
> White is the color of angels' wings and Angel's wings.
> White is the color of brand-new ankle socks fresh out of the bag.
> White is the color of crisp sheets in schmancy hotels.
> White is the color of every last stinking thing you see for endless miles and miles if you happen to be in Antarctica trying to save the world, which now you aren't so sure you can do because you feel like if you see any more whiteness — Wonder Bread, someone's

*underwear, teeth — you will completely and totally lose
your ever-lovin' mind and wind up pushing a grocery
cart full of empty cans around New York City, muttering to yourself.*

That was my first poem *ever*.

Okay, so it's not Shakespeare, but I liked it.

We tied up at the Lucir station's dock, next to a couple
other boats. Awaiting us were a bunch of bright red metal
buildings built up on stilts.

"They're expecting us," said Sue-Ann, motioning to the
first building. "We can go in, meet some people, and they'll
show us to the guest quarters."

"Okay," I said, teeth prepared to clench, prebattle adrenaline starting to trickle into my veins.

There was no green: no trees, no shrubs, no grass, no
weeds. There were also no sidewalks, no trash, no skyscrap-
ers, no cars. It was completely different from anything we'd
ever seen before, and suddenly the phrase "polar opposites"
made a lot more sense.

"This is like being on the moon," Nudge said in an awed
voice. "It's so clean."

"We're explorers," said Gazzy happily. "We might see
stuff no one else has ever seen."

I looked at my flock. Each of them seemed a little nervous and a lot excited. They had a real purpose, beyond
just cleaning their rooms or keeping watch or finding food.
Even if that real purpose was concocted by scientists to
create needless panic in the populace, still. The kids felt as
though they could help. Clearly they just wanted to forget

that this time three weeks ago we'd been fighting for our lives *again*. And, I mean, why would any kid want to forget *that*?

If they really liked being here, really really liked it, would they still come with me when it was time to leave? Because no matter what happened here or how much they felt they were helping, we would still eventually have to leave. We always leave.

This reality check brought to you by Max. You're welcome.

Fang and Iggy were facing away from the station buildings, in the direction of the endless whitescape. Fang stood out against the ice as if carved out of black marble. He turned and motioned me over with a nod.

"Gosh, lots of...white, huh?" I said, bouncing on my heels, already feeling the cold.

"Yeah...," Iggy said in a weird voice.

"You're actually not missing that much, Ig," I told him. "It's not like other places, where there's tons of different stuff to see. Everything here is pretty much white. Lots of sharp white edges."

Fang touched my hand, and I turned to him. He nodded at Iggy.

"I know," said Iggy. "I can see it."

OKAY, I'M GOING to float out a theory here, and maybe it's crap, but I'm thinking that the complete absence of color had something to do with the blind kid suddenly being able to see stuff.

'Cause he really could. I waved my hand in front of his face, and he blinked and pulled away.

"What are you *doing*?" he asked, frowning.

I let my jaw drop open, looking from him to Fang and back, and then Iggy was smiling huge in a way he hardly ever does, and Fang was grinning in a way he hardly ever does, and I felt like skipping around like a ballerina, which, I promise you, I never, ever do.

"What's going on?" Gazzy asked, coming over to us.

"Iggy can *see*," I said, still unable to believe it.

Excitedly Iggy whirled to see the Gasman, and then stopped dead, frowning. He blinked several times.

"It's...it's gone," he said in a hollow voice.

"What?"

"You could see?" Gazzy asked.

Iggy turned around again, his head hanging. He sighed heavily, then stiffened. "No! I can see again! I see the white mountains again!"

So here's the deal: Iggy could see *whiteness*. He could see the shapes of the cliffs and glaciers, the occasional gray rocks jutting out from the snow, the horizon line where land met sky. When he turned around, the ocean, the rocky shore, everything, went blank.

"I'm cold," I said after we'd been standing around looking at Iggy look at stuff for a while. "Let's go inside."

Lucir station consisted of about fifteen metal buildings raised up on steel stilts. Some of them were connected, like stepping-stones, going up the nearest hill. A few stood alone. Most of them had snowcats and bobsleds and ice trucks parked underneath.

We climbed the stairs, and once again Iggy had to rely on touching the hem of my jacket and concentrating on the sounds around him. I could feel him seething with disappointment.

The door of the building opened into an air lock. We took off our jackets and stuff there, then went through another door into the actual station.

We met the scientists who lived and worked at the station, ignoring their curious looks and unspoken questions. They showed us to the guest quarters, which were in a separate metal hut. It was small but cozy and comfortable, with one room full of bunk beds, four high; a small living room; a bathroom; and a tiny kitchen.

"Hey!" said Brigid, knocking on our door. "You guys want to see some penguins?"

"Yeah," Iggy muttered bitterly. "Make 'em stand against a white cliff."

Fang and I looked at each other. Some of us had had new skills show up lately. Would Iggy's be his eyesight?

And here's another question: When was all our world-saving gonna start?

THE UBER-DIRECTOR'S ASSISTANT looked up from a computer monitor. "The mutants have arrived at the station, sir, as expected."

The Uber-Director couldn't nod, but he blinked. "They're all together? None of them stayed on the boat?"

"No, sir." The assistant gestured to his monitor and pressed a button. Instantly the screen showed a somewhat grainy image of the six mutant children trooping across packed snowdrifts toward the Lucir station. The screen split, and the other half showed a still image taken from inside the dining hall of the *Wendy K*. Quickly the assistant zoomed in on the faces of the small group heading inside the station and compared them with close-ups of the faces on the boat. They matched.

"All six are accounted for," the assistant said.

"Very good," said the Uber-Director. "Send a message to our contact, saying that the schedule will continue as planned."

"Yes, sir," said the assistant, turning back to his computer.

The Uber-Director sent a thought command, and moments later the door opened. A hulking creature almost seven feet tall and easily over three hundred pounds stepped into the room.

"Ah, Gozen," said the Uber-Director.

The assistant stiffened in his chair and slowly sneaked a peek. If the soldiers creeped him out, this Gozen thing positively terrified him. Not only was he huge, but he had a human face patched onto a Frankenstein body. A curved, shiny metal plate covered part of his bare skull where they couldn't get skin to grow. One arm was a foot longer than the other, and the hand had metal spikes grafted onto the knuckle bones. His other arm, tinted faintly greenish as if the circulation had never worked properly, was hugely veined and muscled, the result of injecting human growth hormone directly into the flesh.

The face was human, but when the creature spoke, you could clearly see the bolts in his jawbone right beneath the skin. Just the other day, the assistant had seen Gozen reach out, snatch a songbird from the air, and casually break its neck, tossing the light, brightly colored body aside. The assistant didn't know whether Gozen had morals or ethics or any sense of right or wrong. Mostly what he had been given was extreme, astonishing power.

"Gozen," the Uber-Director said again as the hulking thing stood near him, at attention. "It's almost time. Prepare your troops."

"Yes, sir," Gozen said without moving. His voice sounded like a tape of a human voice, played too slowly.

A chill went down the assistant's back.

Reader's Guide

Maximum Ride: Saving the World and Other Extreme Sports is not only a fun read, but it's also full of thought-provoking story elements that are ideal for discussion groups or for your own exploration. Here are some questions to get the conversation going!

1. For the first time since the flock escaped from the School, Max and Fang disagree about the direction the flock should take. Max feels bound to save the world for the common good, while Fang's priority lies with the safety of the flock. How does this difference of opinion affect the flock? Whom would you side with in their argument?

2. How does the flock react when they discover the Erasers are robots? How do the robotic Erasers differ from their predecessors? What advantage does the flock have over the robotic Erasers? What challenges do they face?

3. Max feels threatened and offended by the popularity of Fang's blog. How does the blog negatively affect other members of the flock? What are the positive aspects of the population at large knowing about the flock and their situation?

4. How does Max's decision to allow Ari to join the flock affect them? Should Max have the right to make a decision that no one else in the flock agrees with? Why or why not? Is Fang justified in his decision to leave the flock? Based on what you know of Max and Fang's history with Ari, do you think both of their reactions are justified?

5. When Fang and Max split up, each member of the flock is forced to make a hard choice. Why do Nudge and Angel stay with Max? Why do Iggy and Gazzy go with Fang? How do their choices affect the safety of the flock? Whom would you choose to go with, and why?

6. Once Fang is away from Max, he realizes all the extra duties Max has had to perform and the pressure she has endured as leader of the flock. What effect does this realization have on Fang? Are there situations in which you have had to lead others? How did they change your perception of leadership? Do you prefer to lead or follow? What are the benefits of each?

7. Max is reluctant to trust Jeb after all he's put her through. How does seeing Dr. Martinez and Jeb together affect Max's feelings about him? In the end, do you feel that Jeb is trustworthy? Would you forgive someone who had hurt you if they had done so in your best interest?

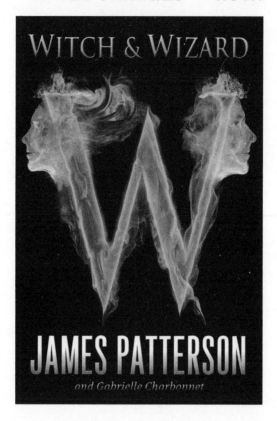

IT'S OVERWHELMING. A city's worth of angry faces staring at me like I'm a wicked criminal—which, I promise you, *I'm not.* The stadium is filled to capacity—past capacity. People are standing in the aisles, the stairwells, on the concrete ramparts, and a few extra thousand are camped out on the playing field. There are no football teams here today. They wouldn't be able to get out of the locker-room tunnels if they tried.

This total abomination is being broadcast on TV and the Internet too. All the useless magazines are here, and the useless newspapers. Yep, I see cameramen in elevated roosts at intervals around the stadium.

There's even one of those remote-controlled cameras that runs around on wires above the field. There it is—hovering just in front of the stage, bobbing slightly in the breeze.

So there are undoubtedly millions more eyes watching

than I can see. But it's the ones here in the stadium that are breaking my heart. To be confronted with tens, maybe even hundreds of thousands, of curious, uncaring, or at least indifferent, faces...talk about *frightening*.

And there are no moist eyes, never mind tears.

No words of protest.

No stomping feet.

No fists raised in solidarity.

No inkling that anybody's even thinking of surging forward, breaking through the security cordon, and carrying my family to safety.

Clearly, this is not a good day for us Allgoods.

In fact, as the countdown ticker flashes on the giant video screens at either end of the stadium, it's looking like this will be our *last* day.

It's a point driven home by the very tall, bald man up in the tower they've erected midfield—he looks like a cross between a Supreme Court chief justice and Ming the Merciless. I know who he is. I've actually met him. He's The One Who Is The One.

Directly behind his Oneness is a huge N.O. banner— THE NEW ORDER.

And then the crowd begins to chant, almost sing, "The One Who Is The One! The One Who Is The One!"

Imperiously, The One raises his hand, and his hooded lackeys on the stage push us forward, at least as far as the ropes around our necks will allow.

I see my brother, Whit, handsome and brave, looking

down at the platform mechanism. Calculating if there's any way to jam it, some means of keeping it from unlatching and dropping us to our neck-snapping deaths. Wondering if there's a last-minute way out of this.

I see my mother crying quietly. Not for herself, of course, but for Whit and me.

I see my father, his tall frame stooped with resignation, smiling at me and my brother—trying to keep our spirits up, reminding us that there's no point in being miserable in our last moments on this planet.

But I'm getting ahead of myself. I'm supposed to be providing an *introduction* here, not the details of our public *execution*.

So let's go back a bit....

James Patterson was selected by readers across America as the Children's Choice Book Awards Author of the Year in 2010. He is the internationally bestselling author of the highly praised Middle School books, *I Funny*, *Confessions of a Murder Suspect*, and the Maximum Ride, Witch & Wizard, Daniel X, and Alex Cross series. His books have sold more than 275 million copies worldwide, making him one of the bestselling authors of all time. He lives in Florida.